The O'Malley Legacy

By
Kate Sweeney

THE O'MALLEY LEGACY
© 2008 BY KATE SWEENEY

ISBN 10: 1-933113-95-2
ISBN 13: 978-1-933113-95-1

First Printing: 2008

This Trade Paperback Is Published By
Intaglio Publications
Walker, LA USA
WWW.INTAGLIOPUB.COM

CREDITS
EXECUTIVE EDITORS: TARA YOUNG AND VERDA FOSTER
COVER DESIGN BY SHERI Graphicartist2020@hotmail.com)

DEDICATION

To all women, regardless of age, shape, or color, who lived, loved and struggled; who in their own way made this world a better place.

Each of us has known such women, whether it be a partner, mother, daughter, sister, teacher, or friend.

Their laughter and tears, heartache and pain echo in our soul.

Their spirit will guide us through life's journey.

This book is dedicated to these women who have traveled before us, and those whose journey has just begun.

ACKNOWLEDGMENTS

As always, to Den who understands the voice inside my head, which is a scary proposition at best, and Kathy Smith; their loyalty and friendship is beyond measure.

To my beta readers, Maureen, Tina, and Tracey.

To editors Tara and Verda, thanks ladies. I still got that adverb thing goin' on.

Finally, to Intaglio Publications, for being a constant in this ever-changing literary world. I have learned a great deal from my publisher, Sheri Payton, and from Denise Winthrop and Kathy Smith. Thank you, my friends.

Prologue

The cold Atlantic wind whipped around her as she stood on the edge of her world, cradling the small babe in her arms. The raven-haired woman kissed the newborn's forehead, then lifted her up to the rising sun.

"Seo m'iníon, Branna Ní Mháille!" she proclaimed her daughter's birth to the gods and goddesses of old. As the baby wailed against the wind, the mother laughed joyously. "Let them hear you, Branna. Look, my darlin'."

She held the infant close to her as she stepped to the edge of the cliff; the vast expanse of water stretched out before them.

"You are *Ui Mháille*. In you flows the life's blood of all before you. You will be in the soul of all that come after you."

The babe cried out and struggled against the warm embrace, as if eager to begin the destiny of the O'Malley women.

Her mother let out a triumphant laugh and held the infant closer. "So it begins, *a stóirín,*" she whispered in the infant's ear. "You are the first, darlin' Branna, but not the last," she vowed as she gazed out at the never-ending sea.

.

Chapter 1

Branna sat on the short stone wall and gazed at the endless ocean before her. She took a deep pensive breath and slowly exhaled. She smiled as she breathed in the clean sea air. The city air in Dublin was not as pristine as it was here in the country. She looked around the green sloping hills, remembering her youth, remembering Reagan Shaunessy.

She immediately shook her head as if to dismiss any thoughts of the woman. Try as she may, it was a losing battle.

"What was I thinkin'?" She sighed and once again looked out at the vast Atlantic. She never should have allowed it to happen again. She should have stayed in Dublin after…

She heard the footsteps on the stone path and knew who it was before she spoke. Her heart raced and her mouth instantly went dry.

"Hello, Branna."

Branna closed her eyes as Reagan's soft voice pulled at her heart. She took a deep breath and clenched her fists to stop her hands from shaking. She turned around and smiled.

"Hello, Reagan," she said, trying to avoid Reagan's crooked smile and deep blue eyes. She still wore that damned old sweater, Branna thought.

Reagan took a step toward her then stopped and jammed her hands deep into the pockets of her wool slacks. She absently kicked at the green turf beneath her worn work boots.

Branna raised an eyebrow. Same old boots as well. "How did

you know I was back?" She stood and leaned against the stone wall, folding her arms across her chest.

"I had a feeling," Reagan answered. She looked at Branna and grinned. "All right, then. I just came from Kathleen. She told me you were back."

Branna hid her smile as she lowered her head. Reagan closed the distance between them; still Branna concentrated on the ground.

"Why did ya come back?" Reagan asked.

"K-Kathleen wired me in Dublin. She said she wasn't feeling too well. So I thought I'd come back."

"Is that the only reason? It would help if you would look at me, Branna."

Branna looked up when she heard the teasing voice. She gave Reagan a defiant glare. "Yes, Reagan Shaunessy, it is. Kathleen, if you've noticed, can't move as well as she used to. She needs me."

"She's not the only one," Reagan said, and stepped closer.

Branna immediately walked away and faced the ocean. She heard the deep sigh from Reagan but said nothing.

"Well, did ya enjoy your little trip back to the big city?"

"Yes, I did. And I'd still be there if—"

"Yes, yes, if Kathleen didn't need you. By God you're a stubborn woman."

"I'm not stubborn, and don't start this again with me," Branna said and brushed the windswept raven hair away from her face.

Reagan watched her and grinned. "You're still as feisty and as beautiful as ever. And you still have the devil of a temper."

Branna glared at her and took a deep patient breath. Reagan kept grinning. "You look lovely."

Branna snorted sarcastically. "I wish I could say the same of you. Must ya wear that old sweater?"

Reagan cocked her head. "What else should I wear in this weather, working the farm? And what do ya care what I'm wearin'?"

"I don't," Branna said too quickly.

Reagan raised an eyebrow. "Perhaps just a wee bit?"

Branna glared at her once again. "You're full of yourself, Reagan Shaunessy."

"And you're not?"

Branna ran her fingers through her hair in an exasperated gesture and turned away from Reagan. She then felt Reagan's hands on her shoulders and fought the overwhelming urge to lean back into her strong embrace.

"I love you, Branna," Reagan whispered close to her ear. "Tell me don't want me to hold you like this." She reached in and swept the long black hair away from her neck and placed a light kiss there.

Branna shivered as she felt Reagan's soft lips; she closed her eyes, remembering not too long ago when they lay in each other's arms after their lovemaking. Reagan gently held her, murmuring words of love as she was now.

She felt Reagan's body press into hers; a moan escaped from deep within. She quickly cleared her throat and pulled away.

"I suppose ya don't," Reagan said in a resigned voice.

"I have to get back to the cottage," Branna said when her voice was steady enough. With her back still to Reagan, she went on. "Kathleen will need breakfast soon and—" She stopped and turned around to see Reagan walking down the stone path.

She said nothing as she watched Reagan's tall figure disappear over the grassy hill. She sat on the stone wall in a dejected heap and put her hands to her face, trying desperately not to cry.

Why couldn't she tell Reagan what she felt deep in her heart? Perhaps Branna didn't even know. However, she knew one thing was certain; Reagan Shaunessy was in her blood whether she wanted her there or not.

They were so young when Reagan professed her love for Branna. Branna was overwhelmed, but what was she to do? She was on her way to college in Dublin. Though she knew little of love, she made love to Reagan that night, and then she left her.

She took a quivering breath and walked back to the cottage. Stealing a glance back, she didn't know if she wanted to see Reagan coming after her or not. She continued down the narrow path.

3

Kathleen smiled as she gazed at the group of islands off the coast of Ireland. *All those years ago.* She took a deep tired breath and looked back at the thatched cottage that had been their home for nearly sixty years. She was grateful she had someone to repair the thatching and paint the cottage to keep it as it was when they first found it. She was grateful Branna had come back from Dublin after she wired her.

Her body ached horribly that morning; she let out a painful groan as she stood by the stone wall. Pulling the shawl around her shoulders, she closed her eyes as the ocean breeze blew through her silver hair. The fragrance of her beloved heather was in the air. Kathleen glanced up at the hill and could almost see her.

Kathleen heard her whistling and opened the Dutch door. Seana came up the cobblestone walk and Kathleen laughed. "Good heavens, what are you doin'?"

Seana grinned, her arms full of purple heather. "Woman of the house. You're finally awake. Where's my breakfast?"

Kathleen put her hands on her hips. "You can't keep taking the heather from the fields, darlin'—"

Seana gave her an incredulous look as she kissed her deeply. "There's so much in that field, I could gather it for you for the next fifty years and it would never be missed," she assured her.

Kathleen reached up and cupped her face with both hands. "Would you gather heather for the next fifty years?"

Seana smiled affectionately, her deep blue eyes rimming with tears. "No, not fifty years, Kath... Forever," she vowed and turned her face to kiss the palm of Kathleen's hand.

Kathleen smiled and leaned heavily on her cane as she noticed Branna slowly walking toward her. By her dejected posture, Kathleen knew she had seen Reagan. She shook her head. "Oh, those two."

Branna smiled as she approached. "Good morning, Kathleen."

"Good morning," Kathleen said. "Did you have a nice walk?"

Branna nodded but said nothing. Kathleen raised an eyebrow.

"And did ya see Reagan?"

"Yes," Branna answered. "I don't expect to be seeing her too soon."

"Don't count on it," Kathleen said and motioned with her cane.

Branna turned to see Reagan on horseback galloping down the path.

"Damn that woman," Branna said and quickly scooted by Kathleen.

Kathleen shook her head as Branna dashed into the cottage. "Two young idiots."

Reagan pulled the black horse to a halt a few feet away from Kathleen and dismounted. "Good day, Kathleen," Reagan said.

Kathleen noticed the heather that Reagan gathered and dropped; she was now cursing under her breath and she picked up the wayward purple sprigs.

"For me?" Kathleen asked and leaned on her cane.

Reagan shot her head up and blushed. "I...Well..." her voice trailed off.

"Branna's inside," Kathleen said.

Reagan walked up to her and kissed her cheek. "Thank you."

Kathleen put a hand on Reagan's cheek. "Don't give up."

Reagan nodded and took a deep confident breath and took her cap off. "How do I look?" she asked in a nervous voice.

"Like you're about to faint. Go on with ya," Kathleen said and prodded her along with her cane. She watched as Reagan walked up the cobblestone path to the cottage and opened the door.

By the time Kathleen made her way to the door and walked in, she heard Reagan's voice booming out from the kitchen.

"You're gonna have to admit it one day, Branna O'Malley!"

"Don't be tellin' me what I have to do, Reagan Shaunessy!" Branna yelled back.

"Well, someone had better. Your high and mighty college education—"

"How dare you! I'd rather be educated than have dirt under my fingernails," Branna said angrily, "from being a pig farmer!"

"They're not pigs! They're hogs!"

5

Kathleen, now sitting by the fire, sighed and shook her head. "Good heavens."

Reagan marched out of the kitchen. "Branna O'Malley is a stubborn, foolish woman, Kathleen," she announced. "Good day to you."

"Reagan," Kathleen said in a soft but firm voice. "Come here."

Letting out a deep angry breath, Reagan grudgingly walked over to Kathleen, who gently tapped the hearth with her cane. Reagan sat down without a word, her long legs stretched out in front of her.

Kathleen noticed the worn sweater and the dark trousers. She raised an eyebrow when she saw the muddied boots. Though she smiled inwardly, Kathleen sported a maternal glare as she looked into Reagan's deep blue eyes. "I've known you all your life. Are you tellin' me, after loving that woman in there for as long as I can remember, you're just going to leave?"

She was shocked to see tears well in Reagan's eyes as she ran her hand through her coal black hair. "I don't know what else to do," Reagan said in a quiet voice.

Kathleen said nothing as she took a tired breath.

"I can't make her love me, Kath."

"True enough. If she didn't love you, that is," she said and grinned. "Go on now. It's time Branna and I had a long talk. It's way overdue."

She prodded the sulking young woman with her cane. Reagan chuckled and shook her head. "Good luck to you with that," she said with a smirk, and walked out of the cottage.

Kathleen glanced over to the kitchen doorway and saw the dark head poke around the corner. "Is she gone?" Branna asked and walked into the living room.

"She is, and if you're not careful, Branna, one day she'll leave and won't come back," Kathleen said sternly and once again tapped her cane on the stone hearth. "Sit down."

"Kath—"

"Sit."

With a deep frown, the brooding young woman sat. Kathleen

smiled as she looked into the stubborn green eyes. Her dark curly hair hung around her shoulders as she swept it away from her face.

"You're a beautiful young woman, Branna—beautiful and intelligent."

"I like it so far," Branna said with a twinkle in her green eyes.

Kathleen narrowed her eyes and leaned forward on her cane. "But you have no heart, darlin'."

Branna leaned back, stunned. She was silent for a moment, then her bottom lip quivered. "That was an unkind thing to say."

"Perhaps, but it's been a long time comin'. I've watched you grow from a baby. You were always full of life and full of the devil, but you haven't let anyone close to your heart, darlin'."

Branna frowned deeply once again. "Just because I don't want to live around pigs—"

"Get over the pigs."

They both heard the baby cry from the other room. Branna sighed and stood. "That was a short nap." She walked past Kathleen and disappeared into the bedroom.

Kathleen quietly called over her shoulder, "You know what I'm saying."

After a moment, Branna came out with Rose, her two-year-old, on her hip. Kathleen smiled as she watched the sleepy child cling to her mother. Rose smiled when she noticed Kathleen. Branna laid Rose down on the couch and covered her with an afghan. She knelt beside her daughter and ran her fingers through the strawberry blond hair. "Go back to sleep, darlin'," she whispered and kissed her cheek.

Kathleen and Branna watched as Rose drifted back to sleep. Only then did Kathleen continue quietly, "You're an O'Malley. You come from passionate, loyal stock."

Branna sat on the hearth once again but said nothing.

"Women who lived and loved—hard at times," Kathleen conceded but went on, "but they gave their hearts for love."

"I know, I know. Aunt Seana told me bits and pieces of our ancestors."

Kathleen heard the dismissive tone in her voice. "If I didn't love you as my own, and think that under that superficial façade was a deep caring woman who was afraid of love, I'd tell you to pack your bags and go back to the city," Kathleen said with more anger than she intended. She stopped and took a deep breath. "I'm going to tell you the story of your Great Aunt Seana." She smiled widely. "Now there was a woman who loved. She loved her life. She loved her country, and she loved me."

She sat back and Branna leaned against the fireplace and waited.

"It was 1943. I'd just left Ireland to work, and found a job in Washington. It was unbelievable there during the war. The world was indeed on a collision course with Germany. There was something in the air. We all knew it, but had no idea what it was. I had no idea Seana would be in the thick of it."

The old officer studied the map of the British Isles. "How in God's name did Lieutenant Neely get his neck broken in a bog?" he asked himself as he puffed on his pipe.

A gentle knock at his door diverted his attention. "Come," he called out.

An officer walked briskly into the room. "Here are the files of the only two candidates, sir," he said and set the files in front of his commanding officer.

Major Jennings groaned. This war was taking its toll. Coupled with the last war, he had seen quite enough. He leafed through the first file and grunted. "No good, Lieutenant. He's got family," he said and tossed it aside. He looked at the other and shook his head. "Damn it... Not qualified." He ran a hand over his forehead and looked up at Lieutenant Bruckner.

"This is it?" he bellowed as there was a knock at the door. "Come," the major barked, and a private opened the door. He walked up to Lieutenant Bruckner and handed him a file.

"I'm sorry, sir. I think you forgot this on your desk." He saluted and made a hasty retreat.

Major Jennings stared at the file, then impatiently motioned for it. Bruckner hesitated and Jennings held out his hand.

"Give me that file." He snatched it from him. *Young whelp.* His eyes widened as he read the soldier's file aloud. "Sergeant S.M. Riordan enlisted three years ago. First in radio school. First in cryptography—speaks fluent French and German. Parents born in Ireland. Lived there for the past ten years," he fumed and turned bright red as he looked at Bruckner. "What in the fuck is the matter with you? Why didn't I see this soldier's file first?"

"Sir, please trust me. Sergeant Riordan is not right for this."

"Sit down, Lieutenant." He took a deep angry breath and pushed the button on his phone. "Get Sergeant S.M. Riordan in here immediately."

They sat silent, as the major glared at the lieutenant through his pipe smoke.

Bruckner let out a sigh of relief when he heard the knock at the door.

"Come," he said, never taking his eyes of the perspiring lieutenant.

Jennings looked up to see a woman standing before him. She was tall with jet-black hair bobbed below her ears. She was dressed in the green winter wool uniform.

"Sergeant Riordan, sir." She saluted.

He returned her salute and glanced at Bruckner, who gave him a sick "I tried to tell you, sir" look.

"S.M.?" he asked sadly.

"Y-yes, sir. Seana Marie," she responded cautiously.

"Sit down, Sergeant," he said. "Damn."

Riordan raised an eyebrow and glanced at Bruckner.

Jennings noticed the look of hatred from the sergeant toward his officer. He took an instant liking to her as he watched her; she was attractive, in very good shape, he thought. With her raven hair and deep blue eyes, she reminded him of someone, someone famous.

The sergeant smiled, and as if reading his mind, she offered, "Tyrone Power, sir."

Major Jennings turned beet red; yet, she was right. She looked like a female version of the Hollywood idol. "Damn," he said again. "I need you to be a man."

9

Seana raised an eyebrow. "Sir, I love my country and I would obey any order given. However, that one is out of my hands."

He chuckled and cleared his throat. He liked her; could this possibly work? "Sergeant, come here." He walked over to the big map; Seana followed and stood next to him.

Jennings watched her eyes darting back and forth. "So what are your thoughts?"

"Well, sir, I'm wondering why those the pins on the map are stuck in Germany and off the eastern coast of France." She pointed to another area on the map and looked at Jennings, who nodded and urged her to continue.

"This tiny strip of islands off the coast of Ireland—the Aran Islands. I've been there. Spent many summers on those islands when I was a young woman."

Jennings continued to watch in silence, as she looked at the map. "There have been several transmissions intercepted over the past few weeks. Something is happening. Am I correct, sir?"

"Continue, Riordan," he said. It was March 1943 and yes, something was happening, he thought.

"Well, we've avoided the conflict in Europe so far, but in the past few months, I've seen Generals Eisenhower and Marshall on a few occasions here in Washington." She stopped and took a deep breath as she looked at the Irish islands once again. "It looks like you've involved Ireland somehow," she said with a shrug.

He wasn't at all sure he should tell her. "Sergeant Riordan, we have a situation here—"

Behind them, Bruckner coughed. Seana ignored him, as did the major.

Jennings continued, "About six months ago, we had an operative stationed in a remote area of the Aran Islands. Now he's dead. Supposedly, he was drunk and fell into a bog."

Seana frowned deeply. "I've been on those islands. A bog, sir?"

He could tell she didn't believe it, either. This was another selling point in her favor. "That's the determination. It was a coincidence, however, that he was to transmit an important code, which we never received."

Seana frowned as she looked at the map. "How is it that Ireland let us use the islands? They're like Switzerland—neutral."

"Exactly," he said, happy to see she was keeping up. "A few years ago, the ambassador to the Court of St. James was—"

Seana grunted. "Joseph Kennedy, the pain in—" She stopped short and blushed horribly.

"Yes, he is. President Roosevelt feels the same way. That's why he appointed him. Unfortunately, he made some rather bad comments about the British and he wisely resigned. However, he is still very, very good with the Irish government. I'll give Joe Kennedy this, he got us in."

"To do what, sir?"

"Our operative was receiving and transmitting information from the French underground and from our people behind the German lines. You're right, Sergeant, there is something brewing. And it's imperative that we keep track of all the noise that's going on."

Seana listened and nodded. "Now that your man is dead, you need someone to take his place."

"Yes, however, I need an officer, and I thought you were a..."

"Man," she added dejectedly and shook her head. She started to say something, then stopped.

Jennings smiled slightly as he relit his pipe, watching her struggle. "Something you wanted to say, Sergeant Riordan?"

"May I be frank, sir?"

Bruckner coughed, seemingly trying to interrupt them—he may as well have been invisible.

"Speak, Sergeant," Jennings said firmly.

"Sir, who do you think is taking care of the home front while the men are fighting? Who's working in the factories, making the parts that build the tanks, ships, guns, and planes? Who then works these arduous shifts only to go home, pay the bills, and keep the house? Take care of the kids, sleep for a few hours and start it all over again—no complaining, no bitching. Who does all these things? All the things that men do and more? However, God forbid, don't give them a gun. Don't let them fight. Well, I'll tell you, Major, some of us want to fight. Some of us can mix it up with the men and get the job done. But in the end, it's up to the men to decide," she said angrily. "This war is changing the world, sir. It's changing everyone." Seana looked out the window. "I'm sorry if I'm out of line, but I'm not sorry for my opinion."

"I agree completely with you, Sergeant. However, I cannot allow a woman to go into harm's way."

Seana didn't even want to look at Bruckner, who was preening like a cat. Jennings then saw her smile. He cocked his head. "Riordan?"

"Major Jennings, I'll make you a deal. You give me until 0700. If my idea doesn't work, I'll go back and stay lost in the steno pool." She glared at Bruckner. "But if you agree, I get my commission and I go."

Bruckner snorted sarcastically. Jennings put up his hand to quiet him, all the while looking at Seana. He stuck out his hand and she took it, giving it a healthy pump. "Deal, Sergeant Riordan. I'm not sure what your idea is, but you have until tomorrow morning at seven."

Seana dashed down to Supply. "I need an officer's uniform, no insignia yet. Winter greens, trousers, jacket and shirt, tie, the works. Size ten," she said, and the supply clerk scurried to gather all Seana required.

Seana impatiently rapped her knuckles on the counter as the clerked hurried. She tossed the money down, struggled into her long coat, and grabbed the bundle and dashed out into the late Washington afternoon. She hailed a cab and gave the Georgetown address.

Chapter 2

Kathleen put the chicken in the oven and set the timer. Pushing the long red curls off her forehead, she took the apron off and glanced at the clock—5:00. Seana would be home soon, she thought. Her mind wandered back to when they first met.

Kathleen sat at the bar, feeling lonely, alone, and a long way from Ireland as she sipped her drink.

"It can't be that bad," a woman's voice said from behind her.

Kathleen turned to see a tall woman holding a bottle of beer. Her hair was black as coal and a lock of the thick mane hung helplessly over her brow. Her deep blue eyes sparkled as she smiled.

"You never know. There's a war on, I hear tell," Kathleen said in a light Irish brogue.

The tall woman, dressed in an Army uniform, grinned widely. "A fellow Irishman, and a native. Excellent."

Kathleen was instantly attracted to Seana, and she didn't know why. They became fast friends, and a month later, Seana told her she was a lesbian. For some reason, Kathleen didn't seem to mind; she didn't know the answer to that one, either. It was confusing. Then it happened: Two months after that, they became lovers. It had been a comfortable, erotic, and wonderful seven months.

The sound of the front door thrown open had Kathleen jumping.

"Kath, where are you?" Seana's happy voice called out.

Kathleen walked out into the living room to see her raven-haired beauty kicking off her shoes, shedding her coat, and unzipping her skirt. "Damn. I hate skirts," she declared as she disrobed in the living room.

"Seana, darlin', why don't you undress in the bedroom?" she asked as she picked up the shoes.

Seana paid no mind as she opened Kathleen's sewing box and picked up the scissors, flexing them maniacally.

"What on earth are you doin'?"

"I'll explain later. Right now, I gotta cut my hair," Seana said, and headed for the bathroom.

"Oh, God, it's happened. The Army has finally sent you around the bend. You've cracked."

Seana rolled her eyes and dragged her along. "Don't be a dope. C'mon, cut, cut."

Twenty minutes later, Seana liked what she saw in the mirror. Kathleen stood behind her and had to agree. "But it is short, darlin'."

Seana didn't care. Her hair now was short, full on the top, she couldn't help that; her hair was so thick. However, it was cut close to her neck and shorter around the sides.

"I like it. You did a good job." Seana turned to her redheaded lover and kissed her deeply, then let her go. "Now scoot, let me shower and I'll fill you in." She slapped Kath's backside on the way out.

Kathleen sat at the kitchen table after dinner and watched Seana as she cleared the dishes. *She is a handsome woman.* The haircut seemed to transform her. She was humming as she placed the dishes in the sink. She seemed freer. Kathleen raised an eyebrow as she watched her hips. Dressed in wool trousers and a dark green blouse, Seana Riordan was a striking picture. Her raven hair was still thick and wavy and her deep blue eyes, shrouded by thick lashes, gave her a sleepy, sensual look. It was her smile, however, that filled Kathleen's heart.

"Do you like being a woman?" she asked casually.

Seana turned to her and smiled. "Yes, I do. I don't want to be a man, if that's what you're thinking, sweetie. I love my gender, although, I cannot abide the skirts and girdles. I love my masculine side, as well as the feminine," she said seductively and sat across from Kathleen.

Seana saw the blush on Kathleen's face and knew what she was thinking. "Come here," she said and pushed her chair back.

Kathleen stood between her legs. Seana wrapped her arms around her waist and pulled her close as Kathleen buried her hands in the thick short mane.

"Sampson and Delilah?" she inquired as she tugged on the wavy hair.

"My strength is not in my hair," she said and pulled her close. "I love the feel of you." Seana sighed, and Kathleen pulled her head close to her breast. Seana reached up and unbuttoned the top of her dress and leaned in. "God, Kath," she murmured against her neck as she nibbled her way farther down, hastily undressing her.

Finally, Kathleen struggled out of the top of her dress, damning the belt. She fumbled with the belt, and Seana pushed her hands away.

"Later," she ordered and took her heaving breast into her mouth and suckled the hard nipple. She then slid her hands down Kathleen's waist and around the back where she grabbed hold of the soft cheeks and pulled her close. Slowly, she lifted the wool dress up to caress the silky undergarments. She smiled inwardly as she kissed Kathleen's breasts, her tongue lazily gliding over the swollen nipple. She pulled the silky undergarments down, letting them slip to the floor, where Kathleen stepped out of them.

"No girdle. That's my Kath." Seana looked up and winked. Kathleen laughed and ruffled her hair. The scent of this redheaded woman wafted up to Seana's nostrils, and all at once, she was ravenous. "Damn, I want you badly," she said in a low voice as she swept the coffee cups out of the way and lifted Kath onto the table, pushing up her skirt.

"Yes, Seana." Kathleen sighed, then cried out as she felt Seana's cool tongue, swiping its way up her inner thigh.

Within a moment, Kathleen was panting and moaning. "Seana, I'm…" She stopped as her body tensed.

"No, sweetie. Not yet."

Kathleen moaned as Seana turned her over and tossed her skirt above her waist. She gasped openly. This was something new. She knew Seana's eroticism had little boundaries—she was crossing one now. It filled Kathleen with anticipation as she balanced herself on her elbows. She parted her legs as Seana stood between them; Kathleen sighed as she felt the wool slacks against her nakedness. "Seana," she moaned helplessly.

Seana leaned over her back and kissed her flawless white skin. "Incredible," she murmured against her back, sending shock waves through Kathleen with every burning kiss. Seana reached her hands around and cupped both breasts. Kneading and tweaking the already sensitive area, Kathleen involuntarily bucked her hips back into Seana. "Was there something you wanted?" Seana whispered, leaning over her, pressing her body against her.

Kathleen groaned and lifted her head and turned, wiping the red hair away from her face. "Seana, please," she almost whimpered, and Seana reached down and stroked the small of her back, across her white hips. Kathleen moaned deeply as she felt Seana's warm fingers slide between her cheeks, stopping by the puckered muscle. Every nerve ending in her body shot through her as she tried to control her trembling. She felt Seana's fingers toying and rubbing around the area, sending her heart rate off the charts. "What are you doin to me?" she asked, her voice a mere whisper.

"Pleasuring you," Seana said against her back. She slid her hand farther down, her fingers saturated with the love that was flowing from her. She easily slipped one finger in, then as she felt Kathleen's warm inner wall expand, she added another.

In long smooth strokes, Seana loved her, controlling the very breath she was gasping. Murmuring her name, Kathleen couldn't believe she was being loved in this sensual way. She bucked her hips into Seana's hand as her body broke into a glorious orgasm.

Seana quickened her stroke, and once again, Kathleen's body stiffened and she came. Seana slowed her rhythm, bringing her slowly, then quickly, controlling her body, until Kathleen could take no more. "No, please, enough."

"Not quite," Seana said in a low voice, her breath too was

ragged; she was amazed that she was completely aroused, nearing her own orgasm without even being touched. She never experienced this with any other lover. She had never loved another, she thought as her heart pounded in her chest.

She took her hand away from Kathleen's breast and encircled her waist, pulling her hips off the table. All the while, her fingers slowly worked within her. Then she reached between Kathleen's legs and touched the engorged clitoris.

Instantly, Kathleen screamed, her walls tightened around Seana's hand as she delved as deep as she could. The orgasmic wave swept through her body.

Finally, she collapsed on the table, completely spent. Her breathing was nonexistent as she felt Seana remove her hand. Kathleen felt an instant loneliness—what control this woman had over her, Kathleen would never be able to comprehend.

Seana carried her into the bathroom as Kathleen rested her head on her shoulder. "I can't move," she whispered, her body still tingling. She reached in and kissed Seana's neck, tasting the saltiness of her perspiration.

Seana set her on the edge of the tub and started the hot bath. "How do you do this to me?" Kathleen asked and tried to unbuckle the dress. She sat there, her upper body naked.

Seana chuckled. "I don't know, actually," she said, confused, as well. She'd never felt this much passion for any woman before. "Here, let me." She finished undressing her.

Kathleen slipped into the hot steamy tub and sighed, leaning back. "You're going to do yourself an injury one day, carrying me like that." She sighed. "Join me."

Seana slowly disrobed as Kathleen watched. Her heartbeat quickened as Seana stood there naked, her tall muscular body glistening from the steam of the bathroom. "Wait. Just let me look for a moment."

Seana smiled and stood there. "Okay, woman. I'm freezing." She slipped in the tub in front of Kathleen, who instantly pulled her back against her breasts. She soaped up the cloth and ran it over Seana's strong but wonderfully soft shoulders and neck.

Seana laid her head against her breast. "Ah, Kathleen, I love the feel of you. You have the softest breasts, much softer and fuller than mine."

Kathleen slipped her arms under Seana's and ran the soapy cloth over her breasts, evoking a gasp from her raven-haired beauty. "It's because you spend so much time at the gym. Don't worry, luv, someday you'll be saggin' with the rest of us."

She dropped the cloth and encircled her waist, kissing the back of her neck. Seana sighed at the feel of her warm lips, seeking and finding that one spot that sent an electric shock down her spine.

"Found it," Kathleen murmured against her neck.

Seana moaned deeply. "Yes. Yes, you did."

Seana was the first woman Kathleen experienced. At first, she was tentative and not sure if she could please Seana. Then as she gained confidence with love and trust, her lovemaking nearly sent the experienced Seana Marie Riordan into convulsions.

Kathleen reached down and, with both hands, caressed between Seana's legs. Seana jumped and sent the water sloshing around.

"Kath," she whispered helplessly.

"Just lay back, darlin," Kathleen murmured into her ear.

Just the sound of her voice instantly aroused Seana once again. Her throbbing grew as the insistent fingers stroked and rubbed. Kathleen had every finger teasing until finally she parted the folds and captured her clitoris between her thumb and two fingers.

"Yes, Kath. God, your touch," Seana moaned and held onto the sides of the tub for dear life.

Seana arched and cried out Kath's name as her body broke into an orgasm that sent the water over the sides of tub. Finally, her body could take no more and she pulled Kathleen's hands up and held them against her breasts. "God, woman."

"Well, you've no one to blame but yourself. You taught me that one." Kathleen kissed her neck.

"You're a quick study. Eddie will be pleased," she said and winced, instantly wanting to take it back. In their time together, they talked little of the soldier who wanted Kathleen. Kathleen didn't know what she wanted. She thought it best not to lead Eddie on, but she was so confused now. Who did she want? Seana or Eddie, who was now fighting in the South Pacific.

They sat in the lukewarm water, saying nothing. They both knew the inevitable. Well, Seana knew. Not being a lesbian, Kathleen would someday find a man and that would be it. It was a tremendous seven months, however.

"Seana," Kathleen started, and Seana stood and stepped out of the tub.

She offered her hand. "C'mon, Kath, we're getting pruney and we need to talk."

Talking was not an option. They lay entwined in each other's arms sometime later. Kathleen rested her head on Seana's chest, her flowing red hair covering Seana's breasts and stomach. Kathleen was amazed at how moments before, Seana tenderly made love to her—quite a contrast to the erotic kitchen episode earlier. This was different. This was love, not sex. That worried Kathleen. "Tell me now. Why did you cut your hair?" Kathleen said sleepily.

Seana told her about her meeting with Major Jennings and explained the predicament. Kathleen listened, lazily swirling her fingers around Seana's breast. "I can't concentrate when you touch me like that."

Kathleen grinned, loving how she controlled this confident woman. She reluctantly stopped. She listened as Seana finished her explanation. "Is that why you cut your hair? Seana, darlin', that'll never work. I agree you look like that Tyrone Power actor fella, but pass as a man?"

"No. I don't think it'll come to that. I just wanted to let him know I can do this. I-I need to feel a part of this war," she tried to explain.

Kathleen reached up and put her fingers against her lips. "I know. You're a good American. You want to be a part of it, and I understand and lo… admire you for it." *Why couldn't I say I love you?* "Where would they send you?"

"I can't tell you that, honey. Well, I could, but then I'd have to kill you," she said seriously.

There was silence for a moment, then both broke into laughter.

"When would you be leavin'?"

"If I get it, probably right away. Kath, look. I just—"

Kathleen sat. "Don't. Don't be telling me that 'this may be our last night together.' Don't do that, Seana Riordan." She cried, then cursed the tears that welled in her green eyes.

Seana reached over and flipped on the light. "Please, don't cry. We both knew this wasn't going to last forever. You and I, well, we have a different idea of love and marriage," she said, and waited for a response. She knew if she stayed any longer with this fiery redhead, she'd fall in love, if she hadn't already.

"I-I don't know if I can live the life you do. I've loved the past seven months," she said, then stopped.

Seana reached over and turned off the light. She then lay back, pulling Kathleen into her embrace. "Sleep, Kath. Who knows, I probably won't get this assignment."

Kathleen heard the disappointment in her voice. She knew Seana Riordan very well. She got what she wanted. Seana had told her once she came from a long line of independent O'Malley women. She heard stories of Seana's ancestors. The O'Malleys who fought for their family—who found their place in the world in which they lived. Strong, brave women, like her great-great aunt Quinlan Stoddard, who helped African slaves before the American Civil War. To Seana, this woman was a goddess, a warrior fighting for what was right. Kathleen smiled, thinking how Seana Riordan was the same way. She loved her country and would fight in any way she could. Kathleen was proud and petrified.

Kathleen held her close, listening to her strong steady heart. With every beat, Kathleen felt Seana Riordan slipping away and becoming a memory.

Chapter 3

Dressed in the uniform, Seana stood in the bathroom and looked in the mirror. "It's got to work."

"I'll give you this. You do look good."

Seana turned to see Kathleen standing in the doorway. With her eyes still full of sleep, she swiped the red hair away from her face; she looked wonderful.

"Good morning," Seana said and wrapped her arm around her waist as they walked to the front door.

"Must you go so early? I wanted to make you breakfast. Now if they do send you straight away, can you call? If you can't—"

Seana's gentle kiss stopped her, and she felt Kathleen melt in her arms. Seana pulled back and smiled. "If I can, I'll call. Who knows, I may be back for dinner," she said, and they looked deep into each other's eyes.

Seana picked up her coat and Kathleen helped her into it; she smoothed the shoulders, then laid her head against her back. She turned Seana around and sported a smile that filled Seana's heart.

Seana smiled in return; everything she felt was expressed in that one smile.

"I loved every minute. Wouldn't change a thing. Not one moment," Kathleen said, desperately trying not to cry.

"Let me go, Kath. Kiss me once, then let me go."

Kathleen kissed her deeply, lovingly. Seana pulled her into a bone-crushing hug, returning her kiss. Then Kathleen did as Seana asked. She let her go.

Seana opened the door and before she changed her mind, was gone.

Kathleen reached for the doorknob, then stopped. She laid her hand against the door and sobbed.

Branna leaned forward, completely enthralled. "Kathleen, I never knew this. Aunt Seana never told me any of this. You must have been devastated," she said and rambled on, "I mean to be left like that and not knowing where she'd be—"

Kathleen held up her weathered hand. "Hold on, such impatience. Heavens, you are an O'Malley. Now I'm forgettin' where I was…" she said thoughtfully, then nodded. "Major Jennings was a good man."

Jennings once again stared at the map. If this worked, it would be a miracle, he thought. He heard the knock at his door.

"Come." He turned, and for an instant, didn't recognize her. Riordan smiled slightly as she saluted him.

He returned the salute. "Well, I'll tell you this, you are tenacious."

"Major, I can do this. This is what I've been trained for, sir. I know those islands. If I keep to myself, who knows? If I'm found out? Who will care? Only you know, and well, Lieutenant Bruckner," she finished and searched his face. "There's no one else and no time to train them. You know I'm right, sir."

He paced back and forth and realized she was right; he picked up the phone. "This is Major Jennings. It's a go," he said and hung up.

He then handed her a folded letter, which she took and read. He needed a levelheaded officer and was grateful she didn't start crying. He picked up a box and walked over to her and saw the confused look on her face. She accepted the box and opened it.

"Those were mine. I've been waiting to give them to a deserving officer," he said, and Seana took out the silver bars. The major took them from her and attached them to her collar.

"I see you're wearing an officer's uniform. Very gutsy, Lieutenant Riordan," he said and stepped back as they traded salutes. "I like guts. You're going to need them. Now don't disgrace those bars or they'll have my hide. If you do, I'll shoot

22

you myself," he said seriously. "Now come here."

Once again, they stood by the map. "You'll take a transport to Ireland. From there, they'll take you to the island. Your gear is already on the transport. It leaves in one hour. Now this is most important: Only Lieutenant Bruckner and I know you'll be our operative. You'll listen, decode, and transmit whatever you hear, French or German. It'll be transmitted to a sub we have cruising the North Atlantic. They'll transmit to us. You can only transmit at night when the sub can reach radio depth. Do this at 2300 each night." He handed her a leather pouch. "These are all the codes. We change them periodically, so as not to be decoded easily. Read them, memorize them."

He took his pipe out and watched her, waiting for some sign of resignation—one inkling that he made a bad decision. Lieutenant Seana Riordan showed no sign as she looked over the papers.

"How will I know my contact on the island?"

He smiled; she was cool and collected. "As you read, you'll see the code used between you. They'll see to it you have everything you need. As I said, a local has relatives on the island, so you should be safe enough. O'Fallon is their name, but you are not to go to them. Only if there's no other way off the island." He rubbed a hand over his tired face.

Seana watched him. "I can do this. I'm not worried."

"Are you scared?"

"Sure. I'm not an idiot...sir," she added and tried not to smile.

He smiled and lit his pipe. She'd be fine. He worried, though, about the death of Lieutenant Neely. "Lieutenant, I cannot emphasize enough your being cautious. I don't believe Neely died accidentally."

"I don't either, sir." Seana's mouth went a little dry.

"You must try and hold out your identity as long as you can. You may look like a man somewhat. We've told our people, who will meet you and have clothes for you. Enjoy that uniform while you can, Lieutenant," he said, and Seana nodded.

"Now you have no family. No one?" he asked.

"Well, there is someone, a-a friend. I know I won't be able to see her, but can I leave her a letter?"

He nodded and slid the paper and pen toward her. "I'll leave you. I'll take it to her myself," he said kindly, then walked out.

Seana sat there for a moment, then dipped the pen in the ink and scratched out a letter to the only woman she'd ever love and keep forever and hold at night for the rest of their lives.

A few moments later, the major walked back in, as Seana was about to seal the envelope. "I've made no reference as to where I'll be. She knows nothing."

"I have to read it, Lieutenant, security."

Seana winced, then figured all was lost. He'd never send her now.

He read it quickly and frowned. Taking a deep breath, he looked her in the eyes.

Defiantly, she looked back into the watery gray-blue eyes, waiting to be court-martialed.

"Seal it," he said as he handed it back to her.

"Thank you, Major," she said gratefully. She wanted to hug him.

He smiled slightly. "It's an upside-down world, Lieutenant Riordan. Women in slacks, working in factories." He sighed.

"Times are changing, sir." Seana sealed the envelope and handed it to him.

"All right. The jeep is waiting downstairs. It'll take you to the airfield. There will be no communication between us, except for the coded pre-arranged transmissions. Should you at anytime feel the need to vacate, do so. We don't want anything falling into the wrong hands. If all goes well, you should be there no more than five months. Destroy everything if need be, then get the hell out of there."

Seana nodded and shook the offered hand.

"If I had a daughter, I'd like her to be like you."

Seana smiled gratefully. Not all like me, she thought wickedly. "Thank you, sir. Could you, would you look in on her from time to time?" she asked and searched his face.

He smiled and nodded. "My pleasure, Lieutenant. Now get the hell out of here before you ask me to adopt her," he said gruffly.

"Get going. Be careful."

Seana walked out of the office, and as she walked down the corridor, she noticed Bruckner walking toward her. Hmm, she thought, she was on equal footing with him now. She stopped as he approached, the typewriters clinked away and the phones rang.

He stopped and looked at her, amazed at the difference. Then he saw the bars on her collar and turned a lovely shade of ash.

Seana put her thumb under the collar to present the bars. "Lieutenant Bruckner, you held me back for nearly two years because I wouldn't sleep with you, you miserable prick."

Smiling, she took a deep breath and happily walked down the stairs.

The typewriters stopped clicking. Even the phones went dead as all eyes were on Bruckner. He turned and faced them with a stony glare as they buried their heads in their work.

Seana glanced out the window, watching Washington fade beneath the clouds. The roar of the transport was deafening, yet she could hear the pounding of loss in her heart as the distance grew between her and Kathleen.

She lightly touched the cold window and whispered, "Goodbye, my adorable Kathleen."

Kathleen sat at the kitchen table, glancing from the phone to the clock. Seana would be coming home now, she thought as she looked outside.

"Twilight, Seana. Our favorite time," she said and closed her eyes and remembered the day.

They sat up on the roof of her brownstone. It was early November as they sat huddled together in the big chair. Drinking hot chocolate, Seana sighed. "I love this time of day."

Kathleen sat between her legs, cuddled against her. "Mmm. Me too, twilight. The gloaming, when the sun's nearly set and the stars are on the rise. The best of everything in one sky. Twilight's own magic."

Seana looked down at the redheaded woman, who was quickly

capturing her heart. "My, you have a way with the words, Miss Burke." She kissed the back of her head. She set her cup on the little table and put her arms around Kathleen's waist, pulling her against her body. "Twilight's own. The best of everything. That's you, Kath," she whispered, knowing she probably shouldn't be saying that much, but not caring.

Kathleen didn't answer at first. She didn't know how to react. She loved being with this woman. However, this was new to her. She didn't trust Seana or her own heart.

"I love—" she hesitated, "this time of day, as well," she whispered, then half turned, curling up in Seana's strong embrace.

Seana looked down through the gorgeous thick lashes and smiled. "You almost said you loved me," she said and grinned like a schoolgirl. Not waiting for Kath's reply, she lowered her head and kissed her, her hand wandering up to caress her soft cheek.

A knock at the door shook her from her reverie. Her heart raced as she jumped up to answer the door. She threw it open.

"Seana, darlin'," she exclaimed happily and stopped as she saw an older Army officer standing there, his eyebrows raised slightly as he removed his cap.

"Miss Kathleen Burke?"

Kathleen nodded, then stepped back. She knew he had come about Seana, and her heart sank.

"Lieutenant Riordan asked me to give this to you. I'm afraid it's my fault. She didn't have time to see you in person." He handed her the letter.

Kathleen took it with shaky hands, tears welling in her eyes. He had said, 'Lieutenant Riordan,' that meant only one thing. "I don't suppose you can tell me where she went."

He shook his head. "You're from Ireland?" he asked, trying to lighten the sadness.

"I am. The west, Aran Islands," she said, fingering the letter.

Jennings immediately frowned, but said nothing. Riordan would not have said anything to this woman. By the look of sadness on her face, he knew he was right.

26

She looked up and searched his face. "Thank you for bringing Seana's letter to me."

"You're welcome," he said awkwardly. "Well, I should be going. Please, try not to worry. She's a strong, self-reliant woman. She'll do fine," he said, smiling, and took her hand. "Goodbye."

"Goodbye, sir. Thank you for your kindness." She closed the door.

Consumed with a numb void feeling, Kathleen walked over to the table and opened the letter. Reading it twice, she wiped away the tears that flowed down her cheeks.

My Darling, Kathleen,

Please forgive me for not being able to see you. Such is this screwy world. I don't have much time, so I want to say this quickly... I love you. I have since the day we met. I know it's not the same for you. This war does indeed do strange things to us all. I need you to know that I've never known such peace and contentment.

Your Eddie is one lucky SOB. Please be happy.

I want you to do something for me. In the bedroom, in my top drawer, there is a cloth package. The note will explain everything, sweetheart.

I will always think of you at twilight... Remember? The best of everything. When I look to the heavens, I will remember you.... Twilight's own.

You were right. I too loved every minute. Wouldn't change a thing—not one moment.

Keep smiling, Kath... My Kath.

Always,

Seana

Kathleen's heart ached so badly, she clutched her chest and let out a heart-wrenching sob. She could barely move when she heard the knock at the door. Jennings stood in the doorway.

Kathleen gave him a questioning look as he glanced at the letter. "That's the way of it, Major Jennings," she said defiantly as she wiped away the tears. "Was there something else?"

"I understand. I am sorry. I thought perhaps, well, if there's anything I can do." He scribbled a phone number down and handed it to her. She smiled gratefully, taking the piece of paper.

After Jennings left, Kathleen sat for some time, blindly staring out the kitchen window into the darkness. Taking a deep sad breath, she walked into the bedroom. She opened the top drawer of the dresser and saw the cloth package and note; she took both and sat on the edge of the bed and opened the letter.

Dear Kathleen,

If you're reading this, it means I got the assignment and can't reach you. I'd like you to do me a favor, sweetheart. This is a family heirloom, a Tara brooch handed down from the O'Malley women you heard me talk about so often. My mother told me I was to give it to my daughter. I'd like you to have it. If something happens to me, please keep this. Marry Eddie, and when the time comes, give it to your daughter. That would please me very much.

You know I must do this. It's deep in my soul and I can't explain it. My grandmother told me once that I was like an ancient ancestor of ours. Branna O'Malley was her name. Apparently, she was some kind of warrior, hundreds of years ago. The story goes—she fought with sword in hand, protecting her love and her family, but you know how we Irish are, we love a good tale. I come from a long line of fighting women, it would seem, and I'm part of it. Please, understand.

I love you more than I can say. I thank Branna's gods and goddesses for the time we had together. Always be happy.

Seana

Kathleen wiped away the never-ending stream of tears. Warrior women, she thought and shook her head. "I had to fall in love with a warrior." She sighed sadly.

She examined the gold pendant. It was indeed a Tara brooch, a circular pendant, with the staff of Tara bisecting it. It looked tarnished, but the blue and green gems around the gold circle still sparkled. She held the pendant between her palms and closed her eyes. Kathleen offered a prayer to God and to Branna's ancient gods and goddesses.

Chapter 4

Seana carried her duffel as she walked through the airfield and smiled slightly; she missed Ireland. It had been quite a while since she'd been back. The memories flooded her mind as she thought of times here with her parents. They were the happy times of her youth before life got in the way.

"Aran Islands are beautiful. Let me take your gear," a voice said from behind her.

Startled, Seana was angry with herself for daydreaming. She looked at the man and realized he couldn't be more that twenty, if that. She pulled her collar up around her neck. "Thanks."

"Jamie O'Fallon." He offered his hand. "This way."

Seana followed, hoping her ruse was working. Not wanting to enter into a conversation with this fellow, she gazed out the window as they drove to the coast.

"Nice weather for this time of year," he said absently.

"Yes, it is," Seana replied in a dismissive tone.

Nothing more was said, for which Seana was grateful. Finally, the driver took a narrow road that led to the seacoast where Seana noticed a fishing boat moored by the rocks. Without a word, she followed the driver the short distance down the beach.

"You can go below, there are clothes for you," Jamie said.

Seana nodded, went down in the cabin, and felt the gentle swaying of the boat as it started toward the islands. She noticed a pair of dark slacks, boots, and a light-colored shirt on the cot; she quickly changed. It was a cool March day, and she welcomed the heavy material. Slipping the big fisherman's sweater over her head, she looked at herself. Good fit, she thought; she could pass for a man in these bulky clothes.

Glancing in the mirror, she realized her thick hair might be a problem. She reached over, picked up an Irish wool cap, and pulled it down over her brow. "Better," she said, and put on the tweed coat, pulling the collar up around her neck.

She examined the leather pouch and looked up when she heard the cabin door open.

"Almost there," Jamie said. "You can leave the uniform. We'll take care of it."

Seana nodded, gathered the pouch, and walked out onto the deck.

The man at the helm steered the boat through rough waters. He looked over his shoulder and said, "It'll work if you don't get too close to someone. You can pass. It's your pretty smile that'll give you away."

Seana held onto the side; she smiled and closed her eyes as she took in the fresh salt air. "Thanks. I'll remember that."

"All your gear is up at the hut already," Jamie said with a smile.

There was something about his smile, Seana thought. His blue eyes sparkled as he took off his cap, revealing a thick mop of reddish hair. He motioned to the man at the helm. "That's Brian."

Seana took his hand as Jamie continued, "Once we get you there, you won't be seeing us till it's time for you to leave. For whatever reason."

"I understand."

They beached the boat and headed up the sandy shore. She looked up at the top of the craggy hill.

"I suppose that's it." She looked at the dangerous climb.

"Well, you weren't expectin' it to be right on shore?" he asked, and the older man laughed.

It took them the better part of two hours to get to the top, then around the rocky passage to the other side. Seana looked back, amazed at how far they had come. The hut was nestled into a grove of trees, partially hidden.

"It's not all that far, just these bloody rocks," Brian said. "It's a perfect spot. Too high for someone to come nosin' around and high enough for all your wireless gear."

Seana nodded breathlessly, not sure if it was from the climb or the anxious feeling in the pit of her stomach. "I've been here before. Long ago. Never this high, though." She looked out at the expanse of the Atlantic. She looked westward—home, she thought, and Kathleen.

"Well then, it's getting dark and I don't want to break my bloody neck on the way down. You're all set and on your own. Good luck," Brian said. "Between you and me, I hope that little Hun bastard burns in hell."

Seana watched as they started down the hill; in a few minutes, they were out of sight. She opened the heavy wooden door and cautiously walked in to the cabin, or more appropriately, the hut.

It smelled musty and damp as she closed the door, and she noticed several kerosene lanterns. She lit one and took inventory of her new home. In all, it was one big room. To the right was a stone fireplace with a big chair in front of it and a side table next to that. On the opposite wall was a desk with a chair. The wireless was already there, waiting to come to life. She assumed Jamie had set it up for her. Next to that was a cot; it could hardly be called a bed.

Beyond that was an old wood-burning stove and a sink with a well-water pump. "Indoor water. That's a plus."

A kitchen table and two chairs situated in the middle of what was supposed to be the kitchen rounded off the room. No back door—one window over the sink and one over the desk. Seana gazed down at the floor; it was made of uneven concrete slabs.

It was…a hut.

She concentrated on her first task and checked out the supplies. She opened one cabinet and found it stocked with canned goods. The other cabinet stored the flour, sugar, and salt, along with three brown bottles with cork stoppers. She took one bottle and peered at the liquid inside. "Hmm," she said and popped open the cork. The heady aroma of whiskey nearly cleared her sinuses. She replaced the cork and set the bottle back with the others.

An hour later, Seana had the place cleaned and organized. Her sleeves rolled up, she looped her fingers in her suspenders and smiled happily. "Now it looks livable."

She had found enough peat bricks to start a fire. Taking a gentle whiff, the pungent aroma filled her senses, instantly bringing her back to her younger years. If there was one thing Ireland had more of than Guinness, it was peat bogs.

Seana glanced at her watch; it was nearly eight in the evening. Her stomach growled and she was exhausted, but she had to get the wireless up and running. Within the hour, Seana had the radio humming and squealing as she flipped through the pages of the leather pouch, looking for the correct frequency. Finding it, she smiled confidently as the French cryptic message came over the wireless.

After opening a can of peaches with her pocketknife, she put on the headphones, sat back, and listened. She decoded what she could, and at exactly eleven o'clock, she tuned into the correct frequency and transmitted to the sub using Morse code.

When she was finished, she took off the earphones and sat back, proud of herself that she could be a part of this war. She stood and stretched as she took the two steps to the cot, collapsed on her stomach, and fell into an exhausted sleep.

Her boss watched Kathleen at her desk, staring at the typewriter. She walked over and leaned against the desk. "Okay, Irish. What gives? You're my best stenographer and you haven't steno'ed in over a week," she joked.

Kathleen looked up at her and sighed. "I'm sorry, Helen. I can't concentrate."

Helen gave her a wary look. "Where's that Army friend of yours? She hasn't been around."

"She's been transferred," Kathleen said almost angrily.

"Can't you call her?"

"No. I don't know where they sent her. She worked in Washington."

Helen noticed how close she was to crying. "C'mon. I need coffee." She pulled Kathleen up.

They sat in the cafeteria, Kathleen drinking a Coke and Helen watching her carefully. There'd been talk around the water cooler about Kathleen and this Army sergeant. Helen never liked talk; she liked the truth. Helen noticed the pendant Kathleen wore on the lapel of her wool blazer.

"That's beautiful. Where did you get it?" Helen asked. Kathleen blushed deeply. "You care for her, don't you?"

"I—" Kathleen took a deep breath and nodded. "Yes, I do. More than I ever thought possible."

Helen raised a curious eyebrow. "Really?" she said in quiet astonishment. "Hmm. And did you tell her this?" Helen asked in motherly fashion.

Again, Kathleen's face turned the same shade of red. "N-no. I, well, that is, we… I mean, Seana is so confident, and I… Well, there's Eddie," she stammered helplessly, and Helen winced, trying to keep up.

"Who's Eddie?" she asked, completely confused. She thought for an instant. "Not that goof with the—"

Kathleen shot her a defiant look.

"I mean, not that young man with the—" She stopped, noticing how nicely her foot seemed to slip into her mouth, shoe and all. She cleared her throat.

"Oh, I don't know. She told me she loves me," Kathleen said loudly and threw up her hands in a helpless gesture.

Helen grimaced and looked around. "Shh. You wanna get us both fired?"

Kathleen gave her a curious look. "Why? Why could we be fired? What difference does it make?" she whispered, answering her own question. To some, it did matter very much.

"Hey, Irish, I don't care, but some do. I don't want to see anything happen to you. If they transferred her, maybe it's for the best," she offered in a soft voice.

Kathleen sat there, staring out the window. It'd been almost two weeks and no word. She really didn't expect to hear anything. Perhaps it was for the best.

For the next three weeks, Seana did her job. Listening, decoding, transmitting—listening, decoding, transmitting. She could do it in her sleep.

On a foggy April morning, she decided to go for a walk. She threw on her coat and cap, pulling it down over her brow, and headed out.

As she walked the path that led away from the hut, Seana looked out over the Atlantic, toward home—toward Kathleen. A pang of loneliness came over her as she dug her hands deep into her trouser pockets and continued down the dirt path. The rugged landscape looked barren and lonely, but to Seana, there was a wild romantic feel to it. She thought of Kathleen, who had lived here, as well. Seana pictured her roaming the craggy hills, tending sheep, her red hair blowing in the breezes.

"It's going to rain, you better get back."

Seana heard the voice behind her and whirled around to see a tall woman standing there. She wore a tweed shawl draped over her head. She was smiling, her white skin contrasted against her long black hair.

Those eyes, Seana thought. They were almost black, but they sparkled wildly. She was annoyed with herself that she had not heard this woman approach. Seana was new at this, but she must be more aware of her surroundings. She didn't want to end up like Lieutenant Neely.

"I don't mind the rain," Seana said, pulling the collar up and the cap down on her brow.

The woman, almost as tall as Seana, cocked her head and glanced at her up and down. "I don't know you, sir," she said, and casually looked around. "Do you know the islands?" Before Seana could respond, the woman looked her in the eyes. "The curlews are nesting."

Seana stared at her, and her heart stopped. Without missing a beat, she answered the code. "Not by the shore," she said evenly.

The woman nodded and smiled. "Maura Flynn." She held out her hand.

Seana reached for it and gave it a manly pump. "Lieutenant Riordan. Nice to meet you."

"Walk with me, Lieutenant," she said in a thick Irish brogue.

They walked down the dirt road side by side. Seana noticed

she was wearing the type of dress that all the island Irish women wore. Long, flowing, almost ankle length, with a white apron. Her light gray wool blouse was tucked in; she removed her shawl, and now her black hair fell across her shoulders.

"Have you got enough supplies?"

"Could use eggs if you've got 'em."

"I'll see what I can do. I'll be stopping up every week or so. Don't contact me. Don't come to town much. You're better off. The less you're seen, the less there'll be questions. How long are you here for?" she asked as she stopped.

"Don't know. They'll let me know," Seana said, pulling the collar up, partially hiding her face.

Maura gave a wary grin. "You're a shy one. Are all Yanks as shy as you?"

Seana glanced from beneath her cap at this attractive woman. "Nope."

Maura was intrigued. "I'd better be goin'. I'll see about the eggs. Good day, Lieutenant Riordan," she said and smiled.

Seana nodded and turned. "Good morning, Miss Flynn," she said over her shoulder and walked up the path.

As she opened the door to the hut, she smiled and said, "Very pretty," as she tossed her cap on the desk and ruffled her hair.

As the weeks dragged on, Seana continued the transmissions. She saw the beautiful Miss Flynn on several occasions—and she got her eggs.

Maura Flynn intrigued Seana; perhaps it was because she was part of this, in a way. Perhaps it was those dark eyes; there was something about her, though.

One April afternoon, Seana was outside the hut, stacking the endless pile of peat bricks to dry for her fireplace. She liked the work; keeping herself in shape on this little island was not easy. She knew every rock and path up and down the craggy hill.

The sun was shining as she ran her arm across her forehead to mop away the sweat as she continued to work.

"You're filthy," Maura's voice rang out.

Seana jumped, then pulled the cap back down on her forehead.

"I like to keep busy," she said, pulling the suspenders up and cursing for not wearing the jacket. She kept her back to Maura as she worked.

"I brought you a little something," she said. "Lamb stew and some homemade bread."

Seana's mouth instantly watered as she licked her lips. Maura walked past her, her hand lightly trailing over Seana's back. A shiver ran down her spine. "Damn," Seana cursed and followed her in.

"Wash up. I'll put this on the fire to heat," she said as she knelt by the glowing flames.

"Miss Flynn," she started.

Maura interrupted her. "Maura," she said over her shoulder.

"Maura, I appreciate this, but—"

"Lieutenant Riordan, you have to eat," she said and walked up to Seana, smiling wickedly. "You're a handsome—"

Before she could react, Maura reached out and took her cap and tossed it on the cot. She looked back at Seana and her eyes widened. "Woman!"

Seana grabbed her by the arm and dragged her to the door. "Thank you. I'd appreciate it if you kept that information under your shawl," she said sarcastically. "I've got a job to do."

Maura wrenched her arm free. "They sent a woman?" she asked and gave Seana the once-over. "Well, you fooled me," she said and nervously put her hand to her throat as she realized what she had almost done.

Seana knew it, as well. She'd done enough flirting in her time to know when it was being done to her. "That was the plan. Now, please, thank you for the stew."

"Lieutenant," she said and stopped. "You are an officer, right?"

Seana nodded and smirked. "But not a gentleman."

Maura walked over to the kitchen chair and sat down.

"Maura," Seana warned seriously.

"Well, I'll be." She sighed with amazement. "Wash up. I'll get dinner ready. Your secret is safe with me," she said, ending the discussion.

The stew was heavenly. Seana ate two bowlfuls, then sat back. "Man that was good."

Maura smiled and cocked her head to one side. "Are you married, Lieutenant?"

"No. I'm not married," she said and smirked again.

Their eyes met and Maura raised a curious eyebrow. "I see. So that's the way of it, Lieutenant Riordan?" she asked, nodding as she understood.

Seana watched as Maura digested the new information. "Strange to you?"

She looked up and shook her head. "We're not all backward, you know," she said evenly. "I'm not anyway."

Maura rose and cleaned up the dishes. Seana's eyes got heavy as she yawned.

"You're exhausted, you need sleep."

"No. I've got a transmission to make."

Maura put on a shawl as Seana opened the door. "I'll be by now and again," she said. "Sir, darlin'," she added and left.

"Sir... darlin'?" Seana repeated as she closed the door.

When she wasn't listening to the wireless, Seana had time to think. She thought about Kathleen and how much she missed her and how much she loved her. She desperately tried not to think about it. Seana ached for her, and on several occasions, the ache got unbearable; self-satisfaction eased the ache temporarily.

She flipped once again through the brown leather pouch that Major Jennings had given her. She took out the page that had intrigued her the first time she read it.

Lt. Riordan,

If for any reason, you feel your assignment compromised, or you feel a breach of security, contact me, in the same way through the sub. However, use this code name: Scorpion.

Your transmission will be sent directly to me. No one else in this office will see it.

Once received, I will understand and do my best to get you out of there.

M.J.J.

Seana sincerely hoped she'd never have to use it. She put the letter in the fireplace and watched it slowly burn. Something made her shiver violently; she rubbed the back of her neck in response. She did not want the same fate as Lieutenant Neely, and she knew she needed to be more cautious. The next day, she'd find Maura and ask her about him. Perhaps she knew something.

Maybe he was drunk and broke his neck. Then again, maybe someone broke it for him.

Chapter 5

The hut was chilly and damp as Seana woke early as usual. As she rekindled the smoldering fire, she heard a noise outside the window. She moved away from the line of sight and looked out. It was Maura, walking by the back of the hut. Seana noticed she was looking around the area, as if trying not to be noticed. She walked to the other window and saw Maura heading to the front door.

The door opened and Seana positioned herself behind it. As Maura poked her head in, Seana grabbed her by the arm and pulled her in, slamming the door. Maura let out a cry as Seana pinned her against the wall.

She glared into her dark eyes. "What the hell are you doing?"

Maura struggled against her. "I was just..." She stopped and continued to struggle. She noticed Seana's shirt was opened nearly to the waist; she was not wearing anything underneath. She swallowed and Seana noticed her gaze but did not let her go.

"You were just what?" She tightened the grip on her arms.

"Let me go. I was seeing if you needed anything." She squirmed and leaned in closer. "Anything at all," she whispered, then leaned up and kissed her.

Seana gasped for a moment, then hungrily returned her kiss. Just as quickly, she pushed her away.

"I can see you need something, Lieutenant." She noticed Seana glance at her breasts.

"Make no mistake, Maura Flynn. I'm here to do a job, and that's it. I don't need any complications," she said seriously, then grabbed her and sat her at the kitchen table.

"Now I want to know everything about Lieutenant Neely," she said and loomed over her. "And I want to know right now."

"You've been told what happened. He came into the village, got drunk. It was a rainy, foggy night. He must have fallen headlong into the bog. You've seen it. It's over eight feet deep. In the fog, no one can tell," she said, looking her in the eye.

For a moment, her eyes faltered. Seana knew there was something behind those dark eyes. "You're lying and I mean to find out," Seana said, not sure if she should show her hand. "He was a trained operative. Getting drunk wasn't his style. I read his file. Something else happened that night." Seana walked over to the door and opened it. "Good day, Maura. Come back when you want to level with me."

Maura shot her an angry defiant look and left without saying a word.

Seana paced back and forth. Neely wouldn't go into the village and get drunk. Especially not on the night he was to send an important transmission. If someone indeed broke his neck, how would he know he was about to send something? If he were alone, as Seana is, how would anyone know? She stopped and looked out the window at the retreating figure of the shawl-covered beauty.

"An Irish Mata Hari?" Seana whispered. She'd find out.

That night, at twilight, Seana threw on her jacket and cap and ventured out for a night walk. About three miles south was the village of Dunmore. A few cottages spotted the hillside, and along the narrow road of the village was a store, a pub, of course, a post office, and a church. That was it.

She walked up the street, seemingly unnoticed, until a hand came out and grabbed her arm and pulled her next to the post office. A hand clamped over her mouth.

"Are you daft? What are you doin'?" It was Jamie O'Fallon.

Seana turned and looked at him. "Geezus. Give me a heart attack, why don't ya?"

"Come with me," he whispered. She followed him up the craggy path to a whitewashed cottage.

As soon as he opened the door, two men stood. "Jamie, are you insane?"

Seana noticed the older man from the boat. The other was the same age at Jamie, but shorter and full of freckles.

"She was walkin' in town."

"Okay. What's going on?" she asked, and Jamie offered her a seat.

The cottage was dark, except for the roaring fire. Seana sat down and waited. The three men exchanged glances, and Jamie shrugged as if to say, "We've nothing to lose."

The other man stuck out his hand. "You know Jamie O'Fallon. I'm his cousin Patrick Burke and this is Seamus."

"Burke?" Seana asked. "Y-you've got relatives in America?"

"A cousin and a brother. My brother lives in New York and my cousin lives in Washington."

Seana's mouth went dry. "Kathleen Frances Burke."

All three men exchanged glances. "Do you know her?" Patrick asked.

Seana nodded, trying to understand. *She's the local who has relatives who'll help us.* She remembered Major Jennings's words. *I could have told her.*

"Yes. This is a strange coincidence. Look, what's going on?" she asked.

"We know your officer was murdered. We don't know by who or why. We do know he was going back to send something to the States he thought was very big. We ransacked the hut after his body was found, but we found no transmission, just the wireless."

"Why? Why are you helping?" Seana asked.

"Ireland is neutral. However, we have relatives in America that are fighting this bastard. We want to help in any way we can. That's why we offered ourselves and let you use the island. Kathleen knows nothing about it. It's an unbelievable quirk of fate that you know her."

"Yes, it is," Seana said, and concentrated on the problem at hand. "Okay, whatever it was that he was trying to transmit, the murderer knew it and killed him. Let me go back and see what I can find. I read his file. He was very resourceful. Maybe you've overlooked something."

"Be careful. Whoever it is probably knows you're looking.

We'll keep an eye out for you," Patrick said.

The May night turned cool as Seana left the cottage and headed back to her hut, with the moon lighting her way. All the way, she had the feeling she was being watched. Once inside, she closed the door and threw the heavy bolt.

She looked around the hut. "Okay. You came back to the hut, knowing you had to send a transmission, an important transmission. It has to be written down somewhere, so what did you do with it?"

She went through every drawer, every cabinet. She looked through the desk. Pulled up the wool loom rug, hoping to find some trap door—nothing. She pulled all the cans from the shelves, opened the cabinet with the flour and poured it out, hoping to find something—again, nothing.

Then she looked at the three bottles of whiskey. She took them out and opened one. The aroma once again filled her senses. Then she opened the other; this time, there was no smell. It was empty. She hadn't checked the other two bottles when she searched the hut for supplies the first day. She cursed herself once again for her ineptness, but the thought then struck her. Why would he leave an empty bottle?

She took it over and held it up to the light. "Lieutenant Neely, you're very clever." She shook the bottle and sat at the wireless.

After retrieving the note from the bottle, she had to read it several times, in amazement. "Oh, shit." She sat there for a moment to collect her thoughts.

It was too early to transmit, so she took the note, placed it back in the bottle, and returned the bottle to its place. She then cleaned up the hut and looked around. All was in order. She threw on her jacket and headed back to Dunmore.

She ran the entire mile, stumbling in the dark, making her way back to the cottage. The glow from the fire was all she saw as she knocked on the door. When no one answered, she peered in and saw Patrick sitting with his head resting on the table.

"Damn it, Patrick," she said and tried the door. It was unlocked, so she stepped in. "Patrick, wake up. I know what happened to—" She stopped as she shook Patrick. He slumped to one side and fell to the floor. Seana knelt beside him. "Patrick?" she exclaimed as she turned him over.

His lifeless eyes stared up at her. It was then she noticed the red marks on his throat. Her stomach lurched as she put a hand to her mouth. "Shit," she cursed. She looked around and slipped out of the cottage and headed back to the hut.

She hid behind the rocks, waiting to see if anyone was at the hut. Satisfied that no one had seen her and there was no one else about, she crept back inside. She steadied herself and took a deep confident breath. She got the transmission from the whiskey bottle, and after memorizing it, she tossed it into the fire. She gathered all the documents she had from the pouch and threw them in the fire as instructed. She watched them burn into ashes, and when she was confident that nothing was being left behind, she sat at the wireless.

Her first transmission was Scorpion. She hastily tapped out the rest of Neely's transmission repeatedly, making sure Major Jennings got it. Then she typed out another, hoping against hope that he'd understand and remember.

Suddenly, she heard muffled voices and frantically typed the last cryptic code, pleading to God that the major would remember. She sent it again and again.

The voices were getting louder, and suddenly, the door burst open. The sound of the gunshot was the last thing she remembered.

It was four a.m. when the phone rang and Major Jennings jumped off his couch to answer it. He was needed at headquarters; he had gotten a personal transmission and his mind raced—there was only one person who would send him such a message.

Once at headquarters, he sat at his desk reading the transmission. He understood everything. It all made perfect sense now—all but the last. He looked at it, trying to understand what Riordan meant. Two words repeated, then nothing. No end of the transmission meant Riordan had to get out of there in a hurry or she couldn't get out at all. His heart pounded as he picked up the phone. "Get security in here now."

Within seconds, two very large military police officers stood inside the door. "Come with me," he said and walked down the corridor to the Cryptography Room. Several tired heads looked up as did Bruckner. The major walked up to him.

"Lieutenant Bruckner, you're under arrest for treason."

"Major, wh-what are you talking about?" he asked nervously as the beads of perspiration broke out on his face. The two MPs stood on either side of him.

"Lieutenant Carl Bruckner, or should I say Carl Bruckheimer. Born in Austria, came over when you were a child, but grew up a Nazi. You've been taking transmissions and sending them back or destroying them. I have all the proof right here. Lieutenant Neely found out and you had him killed. It's all over, you worm."

Carl Bruckheimer stammered and not knowing what to do, he raised his hand high. "H-Heil, Hitler!"

Jennings rolled his eyes in disgust and punched him dead in the face. "Get this piece of shit out of here."

The two smiling MPs dragged him out of the room.

As he returned to his desk, he tried desperately to remember the last two words of Riordan's cryptic message. He knew those words. Where did he know them from? His tired eyes darted back and forth. "Damn." He took off his jacket and rolled up his sleeves.

Pain seared through Seana as she regained consciousness. She was lying on her side in complete darkness, with her hands tied behind her back. Seana knew she'd been shot—that was a given. She didn't know where she was. Tape covered her mouth, and she felt blood trickling into her eyes. She tried to move. Letting out a deep groan of pain, she stopped struggling.

She was lying on cold earth and could smell the salty sea air. As her eyes tried to focus, she looked around and realized she was in some sort of cave, but where? How long had she been there? Did Major Jennings get the transmission? She thought of Kathleen. Cursing the tears that sprang into her eyes, the pain shot through her, and she faded into unconsciousness. The beautiful face of Kathleen Burke was the last thing she remembered.

44

Once again, the muffled voices were around her. One was distinctly a woman's voice, the other a deep male voice. They were arguing and standing near her. She tried not to move as she listened.

They both spoke German as Seana strained to capture the conversation. She heard, "She knows. She must know." Seana knew they were talking about her.

Yeah, I know, you scum. The pain seared through her again, and she let out an involuntary groan.

Suddenly, there was a light shining in her face. She closed her eyes against the bright light and was hauled off the ground and thrown into a chair. As the tape was ripped from her mouth, she cried out in pain. Taking short breaths, Seana tried to collect herself.

"Lieutenant Riordan, you are very clever," a man's voice called out in a thick German accent.

"Let her be."

Seana's eyes widened and she let out an ugly laugh. It was Maura Flynn.

"Let her be? No, I'm afraid it's beyond that. You will tell us what you know, Lieutenant. I promise you that." The man slapped her across the face, nearly knocking her out of the chair.

"For the love of God, she knows nothing."

"She knows. Her transmission was intercepted, you idiot. The last two words, we do not understand. It has to do with the invasion. Tell me, Lieutenant, and I promise a quick death," he said, and Seana looked up, trying to focus.

What invasion? Her mind raced, filing through all the transmissions she'd decoded in four months.

Seana, trying to keep focus, watched as he lit a kerosene lantern and set it on the table; he leaned against the table. His features were coming into view through a cloud of cigarette smoke. He was a tall heavy man with graying hair.

"Hitler?" Seana asked lightly, and the man's smirking face turned to an angry frown. He slapped her again. Seana tasted the blood in her mouth as she spat in his direction.

"Seana, tell him. What's the point now? He'll find out, please,"

Maura said and knelt next to her.

Seana looked down at her and gave her an ugly smirk. "You let them kill Lieutenant Neely. You knew, and now, you'll let him kill me. It's too late. Lieutenant Bruckner, oh, pardon me, Carl Bruckheimer, as we speak is probably being shot as a traitor. I hope so anyway," she said thickly. She was losing consciousness again. She glanced down at her side; her sweater was bloody. "Did you shoot me?" she asked stupidly.

The German tossed Maura aside and stood over Seana. "Uh-oh," she said and looked up. His big arm swinging down put her into darkness once again.

Major Jennings sat drinking his coffee. Stacks of transmissions covered his desk. He and Corporal Harris had spent the last five hours trying to find the connection.

Finally, Harris sat back and rubbed his eyes. "Maybe we're going about this all wrong. I know Seana, um, Lieutenant Riordan. She would pick something that only you would know, sir. Maybe something she'd told you. It means something. Somehow, these two words are connected with the island and the mission. What's the common thread? Only you know it, sir."

Major Jennings walked over to the window and looked out. *Something she told you. Only you would know... Two words were connected.*

He repeated the words as he looked out at the city. Then, it struck him like a thunderbolt. He clapped his hands together. "Sonofabitch." He slapped the corporal on the back. "Son, tomorrow, you'll be a sergeant. Get me a driver now."

He grabbed his coat and ran out of the building. "Georgetown," he ordered as he ran down the steps to the awaiting jeep.

Jennings ran up the steps, two at a time. He rang the bell and knocked at her door until it was opened.

The redheaded woman smiled for an instant. A frown settled across her face. "It's Seana, isn't it?" she cried, and he ushered her into her living room.

He explained everything, knowing he was breaching security,

but there was a possibility that Riordan might be dead. He, of course, did not tell this to Kathleen Burke, who sat there wide-eyed and shivering.

"Why are you telling me this?" she said anxiously. "Oh, God, she's dead. You're telling me this because—" She stopped, and he took her hands.

"We don't know that for sure. I'm telling you this because her last two words were 'Twilight's own.' She repeated it several times, in fact. I remember those words in her letter to you. Why would she do that? Miss Burke, you said you were born on the Aran Islands. I think Seana feels there's some connection with you. Do you have family there?"

"Yes, a cousin only." She stopped, and her eyes were wide with terror. "Major, something's wrong. You haven't heard from her at all?"

"Not since last night's transmission. I'll wait till this evening."

Kathleen stood defiantly. "I won't. I know those islands. If Seana is there, I'll find her." She headed for her bedroom.

He reached out and grabbed her arm. "I can't let you do that. It's much too dangerous, and we don't know who's behind this. It could be your cousin."

Kathleen wrenched her arm free. "Then I'll deal with it. I'm not leaving Seana alone and running. You can help me, or I'll go find someone who will."

He raised an eyebrow. "Threatening the United States of America?"

"To get Seana back safe, I'd threaten the president himself," she said and marched into the bedroom.

He sighed and rubbed his forehead. "I should have been a farmer. My mother wanted me to stay on the farm, but no, I wanted to be a soldier."

"So did Seana," Kathleen's voice called out.

He looked up as she entered the room. She was wearing trousers and a tweed jacket. She pulled her red hair back and tied it with a scarf. He smiled slightly. "Don't you women wear dresses anymore?" He obediently followed her out the door. He

47

commanded hundreds of "men." They all followed orders. Things were organized, thought out. Now he followed this fiery redhead like a puppy dog.

What was this world coming to?

Seana regained consciousness, and again she was lying on her side, wet, cold, and in a good deal of pain. She struggled for what seemed like hours, trying to loosen the ties behind her back.

Miraculously, one hand began to come free. Wincing in pain, she freed herself. She waited for a moment to let the blood flow as she flexed her arms and legs. Her body felt stiff and achy, but she knew she had to get back to the hut and the backpack with the first aid equipment. Finally, she got to her knees, clutching her side. She felt the sticky thickness and winced as she got to her feet. Unsteady for a moment, she knew she had no time to waste. She didn't know how long she'd been out or what day it was, but she knew she needed to get the hell out of there.

As she stumbled through the dim opening to the cave, she shielded her eyes against the setting sun. "Twilight," she said as she stumbled away.

For the next hour, she ran, stumbled, and crawled as far away from the cave as she could. She heard the rush of the Atlantic surf, and by the setting sun, she knew she was on the opposite side of the island. She'd never make it back over the tall craggy hill, but she had to try. She hid herself behind a thicket bush and sat against a rock. Stifling a cry of pain, she pulled her hand away and noticed it was covered with blood. "Shit," she cursed and gingerly pulled up her blood-stained sweater.

The bullet must have grazed her side. There was a long welt-like wound caked with dried blood, but slightly oozing, which ran along her ribcage. She leaned her head back against the rock and closed her eyes. "I am not gonna die," she whispered firmly and felt her hot forehead. "I may go into convulsions, but I'm not gonna die." She laughed as she closed her eyes.

She was lying with Kathleen, her perfume wafted over her as she held her close. "Kath," she said as her lover kissed her cheek.

"Lieutenant, darlin'," Kath whispered. "Get up now... You've got to get up!" the insistent voice kept telling her.

Suddenly, Seana jerked and woke. She looked around and realized it was a dream. She glanced at her watch. It was nearly sunrise. She needed to get back to the hut and wireless.

The plane landed at Shannon Airport, and Kathleen grabbed her bag and headed out. She took the train to Galway and took the next ferry across to the islands.

"Fine spring day," a man said and stood next to her.

"Yes, it is."

"Relatives on the island?" he asked and offered his hand. "Kathleen Burke?" Kathleen nodded and shook his hand.

"Jamie O'Fallon. They said I was to meet you. I don't know where she is. I've been to the hut for three days straight. I haven't seen her. I'm sorry." He told her about Patrick.

Kathleen put a hand to her forehead but refused to think Seana was dead. "She can't be."

"You stay at Patrick's place. He'd have wanted that. I'm sorry. The funeral was yesterday," he said sadly.

Kathleen reached up and touched his cheek. "Thank you."

As the ferry docked, Jamie turned to Kathleen. "You remember where it is?"

"I remember, not to worry," Kathleen assured him.

"Good. I'll leave you here."

The long walk to Dunmore was quiet and eerie. Kathleen made her way to the cottage and opened the door. She remembered this house; she had visited many times. She looked around and a shiver went down her spine.

"Seana was here," she whispered. She changed and dressed in the clothes of a typical island woman. The light wool frock fit nicely. Then she slipped on a pair of sturdy shoes and threw a tweed shawl over her shoulders. She looked at herself in the mirror and saw the picture of an islander. She smiled as she pinned the brooch to the shawl.

She set out to find Seana—knowing, willing her to be alive.

"I told you to watch, you idiot," he spat out and shoved her aside. He bent down and felt the sticky blood on the floor. "She won't get too far, not with a bullet in her side."

Maura glanced around in terror. Seana Riordan was still alive. Maura knew she'd be looking for her.

"She's too far from the hut. She'll never try to make it back there. She'll probably die in one of your bogs. God, I hate this country," he said and took a deep breath. "Well, don't stand there. This is your island. Go find her."

He pushed Maura and followed her out of the cave.

Kathleen walked through town and stopped at a cottage at the end of town. She remembered Mrs. O'Keefe. As always, her front door was open; Kathleen found her sitting at the kitchen table.

"Mrs. O'Keefe?"

The old woman looked up, frowned for a moment, and smiled in recognition. "Kathleen Burke." The next few sentences were in Gaelic, and Kathleen finally put up her hands in defeat.

"Easy, Mrs. O'Keefe. It's been quite a while for me and the Irish doesn't come too quickly."

"I'm sorry about Patrick. Bad business. Is that why you've come?"

"Partly. Tell me, have you seen anything unusual goin' on?"

"Unusual? What are you after?"

Kathleen took a deep breath and bit at her bottom lip. She briefly explained.

Mrs. O'Keefe raised an eyebrow. "That American officer was a woman?"

Kathleen's heart ached when she used the term "was." "Yes, and I need to find her. Patrick was working with the Americans. I had no idea that Seana, um, Lieutenant Riordan was involved. Now she's missing and I'm desperate to find her."

Mrs. O'Keefe searched Kathleen's blushing face, and she looked at her hands. She reached over and put a hand under Kathleen's chin, lifting her gaze to her own. She smiled and clicked her tongue. "You've got the look, Kathleen. God help you. Now I haven't seen your woman in three days. I saw her at Patrick's, after that..." Her voice trailed off. "Though I know Maura Flynn spent a good deal of time at that hut."

Kathleen raised an eyebrow. "She did, did she? Do you know where this woman is?" Kathleen asked as she cooled her temper. Jennings had said Maura might be involved somehow. She needed to keep a level head about her.

"I know she lives on the other side of the island," Mrs. O'Keefe said.

"Jamie said she lives in Dunmore."

"Her aunt lives in Dunmore. Nasty old woman, but Maura's from Aransmore on the other side."

Kathleen paced back and forth, biting her lip. It was worth a try. "If you see this witch, please don't tell her we talked."

Mrs. O'Keefe winked. "Never saw you at all."

Chapter 6

Kathleen took as much food as she could and a thermos of water. Not knowing what to expect, she prepared for the worst and took some bandages and a bottle of antiseptic. She thought of Patrick's death and how he and Jamie were involved with Seana. Patrick was murdered and now they were after Seana. Kathleen needed to concentrate on finding her; she gathered everything and headed out the door.

It was nearly noon, and it would take the better part of the day to get across the island. There were no cars or horses, so walking was the only way.

It took her several hours as she followed the road that wound up, down, and around to the other side of the island. She looked around, knowing the barren landscape would not hide a thing, but she also knew Seana would try to stay out of sight.

By late afternoon, she had reached the other side of the island. The day had become chilly and she lifted the long woolen shawl over her head and around her shoulders. The pack was slung over her shoulder, and she cursed her shoes, as sturdy as they were, for slipping on the wet rocks. Still, she'd made good time. As she walked down the narrow path, she was hoping against hope she'd find Seana.

Suddenly, someone grabbed her from behind. A strong hand clamped over her mouth and the other around her neck. "You fucking bitch. Give me one good reason why I shouldn't snap your neck like a twig," a painful, familiar voice whispered angrily.

"W-well, I've come three thousand miles to save you, that's one," she choked out. She felt the hands slacken and she whirled around, letting out an incredulous cry. "Seana, my God!"

Seana stood there swaying, holding her side, staring as if she were seeing an apparition. "Kathleen?"

Kathleen caught her, as she was falling backward. "Seana, you're alive," she exclaimed and held her around the waist.

Seana cried out in pain and stumbled back. Kathleen pulled her blood-stained hand away and stared at it in disbelief. Seana fell back and sat on the stone wall, slumping forward. Kathleen pulled her bloodied face up and looked into her feverish blue eyes. "Seana, what have they done to you?"

"I can't believe you're here. What in the hell are you doing? God, get going. Get out of here," Seana said thickly and tried to push her down the road. "Damn it, get out of here."

Kathleen felt her hot forehead. She took a deep breath and ignored her ramblings. "C'mon, we've got to get you back."

"No. Listen to me," Seana said in a clipped tone as she held her side. "Can't go back. They're looking for me. I got away. Kathleen, leave me. Go back to the States. God, if anything happens to you," she whispered, then put a hand to her cheek. "I cannot believe I'm actually touching you." Her eyes filled with tears as she shook her head in disbelief.

"Seana, I have food and water. Come with me, I know where to go. No one will find us." She hoisted her off the stone wall.

Seana put an arm around her shoulders and looked down into those green eyes she thought she would never see again.

"My God, you're a heavy one." Kathleen grunted as they made their way down the road, stopping occasionally. What should have taken twenty minutes took the better part of an hour. However, Kathleen was true to her word. The alcove was off the road by almost a mile, and hidden behind a thicket bush.

Seana crawled behind the brush and let out a cry of pain as she lay back against the rock. "So many rocks in this country," Seana said; she tried to laugh but only succeeded in coughing.

Kathleen followed and knelt beside her. She took out the thermos and Seana grabbed for it. Kathleen gently pushed her hands away. "Slowly, darlin', not too fast."

"Thanks. I think I've been shot." She tried to lift her sweater.

"Let me, lie still," Kathleen said, sucking in a breath as she looked at the wound.

"I think I was grazed by the bullet," Seana mumbled; she was fading fast.

"I think you're right. Lie back."

Seana groaned as she stretched out and looked up into her green eyes. She winced as Kathleen lifted her sweater and struggled to get it off her.

Her shirt was covered with blood and Kathleen held back her tears as Seana reached for her. "Don't cry now. I'm fine."

Kathleen only nodded as she unbuttoned the shirt and pulled it out of the slacks.

"You don't know how many times I've dreamed about you doing this. Minus the blood and being shot, of course," Seana mumbled.

Kathleen bent down and kissed her lips. They were feverish, dry, and all together wonderful. "Now stop your talk."

She took out the bottle of antiseptic, along with a huge amount of gauze. "This might sting." Nodding, Seana took a deep breath and held it.

Kathleen doused the wound and Seana bit her lip, trying not to cry out, yet she lay perfectly still. "You've got to sit up, darlin'," she said. Kathleen made sure the wound was cleaned. She wound the bandage around her stomach.

"Tie it tight," Seana said through clenched teeth.

When Kathleen was finished, Seana was soaked with perspiration as she leaned against the rock wall. "Well, that hurt," she said between breaths.

"I'm sorry," Kathleen said and touched Seana's dirty cheek. "You're filthy." She lifted her frock and ripped part of her slip off. "Just like the movies." Kathleen poured water on the tattered cotton and cleaned her face and neck.

Seana winced as she touched the cut on her forehead. "I never thought I'd see you again." She reached over to touch her pale cheek. "My Kath," she whispered and started to shiver uncontrollably.

"Seana!" Kathleen exclaimed as she got Seana to lie down.

54

She felt her forehead, amazed at the heat generated beneath her fingers. Kathleen stripped the damp shirt off her, mindful of the bandage, and covered Seana with a woolen shawl.

"Please, God. Don't let her die," Kathleen whispered as she forced water down Seana's throat. Kathleen slid under the shawl at Seana's uninjured side and held her close, wrapping her arm around Seana's bare chest.

Seana mumbled helplessly through her feverish sleep. Kathleen held her and prayed to every saint that came to mind as she kept a cool cloth on Seana's forehead.

When she woke, Seana eased herself away from the slumbering redhead and sat up. She felt her side—no blood, that was good. Kathleen did a good job of fixing her up. She was now ravenous. She tried to stand but only got to her knees.

"Lie down, for the love of God," Kathleen said and pulled her back. She loomed over Seana and kissed her deeply. "Now, are you hungry?" Kathleen opened the pack. "I've got bread and some cheese."

Seana lay there, watching her. She smiled, watching her fuss to fix the meal. "Come here," she said firmly and smiled when she saw Kathleen shiver.

"None of that now, Seana Riordan. Eat." She thrust the bread in her hands.

Seana gave a disappointed grunt and sat up. She took the bread and cheese and ate voraciously and drank an entire cup of water. All at once, she was exhausted. "We've got to get out of here. I've got to get back to the hut."

Kathleen held her down. "You've got to rest awhile."

"Hey. What are you doing here? How did Major Jennings allow you to—?"

"Allow is it? I'll have you know that I'm a grown woman."

"No kidding."

"And can come and go as I please. Allow, indeed!"

Seana reached up and pulled her into her arms.

"Seana, your bandages."

Seana put her fingertips over her soft lips. "Keep still, woman.

I haven't the strength to make love to you, but at least," she whispered against her lips, "I can kiss you."

Long moments later, Seana looked into the green eyes. "Now answer my question. What are you doing here?"

"Major Jennings remembered your code and came to me. That is what you intended, correct?"

"Yes, but only for you to tell him that you had Patrick here. Not for you—"

Kathleen reached up and put her fingertips against Seana's lips. "He said the same thing, but who knows this island better than me, tell me that?"

"I know, but all this way. It's so dangerous for you to be here," she said angrily as she ran a hand through her hair.

"And would you not do the same for me?"

Seana looked into the jade pools. *Yes, but I love you.* "Why? Why did you come?" Seana asked as she searched her face. "Jamie could have found me. Someone would have."

Kathleen swallowed with difficultly. "W-well. I-I thought—"

"Tell me. Tell me why."

"You see, I was—" She stopped and swallowed.

"Please, Kath. Tell me why."

Seana's voice was a mere whisper, sending a shiver through Kathleen's body. "Because, Seana Riordan, I love you. God help me, I'll love no other." She reached up, cupping her face. She was shocked at the look of joy and gratitude on Seana's face.

Tears sprang into her deep blue eyes, and with one blink, she sent them spilling over her cheeks. Kathleen was amazed at the effect those three words had over this strong, confident woman.

"I never thought I'd be this lucky. Not in my wildest dreams, and believe me, I've had some wild ones," Seana said, choking back her tears. "C'mon, we've got to get out of here. Somehow I've got to stop them."

She let go of Kathleen and stood, flexing and testing her legs. "Okay, you know this place. You lead us out of here."

"Did I hear you correctly? You've got to stop them? They almost killed you." She threw up her hands in a helpless gesture.

56

Seana smiled affectionately and winked. "But they didn't. Thanks to you."

Kathleen clutched at her shirt in a desperate gesture. "Let's go. Leave now. Jamie can get us on the ferry. We can stay in Ireland and—"

"Kath, listen to me. That German agent and Maura are running loose on this island. They killed Lieutenant Neely when he found out that Bruckner was a German spy. Do you know how many Frenchmen have been killed because of him? Don't ask me to walk away from this. Jamie will take you back to Ireland. I'll come and get you when I'm done here."

"You don't want me here?" she asked in a voice that broke Seana's heart.

"I want you safe, don't you understand?"

"Tell me... Tell me you don't want me here. Tell me it's all right for me to come and rescue you, but you don't want me around any longer. Tell me that and I'll go, but I won't go to Ireland. I'll go and you won't find me.

"You said you loved me in that letter. Just now, I said I loved you. Are you telling me now that you're gonna leave me again? How safe will I be without you? If something happens to you, it happens to me. Isn't that what love is? You said once we had a different idea of love and marriage. Is this your idea of love?" she asked, and looked Seana in the eye.

Seana took a deep breath. "No. I never want you out of my sight again. I do love you. C'mon, let's get out of here."

It took most of the afternoon as they made their way down the dirt road. Kathleen glanced at Seana, who was sweating again.

"Seana, you need water." Seana nodded and eagerly drank from the thermos as Kathleen checked the bandage. The wound was bleeding. She worried that Seana was doing too much, too fast.

As if reading her mind, Seana smiled. "I'm fine, but we have to keep moving. I don't like being in the open like this, and I have no idea where they are." She motioned Kathleen forward without another word.

Once back in Dunmore, Seana was breathing heavily and

sweating profusely. They made their way to Patrick's cottage. Jamie was waiting there. "Thank God. I honestly thought you were dead."

"I felt like it, believe me," Seana said.

Kathleen guided her to the chair by the fire and lifted Seana's shirt. "I'll change the bandage."

Jamie handed her a cup of tea and a wedge of bread, lavished with jam. Seana leaned back and gratefully accepted both.

"You've got to go back to the hut, don't you?" Jamie asked.

Seana nodded and winced as Kathleen changed the bandage. Kathleen gave her a worried glance but said nothing.

"Have you seen anyone around, who, well, doesn't fit?" Seana asked and nodded gratefully as Kathleen finished.

"No. Maura Flynn was asking about you, but I played dumb," he said proudly. "I don't think they'll come into the village."

Seana gave him a curious look. "Why not?"

He smiled happily. "Well now, we all took a vote. Mrs. O'Keefe started it. Wait—they're coming," he said and opened the door.

Seana stood painfully and closed her blood-stained shirt. Kathleen stood next to her, anxiously holding her hand.

A few villagers entered the cottage; the old men took off their caps as Mrs. O'Keefe made her way through the gathering. Seana was confused as she watched them.

"We're not part of this war. America never has helped us. No one has. However, I have a nephew in this war. Tom here has a grandson, an American pilot. Jerry has a couple cousins, and of course, you two fine women. We don't like strangers coming and killing. That Lieutenant Neely was a good young man. It's time we got them out of here."

Seana smiled and squeezed Kathleen's hand.

"Tell us what you need," one old man said.

"Thank you," Seana said. "Okay, here's what I've come up with."

They all stood around and Kathleen watched Seana as she spoke. "I've got to get back to the hut to see if the wireless is still there; another transmission has to be sent to Washington, and it has to be done at eleven tomorrow night. Now you can keep your eyes open. I can make my way back to the hut and send it off. I'll have to stay there and wait for the answer. I'm sure they'll do their best to get me an answer straight away."

Mrs. O'Keefe ushered the villagers out, then pushed Seana into the chair. She raised Seana's shirt and examined Kathleen's work. "Not bad. Jamie, go to my cottage, get the mixture for the poultice," she said, and Kathleen gave her a worried look. "You did fine, girl, but there's an infection. Now get into bed." She jerked her thumb toward the bedroom.

Seana gaped at both women. "Ladies, look, I have to—"

"Get her into bed," she said to Kathleen.

Seana lay back, sweating. Her side burned like someone was driving a red-hot poker into it.

"It burns, am I right?"

Seana only nodded. Kathleen placed a wet, cold cloth on her forehead and bathed her face.

When Jamie returned, Mrs. O'Keefe mixed what looked like brown and green sludge together in a bowl. Kathleen took a whiff and grimaced. "Good Lord."

"Stinks, but it works. Now this is going to feel cool, but then it will itch like the devil himself. You can't touch it. It has to stay on till morning. It'll draw out any infection you have. You must not move or touch it," Mrs. O'Keefe said again. "Turn her on her side."

Kathleen turned Seana, who tried to help, but only cried out in pain. Quickly, she lathered her side and back with the putrid thick poultice. Seana sucked in a breath at the feel of it against her wound. Kathleen winced for her and held her hand.

When she finished, she bound her stomach tightly. "Take a deep breath, love," she said and tied off the bandage.

Seana let out a breath and laid back. Kathleen smoothed the damp hair off her forehead and kissed it. "Sleep now, darlin'."

"Take off those filthy clothes. She'll be sweating tonight, Kathleen. You must stay with her. Make sure she doesn't move too much and tear it off. By morning, she should be much better. Mind me now," she warned.

Kathleen assured her as she walked her out. She noticed outside the cottage that several men stood guard.

Seana was awake when she walked back into the room. "Hi."

Kathleen smiled. "Hello. How do you feel?"

"Like a trussed-up Christmas goose," she said in a tired voice.

Kathleen wrung out the cloth and placed it on her forehead. "You need to sleep, but first, I've gotta get you out of these disgusting clothes." She unbuckled her belt. "Not one word out of you, Seana."

Kathleen stripped off the blood-soaked trousers. She washed her as best she could without becoming completely aroused. She knew she was turning red when she looked up to see Seana smiling wickedly. "You're in no condition," she said and pulled the quilt over her naked body.

She blew out the lantern and Seana watched her as she disrobed in the moonlight. "My God, you're beautiful." Seana sighed.

Kathleen slid under the huge quilt. "It's your feverish state, Lieutenant," she said wickedly and rested higher on the pillows. She pulled Seana closer, so her head was resting on her breast. "Sleep now." She kissed her head.

"Thank you. I'd have died out there."

"Shh, none of that now. You're safe and we're together."

There was silence for a moment. "What about Eddie?"

Kathleen smirked. She could hear the satisfaction in Seana's voice.

"Well, he came back on leave and we…"

Seana shot a look up at her. "You what?" she asked angrily.

Kathleen gave her an innocent look. "Don't 'you what' me, Miss Riordan. Just how well do you know Maura Flynn?"

Seana smiled, seeing the game. "Well, that's different. She kissed me and—"

"She what!" Kathleen bellowed and sat up.

Seana winced and grabbed her arm. "Kath, Kath, the poultice," Seana scolded and pulled her back down.

They lay in the quiet darkness for a moment. "The next time

we're naked and in bed, watch out, Kathleen Burke."

Kathleen kissed her head. Seana was already sound asleep.

During the night, Seana was in incredible agony. After what seemed liked hours of Kathleen trying to keep Seana from ripping the bandage, Seana finally quieted and drifted off to a more peaceful sleep. Kathleen kissed her forehead, which was now cool and dry.

She heard wild ancient music playing in the darkness. "Are you gonna lay there, woman? You're the O'Malley now. Get on with you and finish this. You're the O'Malley," the low disembodied voice urged.

Surrounded by fog, she looked around and saw a figure with long black hair brandishing a long sword, floating through the dense fog. Seana walked slowly toward the figure. "I'm trying," she said, never taking her eyes off the figure.

As she walked closer, she reached out to touch the figure hidden in the foggy mist. It had to be her, Seana thought. As her fingers met warm skin, the figure walked out of the fog. It was not Branna O'Malley's face she saw, but her own image staring back at her.

"You must finish this. You're the O'Malley."

Seana woke with a start. She frantically looked around the room, breathing heavily. It was a dream—just a dream.

Her mouth felt like a desert. She slid out of bed and sat on the edge, amazed at how much better she felt. No burning and no fever, but she was starving.

"Get back into bed," Kathleen mumbled behind her.

Seana laughed and winced as she lay down on her good side and watched her. "Good morning. Was I a handful?"

"Yes. You almost knocked me off the bed several times," she said tiredly, then turned onto her side to mirror Seana.

Seana continued to watch her; she looked exhausted and beautiful. "My hero." Seana leaned over to kiss her cheek.

"Seana," she warned halfheartedly. Actually, Kathleen ached for her touch. It'd been four long months of dreaming.

"It's been too long, Kath. Shh." Seana put her lips against her. "I need to feel you. I need to touch you." Her hand slowly cupped her white breast. Kathleen moaned; how she longed for her touch.

Seana kissed her deeply. Her tongue parted her lips and quietly found its home. Both moaned as Seana slowly loved her. With just a kiss, she loved her.

Her kiss was warm and gentle—no urgency, no great eroticism. Just a kiss from the woman Kath loved. Her heart was pounding as Seana's hand almost reverently passed over her hardened nipple, barely touching it. Kathleen's hips twitched at the familiar, yet almost virginal touch.

This was not the sexual Seana Riordan, the lesbian who seduced and won her almost a year earlier—this was the woman she loved. Kathleen looked into Seana's eyes and saw the pain etched in her brow.

"That's enough with you." Kathleen gently took Seana's hand away from her breast and placed a kiss against the palm of Seana's hand. "You need more sleep."

Seana nodded tiredly and allowed Kathleen to pull her close to her breast. "I love you," Seana said as she drifted off to sleep.

Kathleen barely heard Seana, but in those words, Kathleen found peace, a peace she never knew existed.

Chapter 7

As they were sitting around the kitchen table in the late evening, Seana and Kathleen heard the knock at the door.

Mrs. O'Keefe walked in and looked at the two of them. "Well then. I take it, it worked."

"Like a charm, thank you. I feel wonderful," Seana said as she ate the remainder of the soda bread.

Mrs. O'Keefe gave her a wary grin. "Let me see," she said, and Seana stood obediently and raised her shirt. "Very good, ya might want to keep it on for—"

They looked to the door as Jamie walked in, looking grim. "We've got company. Two blond men just got off the ferry. They're headed toward the hut."

Seana jumped up, and Jamie stopped her as she headed out the door. "Hold on now. Tom and Seamus are watching them."

"You've only seen these two men? No sign of Maura or anyone else?" Seana asked.

"No. Everyone's been watching. We've seen nothing of anyone else," Jamie said. "Do ya think these two killed Patrick? And Lieutenant Neely?"

"I don't know, possibly, but you said you just spotted these two." Seana slammed her hand on the table. "Damn, I've got to get to the wireless, Jamie." She glanced at her watch. "It's after ten."

He grinned widely and opened the door. Three villagers walked in with all her equipment. Seana was stunned, but grinned and slapped Jamie on the back. "Good work. It'll take me a few minutes to get it hooked up. The only problem is we're in a valley." She had an idea. "All I need is the radio and receiver. I can tap out a message." She picked up the radio and winced; it was heavy. Everyone watched as she disappeared into the room; she came back, carrying a canvas knapsack. "Please fit," she begged as Jamie understood and helped her load the radio into the pack. It barely fit. Seana raised the antenna and Jamie followed her outside.

She turned on the radio, and it squawked to life. Turning the dial, she barely got a frequency. "On the top of that hill, we'll be fine," she said and pointed.

"Right. We'll leave straight away. I'll carry it. You transmit and we'll be done with it. The villagers will keep an eye out for our visitors," Jamie said.

Seana agreed. "Let me get dressed." She started for the bedroom, then looked back at the sad-faced Kathleen. "Well, don't stand there, get dressed. I'm not leaving you again."

Kathleen grinned, and they disappeared into the bedroom. Mrs. O'Keefe shook her head. "They're both daft."

Jamie laughed and collected the knapsack. He hoisted it over his shoulder. Seana and Kathleen came out, both wild with excitement.

The forty-five-minute trek to the top of the hill left Seana exhausted. "This should be fine."

Jamie swung the pack off his shoulder, and Seana got to work. The wireless came to life and Seana found the correct frequency as she listened with the headset. She took out a pen and began to tap out the message.

Kathleen and Jamie watched in awe as she expertly sent the Morse code. She stopped for an instant, thought of something, and tapped out again. She stopped and put her fingers to her lips when Kathleen started to say something.

The quiet of the late May night was deafening. Seana waited, then tapped out the message again. For what seemed like an eternity, they waited. The cool breeze wafted over them as Seana mopped her brow with her sleeve. "C'mon guys," she whispered, and Jamie gave the night a worried glance.

Kathleen's heart was pounding out of her chest; she was sure both could hear it.

Then it came. The bleeps in staccato rhythm sang out in the dark night. Seana listened and wrote frantically. The bleeps stopped, then started again.

Seana sat there and read the coded message. She was shocked. Jamie and Kathleen watched her in silence. "Holy shit. Okay, let's get out of here. I don't like being—"

"What? What don't you like?"

The deep voice rang out behind them, and Seana whirled around; she stopped when she saw the gun. "Don't be foolish. I won't miss this time."

The stout German came into view. Jamie glanced around, and Seana put a hand on his arm. "Very wise, Lieutenant. I have no desire to kill innocent people, but of course, I will. I only want the message in your hand." He held out his hand.

"This will do you no good, Herr Hitler," she said sarcastically. "It has to be decoded, and I don't have my decoder ring from Ovaltine."

The German's face reddened. "I love you Americans. Even in the face of death, you have a sense of humor." He raised the pistol and pointed it at Seana's chest.

"Let these two villagers go. They only helped because I paid them. They're not part of this," Seana said.

"She's right, my wife and I only helped because of the money. This war is between you two. Not us," Jamie said angrily, grabbed Kathleen, and pulled her to his side. He pinched her waist painfully to keep her quiet.

"I believe you, but we're all getting off this hill, then you can do as you please. As I said, we're not here to kill the innocent. Now move." He motioned with the gun as he stepped back. "Time for another hike. Toward the hut, if you please, Lieutenant." They walked down the dirt path.

They made their way through the craggy pass. Faltering only once, Seana winced and the German laughed. "I see you're still bothered."

Seana turned back to him and stopped. "And I see you're still one ugly kraut," she said and was hit across the face with the pistol.

Kathleen made a lunge for her and Jamie stopped her. "Easy," he whispered. "She knows what she's doin'."

Kathleen stopped and stood as Seana struggled to her knees. "Get up, Lieutenant. I'm not going to kill you, but you will decode the message."

Seana turned and Kathleen stifled a gasp at the blood Seana wiped from her cheek. She winked at Kathleen.

As they approached the hut, Maura Flynn stood in the doorway. She looked wild-eyed as she saw them coming down the road. "Did you get it?" She saw Seana's bleeding cheek. "God, why must you resort to that?" She snatched the message from Seana.

Kathleen and Jamie stood there as the gun was now pointed at them. "Let us go. We want none of this," Jamie said.

"Let them. They all watched as Neely was killed. They'll do the same here. It's not their war," Seana said, mustering all the disgust she could.

Kathleen was frantic. If she left, they'd kill Seana. If she stayed, they'd all be killed.

"Go on, beat it. You islanders make me sick," Seana spat out, and the German reached over and jabbed the pistol in her ribs. Seana buckled and slumped to her knees. "Take her in," she said, and Maura put her arm around Seana and dragged her into the hut.

"Now no one is going to get killed. She will decode the message."

Two blond men carrying pistols walked out of the darkness. The German motioned to both men. "See to it that they get home and watch them. We'll be leaving soon, I'm sure."

Kathleen was near tears as Jamie dragged her along. "Easy, I said," he mumbled, and she relaxed as he put his arm around her shoulder. They walked back to the cottage and the two blond men stood outside.

Kathleen angrily turned to Jamie. "What in the hell are you doing?" she whispered, and he covered her mouth.

"You stubborn fool. As long as Seana stalls them, we have time. Mrs. O'Keefe is keeping watch. I saw her between the curtains. She knows. Now we have to sit tight. It's Seana's only chance."

She slumped into the kitchen chair. "They'll kill her," she cried.

Jamie knelt next to her. "No, they won't. Not if they think she can decode that message."

Kathleen only hoped he was right. Actually, so did Jamie.

"If you keep hitting me, I'll never be able to decode this thing," Seana said as she was thrown into the desk chair.

Maura handed her a cloth and Seana wiped the blood off her cheek again. Glancing at her watch, she sat at the desk and took out the erroneous list.

"You have exactly one half hour to decode that or I start killing villagers," the German said, and Seana shot him a hateful look.

"Do it, Seana," Maura begged, and Seana got to work.

No one had any way of knowing that she already knew what it said. The time for secrecy was done.

Lieutenant Riordan knew what she had to do. She had her orders.

Chapter 8

"Your time is up, Lieutenant."

Seana looked up. "I need more time. Christ, you've waited this long."

That's when she heard it—someone banging on the door. The German whirled around, which was enough time for Seana, who bolted out of her chair and lunged for him. A shot rang out as she tackled him to the ground.

He kicked out at Seana, catching her injured side. She cried out as she fell back. She saw the pistol on the floor and dove for it. The German growled and dove, as well. Now both of them struggled, rolling around on the floor. He reached out and savagely punched her side. Seana's grip slackened as she felt herself lose consciousness momentarily.

Then a single shot was fired. He stared in disbelief before he died. Seana rolled away and got to her knees, holding her side. Maura stood there, holding the smoking pistol.

The door was broken open and Jamie came rushing in followed by Kathleen, who rushed to Seana's side. Jamie wrenched the gun from Maura, who did nothing to stop him.

The villagers took hold of Maura and dragged her from the hut as Seana reached for her. "Wait! No!" Seana gasped as Kathleen helped her to her feet. She ran out the door and stumbled after the villagers. "Wait!" she called out, sagging against the door.

The villagers stopped but still held onto Maura.

"She works for us," Seana gasped, and Kathleen shot her a look.

"But I thought she—"

"I know. I did, too. We all did. That was the message I received. She needs to get back to France. Maura, tell them," Seana said, too tired to continue.

"I work for the French underground. Six months ago, we found many people in the Resistance hauled off. Their hiding places suddenly found out. That's when we suspected a leak in the American radio transmission. I was sent back here to find out. However, the German in there had already killed Lieutenant Neely. So when Lieutenant Riordan came to replace him, I was supposed to find out whether he was a German agent or not— someone was."

She walked up to Seana and held out her hand. "Good job, Lieutenant. You found out and saved so many Frenchmen." She kissed her cheek.

Kathleen raised a protective eyebrow but said nothing.

"What happened to the other two Germans?" Seana asked.

Jamie made a slicing motion across his neck and Seana grimaced. "It was for Patrick," he said, and Seana nodded.

Seana glanced at her watch. It was nearly midnight. "We need to get down to the shore. The sub will be surfacing in an hour. Jamie, get your boat. Miss Flynn needs a ride."

After the trek from the hut to the shore, they stood on the beach, facing west. As ordered, Seana held the naval signal lamp that had been stored in the hut. Off in the distance, they saw the light from the sub, blinking its message. Seana held the lamp and triggered off her response. She waited for a moment until the sub responded.

She nodded and looked at Maura. "Okay. Everything's set. Off you go."

Maura gave her an incredulous look. "You're not coming."

Seana shook her head. "I've got my orders. I have a job to do, so I stay here."

Maura smiled and kissed her. "Thank you. You've helped more than you know. When this is over, perhaps you and I—" She saw the set jaw of Kathleen Burke behind Seana. "And perhaps not. Godspeed, Lieutenant Riordan."

"Good luck, Maura." Seana returned her kiss.

Kathleen stood next to her and slipped her arm through Seana's as they watched the boat slowly motoring toward the sub. There was a comfortable silence... for a moment.

"You just had to kiss her, didn't you?" she asked flatly as they walked up the beach.

"Don't start with me, Kath. I'm injured," Seana reminded her.

"Your kissin' days are over."

Seana laughed and pulled her into her arms. She reached out and caressed the gold pendant. "I see you got my letter."

Kathleen grinned and gave her a scathing look. "Marry Eddie, indeed. What were you thinkin'? We'll have to figure out what to do with the O'Malley heirloom when the time comes, which won't be for a very, very long time," she promised and placed her soft hand against the strong cheek.

"Well, we have the rest of our lives to think about it. I don't have any relatives that I know of, but hell, we're in Ireland. Perhaps I can find a distant O'Malley cousin." Seana kissed Kathleen lightly on the lips.

"So my kissing days are over, huh?" Seana asked.

"There's only one woman who'll know these lips." Kathleen placed her fingertips across said lips.

"Really? Anyone I know?" She put her arm around her shoulder as they continued to walk off the beach. "I hope she likes the twilight. Did you know it's my favorite time of day?"

"Is it now, darlin'?" she asked playfully.

Seana nodded. "Yep."

"Twilight's own—when the sun's nearly set and the stars are on the rise. The best of everything in the sky." Kathleen clung to her.

"The best of everything right here in my arms," Seana corrected her and kissed her deeply.

Branna shook her head in disbelief. "You were heroes. You and Seana. I-I can't believe it, Kathleen. Were you given a medal?"

Kathleen raised her eyebrows and laughed. "Medals? The American government couldn't even admit that Seana was involved. It was all hush-hush. Seana didn't want any medals, Branna." She saw the color rise in the young O'Malley's face. "Sometimes, darlin', you must do what your heart and conscience dictate without any accolades, just because it's the right thing to do. The heart always knows."

Branna sported a sour look. "Not always."

"No? Then tell me why you didn't marry Timothy. He was fond of you and you of him," Kathleen prodded. She looked over at the slumbering child, who now woke and smiled at her mother. "She's such a happy baby," Kathleen said with a grin. "She may have his looks, but she has your spirit."

She watched Branna, who smiled as she picked up her daughter.

"Why, Branna?" Kathleen asked.

Branna looked at her. "I-I don't know. Maybe I'm just not suited for anyone. Rose and I are doing just fine."

Kathleen saw the set jaw and rolled her eyes. "Oh, you are a stubborn one." She sighed as she slowly stood and leaned on her cane. "Come, let's go for a walk. It's a fine summer day and I need to move these old bones."

As they walked to the cottage door, it burst open. There stood Reagan Shaunessy, scowling and breathing deeply.

"I forgot my hat," she said angrily and marched to the table and picked up the wool cap. She glanced at the heather and looked at Branna, who held Rose closer. When the baby saw Reagan, she grinned and reached for her.

"Rea," the two-year-old exclaimed.

Reagan sported a smug grin as she walked up to Branna, who was quietly seething. The little girl squirmed and Reagan kissed her head. "Hello, Rose darlin'," she said affectionately. "You remember my nickname."

She looked up at Branna, who swallowed with difficulty, then glared at the smirking face. "It's an easy name."

Kathleen watched as Reagan grinned wickedly, as if she loved the banter. "She said my name before she said mam," she reminded Branna, whose face turned crimson with anger and she glared once again.

"And you can save the glare for the college lasses in Dublin," Reagan said. "It may scare the devil out of them, but I know better what lies beneath the ice." She turned away, stopped, and whirled around. "Damn you," she muttered and grabbed Branna by the shoulders and kissed her deeply.

Kathleen grinned and leaned on her cane, while Rose, wedged between them, screeched with laughter and Branna screeched for another reason; she struggled against the tall Irishwoman. Finally, she let go, and Branna stumbled slightly against the table. The child was still giggling.

"Rea kiss Mam." She laughed and hugged her mother.

Reagan grinned. "That I did, darlin'." She pulled her cap down over her brow. "Good day, Branna O'Malley," she said with a firm nod. "Good day, Kathleen."

"Good day, Reagan," Kathleen called as Reagan stormed out. She laughed and shook her head. "Impetuous pig farmer."

Branna was breathing heavily as she stared at the door. She picked up a bit of heather and fondly caressed the purple sprig. She shook her head firmly as if dismissing a thought and set it back down on the table.

"Come, I think you need that walk now," Kathleen said.

They walked outside in the warm summer air, and Kathleen took a deep breath as they watched Reagan mount her horse and gallop across the glen.

"It's the twentieth century, and the woman is still riding a horse." Branna shook her head.

"And gathering heather for the woman she loves," Kathleen added.

Branna took a deep stubborn breath and kicked at the green turf. They watched Reagan as she rode up the sloping hill. She pulled her horse to a halt and waved. Rose giggled again and waved back.

"It was over seven centuries ago when Branna O'Malley rode over that very hill," Kathleen said.

Branna shot her an incredulous look. Kathleen nodded. "'Tis true. She was the first O'Malley, you know. It's herself you're named after."

As Reagan rode over the hill and out of sight, Kathleen turned to the young O'Malley. "Branna was coming home from Scotland. She was a warrior. Seana's mother told her they called Branna the Irish Barbarian." Kathleen stopped and smiled affectionately. "She came home right over that hill."

"There, Eamon!" his younger brother called out, the sunlight bouncing off his sword as he waved it overhead.

At the sound of Connal's voice, Eamon whirled and saw the gray horse galloping over the hill. The rider, in full battle dress, unfurled a sword from its sheath, waving it in kind.

"Thank God!" he called out.

Horse and rider came to a halt, kicking up green turf. "Thank the goddess Morrighan, you mean, brother," the rider said as she dismounted the snorting beast. Her raven hair was braided down her back; her green eyes sparkled wildly.

"I will give thanks to any god or goddess you choose, Branna. You're here at last." Eamon grabbed his sister in a monstrous embrace. "I have missed you. Is it possible you've grown stronger, woman?"

"I have missed you, as well. Tell me quickly what has happened. Why are we meetin' like this? Is it true?"

"Aye, it is. I sent word to you in Scotland as soon as I returned. Cousin Malcolm has taken over. With father gone and both of us away, he slithered right in, bringing his horde with him."

Branna cursed under her breath. "Did you bury him next to Mam?" Tears sprang into her eyes as Eamon nodded sadly.

Just then, Connal rode up. "Branna!" he cried out as he flew off his horse and into her awaiting arms. "Put me down," he begged as Branna nearly lifted him off the ground.

Branna held him at arm's length. "Who is this fine-looking man? It cannot be our little brother, Connal." She winked at Eamon. "I left here two years ago and kissed farewell to a scrawny little calf."

"He has grown into a fine bull," Eamon said proudly, and touched his sword toward the boy's groin.

Connal blushed and avoided Branna's laughter.

"Be proud, Connal. You're an O'Malley. Enough play now. Have the English finally found our little piece of heaven, brothers?" she asked as they walked through the open field to the edge of the woods.

Eamon nodded. "Aye, they finally came our way. Malcolm, the cur, sold us out for a few coins and a few head of cattle."

"Cattle!" Her nostrils flared in anger. "Our birthright has been sold for cattle?"

Connal's blue eyes widened as he watched his sister rant. Eamon saw his incredulous look. "You were a young boy when Branna rode off with Uncle Brian to fight in Scotland," he said with a grin. "She looks different now, boy."

Branna rolled her eyes but said nothing. Connal nodded in agreement. "You look much more like a warrior than a woman, but I see Mam's soft smile in you."

Branna smiled and gently touched his cheek. Eamon swallowed a tear as he watched his older sister. He noticed she wore the battle dress of the chest armor of heavy leather, a sword sheath draped across her back, and thick leather gauntlets to protect her wrists and forearms. He saw a sizable scar on her upper arm, and for the first time, he saw the heavy bandage around her thigh just above her knee.

"What happened?" he asked.

Branna waved him off. "An Englishman got in my way."

Eamon laughed but noticed the dried blood that had seeped through the dirty bandage. The man's kilt she wore was covered in dried blood, as well. "Take care, sister. Infections may be troublesome."

Branna narrowed her eyes at her younger brother. "Have you turned into a ninny, Eamon?" she asked as her lips twitched.

"Take care, Branna O'Malley," he warned. "You might look and fight like a man, but you're still my sister."

Branna laughed and put up her hands in defeat. "We've better things to discuss than your manhood. Now let's get down to it. First, tell me how this happened, then we will get our birthright back," she vowed in a low dark voice.

They sat by the fire warming their hands. Branna left Connal to tend to the fire as she and Eamon found their meager dinner.

"I cannot believe I am sittin' in the woods right now and not in a hot tub in my own room," she said angrily as they cooked the rabbits over the open fire.

"You've still got a nasty temper. Keep still whilst I think."

"Whilst? What in the devil kind of word is whilst?" Branna asked as she blew on the cooked meat, snapping her fingers against the heat. "You've been readin' too much again, Eamon darlin'," she scolded playfully and glanced at Connal fast asleep, curled up in a ball by the fire.

"I'd rather be educated than eating a dead animal on a stick."

He saw his sister hide her grin as she ate ravenously. He thought of Branna and how easily fighting came to her. Eamon was the middle child and most educated. He was not a fighter; he knew this about himself. Oh, he would fight when needed, but he considered himself a scholarly man. He also knew Branna was their father's pride and joy. She was the fighter in the family, much like Red O'Malley himself.

Her father taught them all how to handle a sword, how to hunt, how to fight. Eamon smiled as he remembered the old redheaded man barking his instructions. Eamon and Branna nearly killed each other learning how to wield a sword properly.

"Just because you're a woman,' tis no excuse to be weak."

"'Tis too heavy for me, Da," said the girl of twelve.

Her younger brother laughed and stopped as his father slapped him on the head.

"Don't be laughin' at your sister. One day, she'll be a better fightin' man than meself. This is O'Malley land, and one day, you'll fight for it. Now again," he barked, and little Branna groaned as she lifted the heavy sword.

Eamon regarded his older sibling, who was deep in thought. In the two years since she left with Uncle Brian, she had grown considerably. Eamon didn't know women could have such muscles. Yet, there was softness in her that reminded him so much of their mother—God rest her poor tired soul. Connal was only seven when their mother, Deirdre, died along with the unborn babe. Eamon remembered their father was devastated. Their mother left the three young children to take care of each other and their father. Deirdre O'Malley would be proud of each of them.

"By the god Brân, what are you thinkin', Eamon? You look deep in thought," she asked as she sat back and finished her meal, wiping her hand across her mouth.

"Must you eat like a pig? And stop callin' on the gods, you heathen."

"You are a ninny," she affirmed with a grin. "And I believe in the gods and goddesses."

"You sound like Mam."

"Have you come up with a solution? Believe me, I'll march right up there and cut off his manhood, such as it is—"

"Branna, can we stop with the killing? Now they've been in the house since Da died. However, Malcolm hasn't made contact with the English yet. There are only a few people in our home now. Liam told me only today there were three, including Malcolm. Connal was away in Galway, I was in Dublin. I got word to you as soon as I could."

"So the English don't know yet that Malcolm sold our birthright?"

"They do not. Liam said a messenger will be sent tomorrow to take the deed to Dublin."

"Can you get to Liam? Have him find out when this rider will be going. I'll intercept him. It'll bide us more time. When I return, we can decide how to get back and reclaim our home."

She stood and moved her injured leg stiffly as she walked to her horse and pulled out large capes for both of them. Eamon eyed the tartan plaid.

"I took it off a Scotsman," Branna answered his questioning glance, "who was doin' his best to take off me head." She tossed one to her grinning brother.

"I take it he dinna argue too much?" he asked, trying his hand at the Scottish dialect.

"Aye, he dinna..." Branna agreed sadly. "It 'twas hard with me sword up his arse."

Eamon groaned at his sister's irreverence. "Good night. It is good to have you home once again, Branna."

76

"Aye, Eamon. It is good to be home in Ireland. We're all we have now, brother." She bent down to kiss his dark head.

Branna sighed and yawned. "Cousin Malcolm the cur— the name fits the thievin' bastard," she said as she drifted off to sleep.

The next morning, they rode to the outskirts of Galway, making sure no one noticed them. This was hard, as the O'Malley clan was well known. It was to their advantage now they were not as widely known as their more wealthy relations—the seafaring O'Malleys.

Since the time of the crusades, the O'Malleys had prospered along with the O'Neil, the O'Flaherty, and such. However, the lesser-known O'Malleys had enjoyed their anonymity and little piece of heaven. That is, until Malcolm O'Dowd got his greedy hands on the papers after their father died. Somehow, Branna had to save her home.

Branna rode atop her steed with a confident air and smiled as she remembered how she acquired the gray Arabian. It was a "gift" from a dead Englishman when she and her uncle battled in Scotland two years before. She named the mare Morrighan, after the Celtic goddess of battle, war, and fertility. Branna chuckled inwardly; fertility was something for which she had no use. She never understood why she was not like other women. Men held no attraction for her but to drink with and fight with. The coupling aspect with a man never entered her mind. She grinned evilly as she remembered a certain Scottish lass—now that was interesting.

"There's Liam. Stay here." Eamon galloped over to his old friend.

After a brief conversation, he quickly rode back. "The rider left an hour ago, heading east. He's a tall fair-haired man on a black steed. Branna, he has a good head start."

Branna grinned wickedly. "Not while I ride Morrighan. You wait in the same place. I will be back before nightfall." She rode off, her heels digging into the gray horse.

Branna knew which road the rider would take. She rode like

the wind as she took an alternate path, hoping to head him off. Sometime later, she came to a stop outside the town of Dunmore. Resting her horse by a stream, she hid well behind the dense woods and watched.

When she saw the rider was alone, her first instinct was to kill him without question. She grimaced at the idea. *It would be my luck to kill an innocent man.* She mounted Morrighan and followed the stream to head him off.

The man pulled his horse to an abrupt stop as she came out of the clearing. Seeing a woman in a cape, he relaxed somewhat. However, the intensity from the green eyes worried him and he put his hand to his dagger. "Good eve, milady."

Branna gave him a smug grin. "Good day, milord. I think you may have something I need."

The man grinned and raised an eyebrow. "By the looks of you, I think you may have something I need," he said with a leer.

English whelp. She smiled and cautiously rode up to him. "I think we might come to an understandin'," she said with a saucy grin.

She reached behind her and pulled out her sword, swinging it in his direction.

Immediately, he let out a cry and pulled his dagger and plunged it into her side.

Branna cried out, mostly in anger for being duped so easily. She pulled back slightly and drove her sword through his chest. She watched blood pour out of his wound and drove her sword deeper.

"You connivin' English bastard!" she yelled and yanked her sword out of his body. "Branna O'Malley," she informed him in a low growl, as he fell from his horse.

She jumped off Morrighan and stumbled as she put a hand to the wound in her side. She looked through his pockets and found the leather pouch. Opening it, she saw the legal documents to their home. She dragged his body off the path and covered it with branches, leaves, and anything else she could find to make the shallow grave. Painfully mounting Morrighan, she took the other horse and headed back to Galway.

Eamon and Connal sat by the same clearing in the woods and waited. It was nearly dark when they heard the horses.

"Branna!" Eamon exclaimed as he saw his sister.

"Did you get it?" Connal asked.

"Aye, Connie, I got 'em," she said and dismounted. She handed the pouch to Eamon. "Is it all there? I hope it 'tis. I buried the lyin' bastard outside Dunmore. Connie, would you like a horse?" she asked with a wink.

The younger man grinned and took hold of the black steed.

"It's all here, Branna. Thank God for you," Eamon said.

"Good. Let's go. I have a feelin' this is the time." She swiped a hand across her brow.

"Are you all right, then?"

Branna gave him a reluctant grin. "Aye, I'm fine. Come, time to pay Malcolm and his English friends a visit."

"O'Malleys once again!" Connal said with excitement and raised his sword. Branna and Eamon followed suit.

"Once again," Branna O'Malley said with pride as she rode to her destiny.

Chapter 9

Branna swallowed her emotions as the homestead came into view. "It's smaller somehow."

Eamon put his arm around her shoulders. "We're the poor O'Malley relations. It's grand enough for me."

"And me," Connal said proudly.

"Aye, it 'tis grand, isn't it?" Branna agreed and winced, her hand flying to her side.

Both brothers rode on either side of her.

"What is it?" Eamon asked. He placed his hand to her side. Branna saw the look of astonishment when he pulled back his bloodied hand. "Why didn't you say somethin'?"

"He pierced the armor, nothing more," Branna said. "Now this is the right time. He won't be expectin' us. You and Connal go around the back. Remember how we sneaked into our rooms when we were children? We'll do that again. I'll go to the front. I'll give you a little time, then I'll scream like a banshee. That'll bring 'em all runnin'. Go now quickly."

"Be careful. We don't know exactly who's in there," Eamon said over his shoulder as he and Connal rode off.

Branna took a deep, painful breath and stuck the bloodied cloth back into the wound. She wiped the sweat from her eyes and waited. Knowing her brothers must be in position, she clicked Morrighan's sides and took off wailing and screaming.

The huge wooden door opened and there stood her cousin, brandishing a sword and looking ridiculous.

"What a silly bastard," she said as she galloped. She pulled up to the front door, blocking Malcolm as he let out a shriek and raised his sword.

Branna dismounted and pulled out her sword at the same time. "Cousin Malcolm, you thievin' whoreson!" She raised the sword over her head.

Malcolm lifted his in defense and in one blow, his sword fell to the ground with a clang. Branna walked up to him and pointed her sword at his neck. She pulled back to deliver the final blow.

"Please don't!" She heard a woman's voice call out.

At the door was a young woman, wild-eyed and petrified. Their eyes locked for a moment. "Don't kill him, he's unarmed," she begged.

Branna tore her eyes away and looked down at Malcolm, who was trembling so much she could hear his bones rattling. For an instant, Branna relented. When she saw him rise, Branna lightly rapped him on the head with the grip of her sword. He folded in a dead faint. "What a fop."

Connal and Eamon came to the door. Eamon was holding a struggling elderly woman, and Connal was laughing uproariously.

"I've found a feisty woman. Might be to your liking."

"Who are you, sir?" the young woman asked, looking at Branna, who raised an eyebrow.

Connal stifled a snort and Eamon slapped his head.

"Let me go, you Irish barbarians!" the elderly woman demanded, struggling against Eamon's grip.

"Barbarians? You compliment us, madam." He offered a slight bow.

Connal knelt beside his cousin. "Is he dead?"

Branna was breathing raggedly as she leaned on her sword. "Not yet," she wheezed and regarded the young woman.

She was shorter than Branna by at least six inches, wearing a frock that looked expensive, Branna thought. She sounded English, as well. Her hair was long and dark. In the dimly lit entranceway, Branna could barely make out the woman's blue eyes.

"Is there anyone else in the house?" Branna asked in a low voice.

The elderly woman spoke. "Yes, so you might as well give up."

81

Branna raised an eyebrow and smiled slightly at the woman's defiant posture.

Connal hoisted his unconscious cousin over his shoulder and started past the young woman.

"What right have you to come in here like this?" the old woman bellowed.

Eamon still had her by the arm and pulled her into the entranceway.

Branna motioned with her sword to the woman, who quickly backed up and headed inside. Branna closed the heavy door and slid the huge plank of wood across the threshold.

"How dare you come in here—?" the woman continued to bellow.

"Quiet," Branna said, and the woman clamped her mouth shut.

"If you promise to keep still, I'll let you go," Eamon said.

"Do as he says, Elizabeth," the young woman said, never taking her eyes off Branna.

Branna could only imagine what was going through the woman's mind as Branna stood there, sweating and leaning on her sword. With the leather gauntlets covering her from wrist to forearm, as well as the bloody kilt and dirty shirt, Branna supposed she did indeed look like a man. She realized wearing the leather chest plate under her filthy woolen cape didn't help matters.

She was staring into this woman's blue eyes. She tore her gaze away and looked at her brothers. All three of them must have looked dirty, tired, and desperate.

"Lady Anne," Elizabeth warned, but Anne put up her hand to silence her.

"I ask again. Who are you, sir?" Anne asked.

Branna smiled and bowed slightly, eliciting a chuckle from her baby brother, who had tossed their cousin unceremoniously on the bench. He landed with a thud.

"Connal, tie Malcolm. I don't want him wanderin'," Branna said in a low painful voice. "Eamon, take Lady Lizzy back wherever you found her and lock the door," she added sarcastically.

"I will not leave Anne," Elizabeth said firmly.

Branna closed her eyes and took a deep calming breath, fighting the urge to slap her.

Anne continued to watch her. "You're injured, sir," she said. "Go with him, Elizabeth."

"We mean you no harm, ladies," Eamon assured them. "We need to rest a while, and I need to look after my—" He stopped and looked at Branna. "—brother."

Anne looked from one to the other. "You're brothers?" She looked from Eamon to Branna. "You could be twins."

Eamon hid his laugh in his cough.

Branna ignored him. "Please don't be arguin' now," she said in a soft voice.

Anne shot Branna a curious look and locked eyes with her for a moment.

Connal walked back into the room. "There's no one else around, the stables are clear. They must have taken the horses. Everything is as we left it."

Branna nodded. "Go see about something to eat, Connie," she said and stumbled forward.

Anne rushed to her side. "Sir, please..."

Eamon let Elizabeth go and took Branna by the arm and said, "Let's get you to your room."

"Your room?" Anne asked and looked at all three. "You're O'Malley? Quickly, get him to his room."

Eamon nearly picked Branna up as he guided her out of the dark foyer and into her old room.

Once at the door, Anne went in first and lit the large candle on the side of the bed. "I-I was sleeping in here," she explained.

Eamon nodded and set Branna on the bed.

"Elizabeth, go heat the water on the hearth. You," she motioned to Eamon, "you know where everything is. Your brother is bleeding. I'll need some bandages. Go."

Eamon looked from Branna to Anne's worried face. "You better know what you're doin'," he warned and left the room.

Anne lit three other candles. The room was dim, but at least she could see the injured man clearly.

Connal came rushing in and stood by the bedside.

"Don't hover. Start a fire, it's going to be chilly tonight," she ordered.

"Yes, ma'am," Connal said obediently and concentrated on getting the peat fire going in the fireplace. In a moment, he had the peat glowing warmly, illuminating the room. He turned back and gave Anne a cautious look.

"He'll be fine," Anne assured him. "I need to get these filthy clothes off him. Give me a hand." She heard the young brother chuckle. "What is all this snickering about?" Anne asked as she and Connal got Branna to a sitting position.

Connal unbuckled the heavy leather armor and eased it off, revealing a dirty shirt underneath. "You'll know soon enough," he replied with a grin.

Elizabeth came into the room with a bowl of steaming soapy water. Eamon was behind her with a basket full of cotton rags.

"Perhaps I should take care of...him," Eamon offered and glanced at his brother.

Anne shook her head. "You're as filthy as he is. Go, both of you. Elizabeth—"

"I know, Anne. Come with me, gentlemen," she said and ushered them out.

Eamon opened his mouth, and Anne pointed to the door. He shrugged and obediently walked out and closed the door.

Anne worked to get the wool cape off the semi-conscious man's shoulder. She tossed it into the corner, then unbuttoned his shirt; she noticed the red stain on the side. She took a sharp intake of breath as the injured man mumbled incoherently.

"Please don't die on me, Mr. O'Malley," she begged as she opened his shirt.

Her mouth gaped open as she saw the firm breasts, milky white against the dark and dirty skin. The color rushed to her cheeks as she swallowed. "Good Lord, he's a woman," she exclaimed, her eyes riveted to the breasts. She took a deep breath to calm her racing heart.

Branna moaned and her eyes flew open. Disoriented, she bolted up.

Anne put her hand on the strong woman's shoulder. "Please, Mr. um, Miss O'Malley, lie back."

"Eamon, Connal," she whispered painfully.

Anne gently laid her against the pillows. "Your brothers are fine. Please, I have to tend to your wound." She soaked the cotton rags in the soapy water.

Branna seemed to be aware of her surroundings. "My room," she sighed and closed her eyes and faded off.

Anne cleaned the wound and placed several bandages over it. This O'Malley woman was indeed lucky to be wearing the armor. Wrapping it around the slim waist was not an easy task; the woman was heavy, but she managed as she tied it off.

She noticed the bandage on her upper thigh. She hesitantly lifted the wool kilt to expose the other wound, which she cleaned and re-bandaged, as well. All the while, Branna muttered through her fever.

Anne knew she needed to get her out of the dirty clothes. She struggled but managed to pull her up and stripped the shirt off her shoulders, mindful of the new bandage. She slipped the kilt off the woman and swallowed with some difficulty as she looked at the muscular thighs and taut stomach. She desperately tried to avoid the dark triangular patch between the injured woman's strong thighs. Quickly, she pulled the sheet up to her waist and concentrated on bathing her upper body.

Branna groaned and shifted painfully, her eyes once again flew open. "Mam?"

Anne knew the Irish term for mother. "Sleep, please," Anne said and bathed her feverish face.

"Mam, I'm sorry I left Connie and Eamon. I had to go. Please, don't be angry with me," she said in a soft brogue. "I'm tryin' to do the right thing." She mumbled something else, as she drifted off once again.

Anne pulled the covers up to Branna's chin and smoothed the hair off her forehead. She thought of taking the leather confinement off Branna's hair, but it would wake her unnecessarily. Quietly, she gathered the bowl along with the bloodied bandages and closed the door.

Eamon and Connal were now in fresh kilts and capes. Both men grinned sheepishly.

"Your sister should be fine," Anne said evenly. "What is her name?"

"Branna," Eamon said, shamefaced. Connal chuckled and got an elbow to the ribs.

Elizabeth was shocked. "A woman? Wielding a sword?" she said in disbelief.

Connal sprang to his sister's defense. "Yes, a woman. And she is a better warrior than all your Englishmen put together," he said loudly. He noticed the fatherly look from Eamon and blushed. "Ma'am," he said apologetically.

Eamon regarded both Englishwomen. "For now, you can stay until Branna figures this out. I'll go and check on her."

Anne waited for a few moments and walked to the bedroom and quietly opened the door. Eamon stood by his sister's bedside. Anne thought she was intruding and turned to go when she heard Eamon's quiet voice. "She looks so young and vulnerable sleeping here as a child. Don't you think?"

Anne walked into the room and stood beside him but said nothing.

"She looks so much like our mother," he continued. He grimaced as he saw the thin red line on her upper arm and lightly traced the scar.

He sighed sadly and kissed her forehead. "You fight so fiercely for this land, Branna. You are the O'Malley," he whispered proudly as they both left the room.

Chapter 10

Branna's throat was burning, and someone was trying to force her to drink. She opened her eyes to see a woman standing over her.

"Miss O'Malley, can you hear me?" the soft English voice whispered. "Please, you need to drink this."

Branna focused on her surroundings; when she realized where she was, she tried to sit. "Eamon, Connal," she mumbled helplessly.

"They're both fine. Please drink this."

Branna relented and eagerly gulped at the cool water.

"Easy, not too fast," Anne said as she held the cup.

Branna nodded and slumped back against the pillows. "Thank you," she whispered and took a deep breath as she faded off again.

The last thing Branna remembered was the cool cloth against her forehead and a worried look in the blue eyes.

When she woke again, the sun was gleaming through the window. She glanced around the room and saw the woman curled up on the long cushioned bench by the fire. A huge tartan cape covered her body. Branna swallowed easily now but knew at some point, she was feverish. Visions of her Mam and Da invaded her dreams.

She moved under the heavy quilt and realized she was naked; she raised an eyebrow and glanced once again at the slumbering Englishwoman. Trying to sit, Branna let out a deep groan she could not stifle.

Anne was quickly at her bedside. "What are you doing?" she

asked and pushed Branna back.

"I'm tryin' to get out of this bed," Branna said seriously, as she struggled. "It 'tis, I'm afraid, a losin' battle," she mumbled and lay back.

"How are you feeling?" Anne asked, wringing out a damp cloth and placing it on her forehead.

"Better. Thank you," Branna said. "What is your name?"

"Warrington, Anne Warrington," she said. "You have been asleep for two days."

Branna's eyes flew open. "Two days? Damn, I must get up. Where's that whoreson Malcolm?" she said through clenched teeth. "Thievin' bastard!"

Anne winced. "Such language."

Branna looked up to see Anne looking at her breasts. Anne averted her eyes. "Y-your cousin is still in constraints in the stable. Connal is looking after him. Eamon is trying to find all the cattle that have been on the loose for over a week."

"I only hope that bastard is lying on a pile of dung," Branna said.

Anne stifled her laugh as she bit at her lip.

Eamon poked his head in as he knocked at the door. "Branna, I heard you all the way from the great hall. You must be feeling better," he said, sporting a grin.

Branna laughed and winced slightly. Anne moved away from the bed, astounded that this woman did not bother to pull up the sheet completely. Her brother did not seem to notice. Anne did not understand these Irish people. In England, a woman would not even been seen in her own room without proper clothing.

"I am. Eamon, get my robe."

Anne shook her head. "You are not getting out of that bed until you eat."

Branna frowned. "This is still my house and—"

As Anne walked out of the bedroom, she gave Eamon a stern look. He was eyeing Branna's robe. "Don't give it another thought, Eamon O'Malley," she said and took the long robe with her.

"You think I won't get up without it?" Branna called after her and collapsed back against the pillows.

88

Eamon winced. "Stop yellin', you heifer. Can you not be civilized?"

Branna gave him a disturbed look. "You have turned into a ninny," she accused as her brother laughed. "What has happened in two days?"

"We still have Malcolm tied up to the stable. He's crying like a wee babe." They both chuckled as Eamon continued. "Connal is watching him. This Warrington woman and her, whoever she is, Elizabeth, have apparently been led to believe that by comin' here... Well, Branna, we have a problem."

Branna raised an eyebrow. "Just findin' that out?"

Eamon glanced at his sister, ignoring the sarcasm. "Did you know Da was in debt?"

"He never let on, but I knew."

"Well, I didn't. Why did you not tell me?" he asked angrily.

"I'm thinking Da didn't want anyone to know. When Uncle Brian told me about his idea to go to Scotland, we decided to do it. Da knew we were goin', but not the reason why."

"Damn it, Branna! I'm a grown man."

"I'm the oldest. It was my decision. Someone had to stay here."

"I was in Dublin, no one told me about anything. If I'd known, I would have never left Da."

Branna sighed and lay back. "What happened?"

"Apparently, our cousin—"

"The thieving whoreson, bastard," Branna offered angrily.

"Aye, aye, let's leave the family lineage out of this for a moment," he said and continued. "Malcolm made a deal with a certain English family. In order for Da to save the land, he had to marry a member of this family. This Warrington family agreed to send their daughter in marriage. We keep the land. They pay off the debt, but would have a stake in our property, as well."

"That's why I went with Uncle Brian to Scotland. Go look in my bags."

Eamon gave her a confused look and opened her leather bag. "How much is here?" he asked in amazement.

"Enough gold to keep our land. That's why I went to fight in

Scotland. Uncle Brian and I were paid to fight—paid to fight the English. I'd have done it for nothin'," she said angrily. "All for nothin'," she added with a sigh. "Did he marry this woman?"

"No, and now that you stopped the rider, we've only Malcolm to contend with. Well, and the Englishwomen."

"Send them back to England."

"I can't do that. I talked with the Warrington woman; she seems to be an innocent."

"English? Innocent? Are you listenin' to yourself? Jaysus, I'll tell her myself!"

Anne walked in with a tray. Eamon sported a smug grin as he watched Anne place the tray on the bedside. "If you eat enough and get more rest, perhaps by tomorrow, you will be able to get up. Of course you will have to stop your barking," she said and blew at the steamy cup of broth.

Branna glared at her smiling brother. "Was there somethin' you wanted to say, Branna darlin'?" he asked sweetly.

"Yes, go find the cattle that are wanderin' all over Galway by now!" she bellowed and winced.

Eamon laughed and walked out of the room. "You've got my permission to beat her, Miss Warrington."

Anne smiled. "It is nice to see such love between siblings." She held the spoon of broth up to Branna's mouth.

Branna opened it to say something, but the spoon stopped her. "I can feed myself, woman," she grumbled and shifted under the covers. However, she dutifully took another spoonful. Realizing she was ravenous, she allowed Anne to feed her.

"Miss Warrington," Branna started, and Anne held up a piece of bread.

"No bellowing until you have eaten, Miss O'Malley," she said firmly, and Branna took the bread. Anne watched as she ate. "Drink this tea, please."

Obediently, she took the heavy wooden cup and drank the strong brew. She stopped, completely fatigued by the effort. Her eyes grew heavy as she tried to concentrate. "Now, Miss Warrington. My brother told me," she slurred as her eyes closed.

Branna let out a contented sigh as she felt the soft hand on

her brow. She felt a pang of regret when she heard Anne close the
door.

Branna had no idea how long she had slept when she
cautiously sat on the side of the bed and stood. Testing her legs,
she realized the wound on her thigh no longer throbbed. Anne
Warrington bandaged the wound with care. Branna cautiously
walked to the dressing area and couldn't help but smile when she
saw a long fur-lined robe on the chair. Though it was near summer,
the mornings were still foggy and damp. Letting out a low curse,
Branna painfully twisted back and forth. She heard the big heavy
door creak open; there stood Anne with her hands on her hips.
    "Miss O'Malley—" she started.
    Branna held up her hand. "Stop nagging, woman," she said.
"I appreciate your kindness. You've done a good deed. Now go
away!" She turned and swayed slightly.
    Anne put her arm around the lean waist and guided her to
a wooden chair by the fire. "You are a stubborn woman, Miss
O'Malley, and you need a bath," she said. "I'll put the water on
the hearth and have Connal bring the basin in here." She promptly
turned and walked out of the room.

Branna lay in the hot steamy, scented water. The large basin
barely fit her long legs.
    "Branna?" Eamon's voice called out.
    She lifted her head and beckoned him into the room. "By the
gods, I have missed takin' a hot soak." She sighed as she pulled
the leather straps from her long raven hair. Ruffling her fingers
through it, she sighed happily, as she put her head back against
the wooden tub.
    Eamon laughed at his sister's inhibitions, sitting in a tub, the
soapy water barely covering her breasts. "You are a woman after
all," he said and held up a pitcher along with wooden mugs.
    "Eamon, you read my mind." She took the wood mug of
mulled wine. Sipping it, she sighed once again. "You did a good
job with this batch, brother."
    "It wasn't me. Miss Warrington thought you might like a bit

of something," he said, and Branna opened one suspicious eye. "Maybe it would ease your foul temper." He laughed heartily at her glare.

Ignoring the idea of the Englishwoman, Branna sipped the warm wine and stared into the fire as she soaked in the steamy water.

"What are we going to do with them?" Eamon asked.

Branna groaned. She took a wet cloth and placed it on her face. "I have no idea," she mumbled under the cloth. "Once I'm up and about, we'll talk. What about Malcolm, is he still in the stable?"

Eamon nodded, and both siblings broke into a fit of laughter. They stopped as the door opened and Connal poked his head in.

Branna removed the cloth from her face and grinned. "Come in, Connie." She waved him in, causing water to slosh over the sides of the basin.

He raised an eyebrow as he watched his sister lounge in the hot soapy water. "How can you sit in there? Don't the cows drink out of it?"

"It's a woman thing, me boy," Eamon answered and handed him a mug.

"Don't you think it odd that we're standing here while Branna is bathin'?" Connie asked, and before anyone could speak...

"Yes, I do! Good heavens, don't you Irish have any propriety? Get out of here," Elizabeth scolded the two men, who looked to their older sister.

"Where have you been?" Branna asked and sipped her wine.

"Taking care of this house and these ill-mannered brothers," Elizabeth said as she ushered them out. For some reason, Branna had taken a liking to this cantankerous woman.

"Ill-mannered?" Eamon asked over his shoulder.

"Leave the wine, Eamon," Branna called after him. Eamon bowed to Elizabeth, who was scowling, and handed her the jug.

Elizabeth shook her head and set the jug on the table. "Letting your brothers see you half-naked," she accused. "I have never in all my life seen anything like this country—women wearing men's kilts, in armor and carrying a sword, riding that horse, astride no less. I tell you, it's shameless."

"You think me shameless, woman?" Branna lowered herself into the tub, getting her head wet to wash her hair. "I have seen too much in the past two years to hide anything."

Elizabeth pushed Branna's hands away and started to wash her hair. "What is your relationship with Anne Warrington?" Branna asked.

"I am her aunt and chaperone," she said as she rubbed Branna's head. She took a bucket of water and doused Branna's head, repeating the gesture and rinsing it several times.

As Branna sat obediently, a feeling of loss came over her; she missed her parents. Elizabeth smoothed her hair back and wrung the long tresses as dry as she could.

Branna looked up and smiled slightly. "Thank you. My mam used to wash my hair like that," she said and blushed horribly at exposing her emotions to Elizabeth. She stood and stepped out of the basin with some assistance from Elizabeth, who now held up the drying sheet for her. Branna wrapped herself in the sheet.

"You call her Lady Anne, why?" Branna asked in a tired voice. She let out a small gasp of pain as she reached for the comb on the table.

Elizabeth picked up the long robe and held it for her. "Put this on, child."

Branna grudgingly slipped into the robe and sat down once again. Elizabeth picked up the comb and began to comb her hair as she stood behind Branna. "I suppose it doesn't matter anymore. Miss O'Malley, we came here thinking something quite different. It is true Anne was to marry your father. Now Anne cannot go back. If she does, without a husband or property, her family will be disgraced. You see your father was not the only man with debts. Anne was sold to your father."

Branna stopped and frowned deeply. *Sold?* She looked over at Elizabeth and sighed. "And you called us barbarians."

"Don't blame my aunt, Miss O'Malley," Anne's voice called from the doorway. She walked over to Elizabeth and knelt beside her. "It wasn't your fault. It was my decision."

Branna watched the exchange between them and shook her

head. She fluffed her long hair behind her head and angrily stood. "I cannot imagine that my father agreed to this."

"No. He did not know, but he had no choice," Anne said. "Malcolm knew he had the upper hand. You were all gone and, well, he knew that his debt was to be paid and he was to keep his land. My father took what little money your father had and the deal was made. I did not know this until I arrived, as your father passed away. I'm sorry."

"So you see, Miss O'Malley," Elizabeth started as she set the comb on the table. "If Anne was to go back to England, all deals would be off and it would ruin my idiot brother. Anne would—"

"Elizabeth, it is done. I cannot ask this family to go through anymore. I am grateful you stopped that rider and got your birthright back, Miss O'Malley. I only hope he won't cause you anymore trouble."

"He won't, not from hell he won't."

Anne gaped at her. "You...you killed him?"

"I did. He was tryin' to do the same to me," she reminded her as she felt the wound on her side.

"Did you have to kill him?"

Hearing the judgmental tone, Branna's mood darkened and her back stiffened. "Yes. What else do you expect from a barbarian?" she asked in a low angry voice.

Anne shot a look into the green eyes.

"If you ladies will excuse me," Branna spat out and marched out of the bedroom.

"So much death in this country." Anne sighed and sat down.

"She is a proud woman, Anne. You must tread lightly," Elizabeth warned.

The next morning, Branna dressed in a kilt and white blouse, a cape once again draped over her left shoulder, held in place by their family brooch; she wore her long thick hair down and flowing.

It was early, fog still engulfing the morning. As she and Eamon walked into the stable, there sat Malcolm.

"Well, cousin. How are you farin' this fine soft mornin'?"

Branna asked as she leaned against the stable door.

Eamon grinned and Malcolm scowled at both of them. "You can't keep me here. Someone's bound to miss me!" With his reddish blond hair tousled and green eyes bugging, he angrily pulled at the leather restraints.

"Who'd miss you?" Eamon asked lightly.

Branna laughed. "Now, Eamon, someone must be lookin' for him."

"You crazy bitch!" he spat.

Branna walked over and hauled him to his feet. "Yes, I am crazy, so don't go too far. I'd just as soon kill you as look at you."

Eamon looked up to see Anne standing by the door. She was dressed in the Irish peasant garb—a long woolen frock with a heavy wool blouse; a dark shawl was thrown around her shoulders.

Branna examined her dress and smiled slightly. "Good mornin'. You look good as any Irish lass," she said in a low voice, and Eamon rolled his eyes playfully.

"Keep your filthy perversion to yourself, Branna," Malcolm said. "She's a lady, not a girl-fucking—" Eamon's right fist to his jaw stopped him.

Anne was shocked as she looked at Branna, who had such a melancholic look on her face it broke Anne's heart. Branna opened her mouth to say something as Anne dashed from the stable.

"Damn you, Malcolm. You just don't want to live, do you?" Branna asked, shaking her head.

Eamon flexed his bruised hand. "Go to her, sister. I think some explaining will be necessary now. I'll keep an eye on cousin here."

Branna walked out into the dissipating fog. She looked around and found Anne standing by the edge of the woods, her arms folded in front of her. Fearing Anne would be upset; Branna winced and walked over to her. "Miss Warrington…" she started.

Anne whirled around and backed up.

Branna stopped immediately and sported an angry look. "I'm not going to molest you, woman," she said. "I apologize if you've been offended. My cousin, well, you know what he's like. I'm

95

sorry," she said awkwardly. Shaking her head, she turned to walk away.

"Is what Malcolm said true?"

Branna turned in a defiant pose. "Yes, it 'tis. Good day, Miss Warrington."

Before Anne could say another word, Branna strode purposefully to the stable. Anne watched her gallop away on the gray Arabian, her raven hair blowing wildly behind her.

Chapter 11

"I think I may faint. Where is that mulled wine you concocted, Anne?" Elizabeth exclaimed upon hearing what happened; she fanned herself with the towel. "Oh, these Irish."

Anne gave her aunt an exasperated look. "Aunt Elizabeth, really. There are women and men like this in England, as well."

Elizabeth opened her mouth to disagree but quickly shut it, realizing it was true. She watched as her niece looked down at her hands.

"Anne, what it is, dear?" When Anne didn't answer, Elizabeth continued, "I have always wondered about you. The suitors, which your father found, were never acknowledged, never wanted. I have wondered why."

Anne sat there, thinking of Branna O'Malley and how sad she looked, yet still proud. She remembered the green angry eyes boring into her that morning and how she wanted to run after Branna to tell her she knew what Branna was going through. Anne understood Branna O'Malley in a way she never thought she could. Her heart raced as she closed her eyes, trying to deny the image of the tall brooding woman.

"Ladies, I must apologize for my cousin," Eamon started as he walked in.

"Where did your sister go?" Anne asked.

"It's hard to say. The last time I saw her that angry, she got drunk and into a fight—"

Elizabeth groaned in disbelief. "Women drinking and fighting."

"Possibly both," he concluded with a grin. "She left her sword behind. That's a good sign." He looked at Anne, who was staring at her hands.

"Her wounds have not yet healed," Anne said.

"Branna can take care of herself, believe me," he said as he watched her.

"I'm afraid I hurt her."

Eamon cocked his head, and Anne felt him watch her. "She's been hurt before. Branna is a unique woman, Miss Warrington. She is both woman and warrior. My parents knew that. She is so much like Da. Strong and brave, loyal and steadfast, but she has our mother's independent spirit. Branna is not, however, a typical woman, as you now know. It is very hard for her. Please don't judge her too harshly."

Both women heard the love and affection in his voice.

"Judge her?" Anne repeated sadly. *How can I judge someone who is like myself?* "Can we go find her?"

"Not if you want to live. She'll be back after she cools off. You must let her be. If you care, that is." He looked into her eyes.

"I care, Mr. O'Malley," Anne whispered, surprised by the sincerity in her voice.

She avoided her aunt's incredulous look and Eamon's wide grin.

The gray clouds darkened the day as the wind whipped around the cliffs. Moiré O'Neill looked up to see a rider galloping toward her. She saw the wild raven hair and shook her head. Branna O'Malley, she thought with a smile; she hadn't seen this woman in two years. A pang of sadness rippled through when she thought of what Branna had come home to.

"Good day to you, Branna," she hailed her greeting as Branna pulled Morrighan to a screeching halt and dismounted. "Welcome home. I'm sorry about your father," she added softly.

"Thank you, Moiré."

Moiré reached up and touched Branna's weathered cheek and kissed her. "Now what brings you here?" she asked, smiling. Her smile faded, and she gave Branna a worried look. "It isn't Eamon, is it?"

"No, Eamon is fine." She smiled at the look of relief on Moiré's face.

"Then what are you doing over here?"

Branna looked at the ground and grumbled. Moiré leaned in to hear. "Come into the house. It's raining, if you haven't noticed." She pulled the brooding woman along.

As they sat in front of the fire, Moiré said nothing for a moment or two until she could take no more. "All right then, out with it. What's put that scowl on your face?"

"I'm not scowlin'. I just came over to see you," she grumbled and leaned forward, warming her hands against the glowing bars of peat.

"Don't give me that. We've known each other too long. Now out with it."

As she explained, she couldn't quite look Moiré in the eye. She stared at the glowing fire as she spoke. She told her of the Englishwoman, why she was here, and the uncertainty of the woman's future.

"Well, that's quite a problem. You O'Malleys get yourselves in more trouble than anyone I know," Moiré said with a chuckle.

For the first time, Branna laughed. "'Tis true, I'm afraid, but don't be laughin' too hard. You'll be part of it one day," she said with a wink.

Moiré blushed to her roots and looked at the fire. "Well then, what are you going to do with this Englishwoman? I take it she has a name."

Branna took a deep soulful breath. Moiré smiled sadly. It had not been an easy life for Branna. She was a strong woman in every sense of the word. Moiré had never seen a woman who could fight as well as any man; she could ride and wield a sword with the best of them. Branna was like a man in a good many ways. Moiré raised an eyebrow as she realized just how much. Though they had never spoken of it, there was an understanding between them when their eyes met.

"I have to protect my home and family, but I can't throw this woman out. I-I have to think of somethin'." Branna let out a dejected sigh.

"You can't do it all on your own. Talk to Eamon and Connal. You'll find the way that is best for all the O'Malleys," she added with a soft smile, "and your Englishwoman."

Branna shot her an incredulous look. She saw the warm kind eyes challenging her. "I-I…She's not…" she started and stopped. Moiré laughed. "I'd like to meet this woman who has you stumbling all over your words."

The door opened and in walked Dermot O'Neill. He was a tall young man with thick dark hair. He smiled when he saw Branna. "Well, Branna O'Malley," he said. "Welcome home. What brings you here on this rainy day?" he asked and shook his wet head. "Did ya kill many Englishmen?"

Branna laughed heartily as Moiré slapped her brother on the shoulder. Dermot waved off his sister, walked to the cupboard, and took down the earthen bottle.

His sister rolled her eyes. "It's a little early in the day, brother," Moiré said seriously.

"Keep still, woman. We have a guest in this house."

Branna laughed and accepted the wooden cup. She raised it to her friends. "I am not a guest, but a friend."

Dermot's smile filled his face as he nodded in agreement.

Moiré shook her head. "Well, if you insist on drinking that swill, have a bit of bread to go with it."

In the early evening, Branna rode Morrighan home through the grassy hills. As she saw her homestead, she pulled the mare to a halt. She smiled fondly, remembering her mother's tale of her birth. How she introduced her newborn daughter to the gods and goddesses of old on the cliffs, on the edge of the world. Her mother instilled such strength in her, teaching her to fight for her family, while her father taught her to fight for the land. It was all she knew.

Now, Anne was there and her heart was lost. She felt compelled to help Anne and Elizabeth, but at the same time, she knew she must keep her home and family intact. She knew by her reaction that Anne did not share her feelings. *What did you expect? To find a woman to share your life with? The gods do not favor you that well.*

She looked out at the expanse of water. "How am I to do it, Mam? What'll I do?" she asked openly and let out a dejected sigh.

They were well into the evening meal and no sign of Branna. Even Eamon was anxious. When the rain came, all sat by the long table in the great room not saying much as they picked at their food.

Connal stood. "We can't just sit here."

They heard the door opening as Connal finished speaking; he made a dash for the door.

"Branna, finally!"

She stripped her wool cape over her head, and Connal took it from her. "You're freezing," he said, and Branna smiled down at her brother. She placed a gentle hand on his cheek. "Connie, you look like Mam." She patted his blushing cheek.

"You had us all worried," Eamon said from the table as he ate.

"I'm glad to see it didn't bother your appetite," she said, slurring her words.

Eamon raised an eyebrow. "You need food, Branna," he said and roughly pulled her down next to him at the long table.

She avoided Anne and Elizabeth completely.

"I'll get you some food," Anne said and walked over to the fire.

Branna ran a tired hand over her face as she watched Anne prepare the plate of stew and set it down in front of her. She reached over and took Anne's hand. Anne caught her breath at the gesture. "I apologize, Miss Warrington."

"You have nothing to apologize for, Miss O'Malley. Please, eat something," she said, and for an instant, their fingers entwined.

Branna realized what she was doing and released her hand. Eamon slid the loaf of bread over to her. She knew he was angry. "I'm sorry, Eamon," she whispered. "I know I worried you."

Anne and Elizabeth said nothing as they watched the tender exchange between siblings.

Connal sat on the other side of his big sister and sliced the bread for her. "Here, this will do you," he said kindly, and she smiled and took the offering. Both brothers watched their older sister, making sure she ate every bite.

Tears sprang to Anne's eyes as she watched. Her family in England was nothing like this.

As Branna finished her meal, she motioned to Connal. "Connie, go get Malcolm and bring him in here." Her voice once again took control.

"What do you have in mind?" Eamon asked.

Branna took her bowl of stew and a piece of bread and sopped up the remains while Elizabeth cringed and Anne chuckled at the Irish barbarian licking her fingers.

"I did a little thinkin' today," Branna said and stood.

As Anne watched Branna, she realized how tall and muscular Branna was. *Why hadn't I noticed this before?* With the sleeves of the wool blouse rolled up, Anne could see the muscles tensing in her arms. Between the dark wool kilt and the high worn boots, her knees were the only thing exposed. Even those looked well muscled to Anne.

"I think I found a way to solve our situation. It appears that your father needs to have proof of your end of the bargain. In other words, money that up until now, none of us had," she said and saw the smile spread across Eamon's face.

"Miss O'Malley, we still don't have the money."

"Miss Warrington, do you want to go back to England? Do you, Lizzy?"

Elizabeth tried not to smile at Branna's familiarity. "My idiot brother got us into this mess. His inability to handle his estate, his indifference toward his own daughter..."

Branna rolled her eyes and leaned on the table. "Is that a no, woman?"

Elizabeth blushed and nodded.

Branna looked at Anne. "And you, Miss Warrington?"

"I-I have grown accustom to this island, Miss O'Malley, to this region, and the people. I would not mind living here."

Eamon grinned and looked back and forth at both women.

Branna smiled affectionately and nodded in agreement. "Then here's my plan."

All eyes were on Branna, who again held their future in her strong capable hands.

"Marry your brother?" Anne exclaimed.

Eamon grinned. "I like the idea so far."

Anne glared at Branna. This was not at all what she expected.

"Do you want to stay? You can't go back. It's the logical thing to do," Branna said.

Anne searched the green sparkling eyes. "I do not suppose it matters that I don't love Eamon," she said evenly and gave the rebuked man an apologetic glance.

Branna raised a curious eyebrow. "I wasn't aware you loved Da, either, but you were willin' to marry him."

"'Tis true," Eamon agreed with a sigh. "I believe I'm much more handsome."

"She had no choice in the matter," Elizabeth said. "There must be another way."

"There's not," Branna said angrily. "I'm doin' my best to get you and my family out of the mess you and Malcolm created. Now you'll marry Eamon and that's final."

She strode to the door. She opened it, and Connal tossed Malcolm ahead of him. "Sit down, cousin," she said. She dragged him over to the end of the long table.

Anne was seething as Elizabeth held onto her arm to quiet her. Branna marched down the long hall and returned in a moment with a leather bag. She had a piece of parchment and a quill.

"Here is the situation, Malcolm," Branna said. "You get your pieces of gold and more. You will write a letter to the Warrington family advising them that their daughter will marry Eamon O'Malley, eldest son of Red O'Malley—"

"I will not!"

"Yes, you will. Sit down!" she bellowed, and Anne abruptly sat. Branna looked down at her trembling cousin. "Write!" she yelled, and Malcolm scratched away. "They will be wed and you will be there as a witness. You will then ride with Liam to Dublin and arrange to leave Ireland on the next ship. You will give the family their dirty money, and I never want to see your putrid face in my home again. If you want to live, that is," she said, her thick brogue accentuated by her anger.

He scribbled and set the pen down with a shaky hand. Branna read it and blew at the drying ink. She placed the O'Malley ring on her index finger, folded the heavy parchment, and took a candle, dripping the thick wax on the edges. She angrily pounded her fist on the parchment, embedding the family crest onto the heated wax, sealing the letter. Everyone jumped as the mugs and plates bounced on the table.

There was a loud knock at the door. Connal opened it and in walked Liam, his cape slung over his head, his ruddy face grinning. "Is it done?" he asked, looking around.

"It 'tis," Branna said and placed the letter in a pouch. She handed him a few pieces of silver. "Take care."

"Not to worry," he said and left without another word.

Branna took a deep breath and faced everyone. "Malcolm, I don't care what you do anymore. If it were up to me, I'd have run you through right on the doorstep. Lucky for you, there was a lady in this house," she said. "Be here in three days. I will have the priest here to perform the ceremony. Go on, get out of my sight," she spat. Malcolm jumped and ran out the door.

She turned to Anne, who gave her a hateful look and walked out of the hall. She took a deep breath and looked at Elizabeth. "Go to her, Lizzy."

"I hope you know what you're doing," she said sternly and walked down the hall.

Eamon was sitting there with his chin lazily resting on the palm of his hand. "I don't suppose it means a thing that I'm engaged to be married to Moiré O'Neill?"

Branna laughed and flopped down on the big chair.

"What in the world are you thinking?" Eamon asked.

She gave him a confident wink. "You are to wed Miss Warrington in three days."

"But—"

"By Father Magnuson, a visiting monk from Donegal," she continued.

Eamon gave his sister a wary grin. "What are you planning?" he asked as he looked into the green sparkling eyes.

Chapter 12

Down the hall, Anne sat in her room and cried.

"There, there, child," Elizabeth soothed.

"How can this happen? How could she do such a thing to me?"

"Well, dear, we did get ourselves into this. Eamon seems like a very nice young man."

There was a knock at her door. "I don't want to see her," Anne said as she dried her eyes.

The door opened, and in walked Branna, standing tall and proud. "May I speak with you for a moment?"

Anne glared at her. "No!"

Branna motioned for Elizabeth to leave, which she did. "You must understand my position. I'm doin' my best here," she tried to explain.

Anne would have none of it. "Your best? To marry your brother off to someone he doesn't love?"

Branna grinned and scratched her head. "I'd marry you meself, but—"

"That is not amusing. As if I'd have you!"

Branna took a few steps, closing the distance between them. "And have you thought about it then?" Branna asked, realizing her mouth suddenly had gone dry.

Anne took a deep quivering breath as Branna stood dangerously close. She looked up into the sparkling green eyes of this woman-warrior.

Branna was breathing hard just to be standing this close to her.

"You...you cannot do this to me. You have no right to marry me off to your brother, and come to my room like this," she said in a low unsteady voice. "You Irish are insane. I hate you," she said as Branna put her strong hands on her shoulders. Anne tried to push her away but found her hands resting against the soft mounds of Branna's breasts. Her fingers were on fire from the touch.

"I hate you," she repeated in a whisper as Branna lowered her head and captured Anne's lips.

"I love you," Branna said.

Anne barely heard her, but she gasped at first contact with another woman's lips. Her mind was reeling out of control. However, her body was trembling as she gently squeezed the soft firm flesh beneath her fingers.

Branna groaned as she deepened the kiss, her tongue slowly parting Anne's lips. Anne moaned as she felt her legs begin to tremble. Her mind caught up to her body and she pulled back.

As Branna's eyes fluttered open, Anne reared back and slapped her hard across the face.

Branna's head snapped to one side, and as Anne raised her hand for another blow, Branna caught her wrist and twisted it behind her back. Anne gasped as Branna had her bent backward against table.

"The first one was free, lass," she murmured in a low voice. Their eyes locked, and Branna gazed into Anne's eyes. "Annie," she whispered.

For a moment, Anne's heart and body ached for her kisses. "You are a barbarian," she said in a calm voice.

Branna let her go and sported a roguish smile as Anne fell against the table.

"Good night, Miss Warrington." She turned and strode out the door, closing it behind her.

Anne sat rubbing her wrist as Elizabeth ran back into the room. "I heard it all the way down... well, I was listening at the door. Did you slap her?"

Anne took a deep breath. She stood on shaky legs and sat down again. "They're all insane," she said and put a trembling hand to her forehead, trying to dismiss the soft feel of Branna's lips against her own.

Over the next two days, Branna avoided Anne completely.
She would gallop away in the morning and not come back until
late at night.

Eamon watched both women. Anne looked heartsick. Branna
was brooding and angry. He wondered if this was a good idea of
Branna's.

"Eamon, I-I want you to give this to Anne," Branna said in a
tight voice.

He gave her a curious look as he took the cloth-wrapped
bundle. He opened it and his eyes grew wide. "Branna, Mam gave
this to you—"

"Yes, to have when I marry and give to my daughter. We both
know that's not going to happen."

"It's the family brooch. This is not what Mam had in mind. I
can't do this." He pushed it back into her hands.

"Eamon, damn you, must you always argue with me? Now
take it and give it to Anne. I-I want her to wear this."

Eamon took the brooch and shook his head in confusion.

"She has to have something from you. It would look odd if
she didn't."

Then he grinned and nodded. "I understand. You had me
worried there," he said with relief.

Father Magnuson was an old monk with a ruddy smiling face.
He stood in front of the fireplace along with Branna, Eamon, and
Connal, who were dressed in their best O'Malley colors of dark
green kilts and capes. Branna stood beside Eamon as the oldest.

Malcolm was there, as was Liam and select townspeople as
witnesses. There was silence in the great room when they heard
the door open.

They all watched as Elizabeth preceded Anne down the hall
from the bedroom. Branna could tell Anne had been crying;
Eamon and Branna looked into each other's shameful faces.

When Branna saw Anne, her heart skipped a beat. She actually
stopped breathing.

Anne was beautiful. She wore a simple light-colored woolen frock with the O'Malley cape lightly draped across her shoulders. The family gold brooch pinned the cape in place.

Eamon gave Branna a glance. "Breathe, sister. I'm the one gettin' married," he whispered.

Branna frowned, wanting to stop this if only to get the sad look off Anne's lovely face.

Anne smiled slightly as Eamon took her hand in his.

The priest smiled and started. He spoke in Latin as he performed the ceremony.

Please stop this, Anne eyes begged as she glanced at Branna.

Branna tensed her jaw, as well as her fists, to avoid crying out.

As Malcolm witnessed along with the other townsfolk, both made their commitment and signed the documents, then Eamon kissed Anne on the cheek.

Immediately, Branna walked over to Malcolm. She tossed a pouch of jingling coins at his midriff.

"Heed my warning," she said in a dark voice that made Malcolm nod furiously. She motioned to Liam, who grabbed him and headed out the door with Connal following.

They all waited in silence until Connal came dashing back. "Liam's got him riding so fast, he's nearly off the horse."

Everyone laughed and congratulated one another. Branna saw the tears welling in Anne's violet eyes and took a deep breath. As the celebration started, she watched as Eamon put his arm around Anne. She quietly walked away.

After a few hours of celebrating, the band of people went on their way. Father Magnuson had too much poteen, and Anne and Elizabeth thought that was peculiar for a monk.

"Oh, these Irish." Elizabeth sighed. Anne smiled in spite of the situation.

Finally, with everyone gone, Eamon and Anne were left sitting alone at the long table. "You look beautiful," he said.

She smiled her thanks. "You look handsome, as well."

"Not as good as Branna, though, am I right?" he asked, and

Anne's head shot up with an incredulous look. "Thought as much."

"Poor Eamon. I am sorry," she said sadly. She fondled the golden brooch she still wore. "This is beautiful, thank you. I know it's a family heirloom. I-I really shouldn't be wearing it."

Eamon smiled and leaned in. "Branna wanted you to have it. My mother gave it to her for her wedding day."

"Then I really should give it back to her," Anne said in a quiet voice. Her heart ached as she thought of Branna.

"I think you're right," Eamon said firmly as he stood and took her by the hand.

Anne hesitated for a moment but took his hand and followed him out of the great room and down the long hall to her fate.

Chapter 13

Anne looked confused as Eamon stopped at his sister's bedroom. He laughed at the confounded look as he opened Branna's door.

There stood Branna tall and proud.

"But..." Anne said.

Eamon pushed her through the doorway. "Good night, my sisters." He closed the door.

Anne could not move as she looked at Branna standing there in her dark green kilt and cape. Her hair was pulled back in a long braid, her green eyes sparkling.

"I don't understand," Anne said.

Branna offered her the chair by the glowing fire. Anne sat and shook violently. Branna stripped off her wool cape and wrapped it around the smaller woman.

"Th-thank you," she murmured as her heart beat out of control.

"I'm sorry I had to lie to you."

Anne gave her a curious look but said nothing.

"I had to figure out a way to get Malcolm out of Ireland and have you safe with me forever."

Anne pulled the wool cape around her. "But I can't be with you forever. I'm married to your brother," she said in her quiet English voice. Branna chuckled, and Anne shot her an angry look. "How can you laugh at this? This is my life. You—"

Branna knelt in front of her, took her hands, and grinned. She kissed each hand, eliciting a quiet gasp from Anne. "Don't be callin' me a barbarian now, luv. You're not married to my brother."

"I vowed to be his wife in front of a priest," she reminded her.

Branna grinned again. "You pledged your vows to a fisherman from Donegal, Seamus Magnuson. His wife was one of the witnesses," she said and couldn't help herself. She laughed openly at the shocked look on Anne's lovely face.

"The witnesses? The people from the village. They knew? You mean we were never married?" she asked in a screeching voice.

Branna shook her head as she grinned. "No, Eamon is engaged to Moiré O'Neill. They're to be wed next spring. He's probably over there right now, catchin' holy hell from Moiré," she said, laughing. She stopped abruptly as Anne backed away and walked over to the fireplace.

"This is all too much," Anne said as she stared at the dancing flames. "I don't know what to think—what to feel."

Branna walked up behind her and placed her hands on Anne's shoulders.

Instinctively, Anne leaned back against the strong warm body. She felt the soft kiss upon her head and closed her eyes, but still she hesitated. "Branna, please," she nearly begged as her heart pounded and her body trembled.

Branna turned her around and smiled. "Enough for one night. I don't want to scare the life out of you."

Anne blushed and lowered her head. Branna placed her fingertips under the soft chin and lifted Anne's face. She gazed into Anne's eyes. "Never be afraid of me."

"I'm not afraid, but this is all so—" She stopped and took a deep breath as she looked up into the green eyes. "Can this be? Can we love each other like this?"

Branna let out a nervous laugh. "By everything sacred, I hope so."

Anne chuckled along and Branna pulled her into her arms, kissing her forehead. They stood there for a long moment; each seemingly lost in her thoughts, until Branna pulled back, took Anne by the hand, and led her out of her room and down the hall.

She opened Anne's door and stepped back. Anne smiled and put her hand on Branna's cheek. "Thank you." She unpinned the Tara brooch and handed it to Branna. "Keep this safe."

Branna raised one eyebrow. "I'll keep it until it's time for you to wear it—always," Branna replied. "And you're welcome. For now." She pulled Anne into her arms, and as she lowered her head, she stopped. "You won't be slappin' me, will you?"

Anne grinned and pulled Branna down to her. "No, I will not," she said against her lips.

It was a gentle kiss, and though Anne did not want it to end, she pulled back and took a deep breath. Her body was trembling as she looked up. "What are we going to do?"

Branna stepped back and Anne smiled as she noticed Branna's body trembling.

"We will figure it out, but right now, I will say good night before I get slapped again." She offered a cocky smirk and bowed slightly. "Pleasant dreams."

"Sleep well." Anne sighed and slipped past her, quietly closing the door.

As the days turned into weeks, Branna courted Anne; Anne had a feeling Branna had never courted another woman in her life and was used to getting her way.

One morning, they strolled together along the edge of the woods. Anne silently walked beside Branna, who picked up a stick and absently hit it against the trees.

"You have a good deal of property, Branna."

"I suppose," she mumbled.

Anne glanced at the brooding woman and hid her grin. In the past few weeks, Anne's feelings for this woman intensified. She had no idea how to love Branna, but she knew she did indeed love her. She wished she were as confident as Branna O'Malley. Anne looked at her now and stifled a giggle as Branna frowned deeply.

Anne stopped and faced Branna. "Well, are you going to kiss me or not?"

Branna whirled around to her and dropped the stick. She

grinned and pulled Anne into her arms. "Are you sure?" she asked with a wide grin.

Anne nodded and started to say something, but Branna's tender kiss stopped her. She gasped and held onto Branna's shoulders, returning her kiss with passion. So much so, it left both women breathless as they pulled back. Anne staggered backward as Branna let her go. "Good God, Anne."

Anne could only nod furiously in agreement. "Indeed, Branna. Indeed."

Branna took her by the hand. "Come with me. We'll take Morrighan for a ride. That should cool us off."

Anne laughed as she allowed Branna to drag her along to the stable.

Morrighan galloped along with Branna at the reins and Anne happily sitting in front of her. They came to a halt under a grove of trees at the cliff's edge.

"Clew Bay," she said breathlessly, as she slipped off Morrighan's back and helped Anne. After removing the saddle, she slapped her flank, sending the Arabian horse running.

They sat side by side, leaning against a tall tree watching the ocean. Branna reached over and took Anne's hand in her own. "We must talk about this, Annie," she said in a low commanding voice.

Anne took a deep breath. "Yes, we must." She half turned to face Branna, who was frowning. "Don't frown so."

"I'm worried, worried that you may want to go back to England and—"

Anne placed her fingertips across Branna's lips. "I'm not going back to England. I have no life there."

Branna took a deep calming breath. "And where is your life?" She looked into Anne's eyes, now filled with tears.

"I'm looking at my life."

The grin that spread across Branna's face filled Anne with such peace, she nearly cried out.

"Are you now?" Branna asked with a cocky grin. She leaned over and kissed Anne. "That's good to know. For I've found everything I'll ever want, right in that kiss." She pulled back and unpinned the Tara brooch from her cape and pinned it on Anne's wool frock. "I told you I would keep it safe until you were ready to wear it always." She caressed the brooch that Anne now wore. "It will please me that you wear this."

Anne sniffed back the tears of happiness. "Then I will always wear it."

Branna smiled and nodded. "My mother gave that to me when I was younger. She wanted me to give it to my daughter, so it can be passed down from generation to generation," she said and took a deep worried breath. "That will not happen, but I wanted you to have it. You're my family now, and though I cannot marry you, I want you to have it always."

Anne smiled and kissed her tenderly. "We may not have children, but we have love. I-I do love you."

"Oh, Annie," Branna sighed as Anne ran her fingers through her hair. Branna pulled back and offered her hand; she pulled Anne to her feet.

"We'd best be getting back," Branna said and whistled for Morrighan.

Later that night, they walked down the long hallway. Branna stopped by her door and gently held Anne back when she started for her own room. Anne looked up into the green eyes filled with desire and swallowed convulsively.

"I want to make love to you tonight," Branna said and opened her bedroom door.

Anne followed without a word. She stood in the center of the room as Branna started the fire. She nervously clutched her cape around her and watched Branna light the large candles by the bedside.

Branna stood by Anne and smiled down into her eyes. She caressed the brooch on Anne's cape. "I never thought I'd find someone to give this to, luv."

Anne moaned deeply as Branna slipped the plaid cape off her shoulders. Then steady fingers slowly unbuttoned the wool blouse, pushing it off her shoulders, as well. Anne sighed and shivered with anticipation as Branna lowered her head to kiss the hollow of her neck. Anne was shivering as Branna removed the remainder of her clothing. Anne felt extremely vulnerable, but she trembled with anticipation as she stood naked before Branna.

Branna pulled the heavy quilt back and lifted Anne in one easy movement, gently lowering her to the middle of the large bed. Anne watched as Branna unbuttoned her wool shirt and slipped it off. The kilt was next.

Anne's heartbeat pounded in her ears at the sight before her. Branna had a beautiful body. Even with the wounds that were now healed and battle scars, she was a remarkable sight. Her broad shoulders flexed as she reached behind her head to loosen the braid. Anne gasped openly as the raven hair tumbled around her shoulders. "My God, Branna, you are magnificent," she whispered in awe.

Branna smiled and slid in next to her. Both women caught their breath as their bodies touched for the first time. Branna loomed over Anne, her long black hair flowing. She lowered her head again, capturing the perfect lips in heated but tender kisses.

Anne was moaning and gasping as every fiber of her body seemed to be lit from within. Branna reached down and lightly touched her heaving breast. Anne cried, but Branna smothered the sound in a warm kiss.

Branna lightly flicked her nipple, causing her to cry out once again and arch her back into the touch. Anne's head was reeling when Branna's lips traveled farther, lightly kissing down her neck to the pulse point. Anne could feel the blood coursing through her veins as Branna sucked on the tender flesh. Anne writhed beneath her as experienced, but gentle, fingers toyed and teased her aching nipple.

"Oh, my God," Anne sighed.

Branna lowered her mouth to Anne's plump breast. Anne called out her pleasure as she entwined her fingers in the black mane, holding Branna in place. Branna hungrily fed on the aching breast, suckling the nipple, rolling it between her teeth as she nibbled.

Anne was whimpering with need as she instinctively parted her legs. Branna slipped her fingers lower, teasing velvet-like curls.

"Yes, Branna. Please."

Branna continued to suckle one breast, then the other. Her fingers dipped lower, and she moaned against Anne's breast. Anne bucked her hips, and her heart nearly leapt out of her chest as the strong fingers slid up and down the length of her. Anne cried out and her body shook uncontrollably with each pass of Branna's fingers.

"I'll die, Branna," she yelled, her fingers still entwined in Branna's dark hair.

Anne's body quivered beneath Branna's, and on the third heavenly pass, Anne screamed out her orgasm. Branna continued until Anne's body went limp. Her body was quivering and her heart racing.

Anne was nearly faint as Branna pulled back and touched her cheek. Her eyelids fluttered open to see the bright green eyes filled with tenderness.

"I adore you," Branna whispered.

Anne woke slowly. She was on her side and felt the long arms of her warrior holding her in a warm secure embrace. She sighed and nestled back into the warm body. Anne found that Branna's upper arm made quite a nice pillow as she turned her head slightly to kiss the warm hard muscle, amazed to find the soft skin beneath her lips. Anne smiled happily as she thought of this woman, who could be so forceful and gruff, then so exquisitely gentle and feminine as she was the previous night. She was still smiling as she faded off to sleep once again.

Branna sighed in her sleep and pulled Anne closer, her arm wrapping around her waist. One hand wandered up to cup Anne's breast; Anne covered Branna's hand, holding it in place.

"I will need that hand back at some point, madam," her low sleepy voice rumbled out.

Anne chuckled and turned around to face the smiling green eyes. "After the way you loved me, I cannot make any promises."

"Did you sleep well?" Branna asked as she reached up to push the errant brown strands away.

"I slept very well. I'm sorry for falling asleep, however. I-I wanted to please you, as well."

Branna grinned widely. "Ah, you have no idea how much you pleased me last night."

Anne leaned over and Branna naturally rolled onto her back. Anne gazed at the long, lean, battle-scarred body. She reached over and caressed the mark on her upper arm.

"How did you get that?" she asked as she traced the outline with her fingertips.

Branna took a deep breath to calm her racing heart. "Last year. Edinburgh. I-I don't really remember now."

Anne grinned and traced her fingers up to the jaw line and found a tiny scar hidden under her chin. "Hmm. How about this one?"

Her feather-like touch made Branna grateful she was lying down. "Eamon was chasin' me, I slipped and fell."

Anne saw gooseflesh break out on Branna's skin. She reached up and placed a light kiss on her chin, then traveled up to her dry lips.

Branna moaned as she eagerly sucked Anne's probing tongue into her mouth. After several minutes, Anne pulled back breathless, and Branna noticed a doubtful look flash through the violet eyes. "Any way you touch me, Annie, will be heaven," Branna assured her. Anne still looked doubtful, and Branna took her hand and placed it on her breast.

Anne gently kneaded the small firm breast. It was soft and not as full as her own. She watched Branna, who had her eyes closed and a faint smile on her lips.

Anne slowly teased the nipple and was amazed at how hard it became under her touch. She knew Branna was enjoying it; the perspiration was now evident on her upper lip, as well, and her breathing was ragged and shallow. "Is this all right?"

Branna couldn't answer; she nodded and waited. Anne licked her lips and lowered her head to Branna's breast, amazed at the soft skin against her lips. Branna let out a groan as she felt the innocent tongue lapping across her hard nipple.

After a few moments of torture, Anne pulled back to see Branna panting wildly. Anne knew she was trying to control herself and not rush her, but Branna looked pained. "Branna, help me. I don't know how to touch—"

With that, Branna took her hand and placed it where she desperately needed it. She guided the fingers for a moment and let go. "That's it, luv, just like that. It's heavenly," she said as Anne continued to stroke back and forth.

Anne lowered her head and once again took the aching nipple into her mouth and suckled it past her teeth. Hearing the cry from Branna, Anne repeated raking her teeth across the rock hard nub.

"Yes, Annie! Yes," Branna rasped out her encouragement.

She bucked her hips, and finally, Branna arched her back and her body stretched out as tight as a bow. Then the first wave rippled through her body, and she was helpless to stop it.

Another wave crashed over Branna as she cried out. "My God, Annie!" She slowly regained control of her body while her heart still raced.

Anne eased her fingers away and rolled onto her back, taking Branna's quivering body with her. She wrapped her arms around the broad shoulders and caressed her back, making lazy circles with her fingernails.

"You swear by the goddess Aine that you have never touched another woman before?" Branna asked in a tired happy voice.

Anne nodded and blushed horribly. Branna laughed and nestled her head against her plump breast. "Then by the goddess of love, I am a lucky woman."

Chapter 14

Weeks passed as Branna and Anne lived in bliss. Elizabeth had no idea what to make of the situation.

"The Lady Anne and I are goin' for a ride on Morrighan," Branna said and playfully pulled the screeching woman out the door.

"It doesn't seem strange to you?" Elizabeth asked both brothers.

"It truly does not. I suppose it's because Branna has always been so strong, so much like a man, we forget she's our sister and a woman," Eamon said.

"Don't they both look normal together?" Connal asked.

Eamon nodded, and Elizabeth had to admit the women looked like they were meant to be together.

Later in the morning, both women were laughing when they walked into the great room. Connal was sitting there, looking petrified. Elizabeth looked as if she was going to faint, and Eamon looked ill.

"What in the devil is wrong with all of you? It's a fine summer's day and—"

"Henry Sussex is here, Anne," Elizabeth interrupted, and Anne nearly collapsed into the chair.

"What is a Henry Sussex?" Branna asked, trying to find something to keep her bright mood. It would not be. She looked at Anne. "Luv, who is this man?"

"He's the man my father wanted me to marry in the beginning," she said as her face lost all its color.

Branna put her hands on her hips. "Well, darlin', he can't have you," she said with a grin.

Eamon gave her a pained look. "He thinks I'm her husband."

"Good, that's what we wanted," Branna said, getting a little angry. She noticed his bloodied cheek, and her eyes grew wide. "Tell me what happened."

"He got Eamon angry and Eamon insulted him in front of Charles Wolfingham," Elizabeth tried to explain.

"So? He's insulted. Why is everyone so damned glum?"

Anne reached up and placed a hand on her arm, instantly calming her.

"He challenged Eamon," Elizabeth said. "Told him to meet him at dawn in the clearing. He can pick his weapon. Since he was told that the O'Malleys are excellent swordsmen—"

"What?" Branna bellowed.

"I know what he's up to," Anne said flatly.

Branna was breathing heavily and trying not to see the worried sick look in Eamon's eyes; she looked down at the woman she loved.

"He wants this land. He wants me," Anne said and avoided her look.

Branna glanced around at all four defeated faces. She put her hands on her hips in a defiant pose. "Well, he can have neither!"

"My only chance is to beat him tomorrow morning," Eamon said in a low voice.

All three siblings knew it had been a long time since Eamon wielded a sword in battle. He was no match for Sussex.

Branna paced back and forth in front of the fire, thinking of a way out of this. She looked at Anne, who looked so forlorn, and Eamon, trying to muster all the strength he could, that it broke her heart—then it angered her.

She knew what she must do to take the final step to ensure the happiness and future of the O'Malleys.

"Listen to me," Branna said in a stern voice. They all looked up at her with hopeful eyes. She looked at Elizabeth. "Lizzy, you know this man and the Charles bastard, am I correct?" Elizabeth nodded. "He wants the land and Anne. This is true?" Again, she nodded. "Then this is the way it will be done."

Branna left to retrieve parchment and a quill. She sat down at the long table, scribbled her plan and blew at the paper to dry the ink, and slid it across to Eamon first.

He read it and looked at her in amazement. He handed it back to her and she gave it to Anne, who read it and was shocked. Connal and Elizabeth had the same reaction.

"How in God's name will this work?" Eamon asked, completely at a loss.

"Connal, you will take this to Henry Sussex, what a ridiculous name, and await his answer. I'm sure his arrogance will say yes. Off with you now," she said and pushed the boy out the door.

Anne sat there gaping at the woman she loved. "Let me understand. You're offering your birthright, and me, if Henry kills Eamon," she said, trying not to believe Branna hadn't gone mad.

"Yes, however, if Eamon kills this Henry bastard, Charles Wolfingham leaves and never returns to Ireland."

"Branna, I can't kill him. I may be able to injure him—"

"You won't be fighting him," Branna said in a confident voice.

All three sat there for a moment to digest what she had said. Elizabeth was the first to speak.

"That's why you put that stipulation about full battle dress," she said, and Branna nodded.

"No," Eamon said, shaking his head. "I will not let you do this. I have to fight my own battle. I may not win, but I have to fight."

Branna stood in front of him and smiled. "What was the first rule Da taught us?"

"No—"

"Eamon," she urged in a gentle voice.

"Choose your battles wisely. If you can't, then battle them wisely," he said obediently.

"What is the wisest way to fight this battle?"

Eamon looked up at her and pulled her into a fierce hug.

Anne watched, still not understanding. Eamon let his sister go, and Branna slapped him on the back.

"Now we look alike, and in full battle dress, no one will tell us apart. I'll put my hair up under the headgear."

Anne now fully realized what was happening. She strode up to Branna and turned her around to face her. "You are not fighting Henry Sussex. Branna, he is very, very good."

Branna cocked her head and put her hands on her hips. "Well, Lady Anne, I am very, very good, as well. And what's more…" She grinned evilly, "…I'm better."

When Connal came running into the house, they all whirled around to him. "It's done," he said breathlessly. "He took the bait, full battle dress."

Branna took a deep breath and nodded. "It's done," she said in a firm steady voice.

They lay in bed that night, Branna staring at the ceiling, Anne cuddling close to her side.

Anne's head rested on Branna's breast, listening to the strong steady rhythm of her heartbeat. She prayed to God that she would be listening to it the next night.

"Is there no way I can talk you out of this?" she asked as she caressed the taut abdomen.

"Would you really want to, luv?"

"To keep you alive? Yes," Anne replied in a quivering voice.

Branna rolled her onto her back and gazed down into the violet eyes that now looked black in the shadow of the firelight's glow. She saw the pleading look.

"I would not be alive, luv. You'd be livin' with a ghost. For I'd surely be dead to you," she assured her. "I am not like Eamon or Connal. Da knew it. That's why he taught me. That's why I learned and Eamon did not. He's a gentle soul, Eamon is. It's in my blood and deep in my soul. Don't ask me to stop bein' what I am," she said in a steady voice. "I need you now, luv. I need your strength, not your indecision, not your worry. I need your strength, Anne. I'm beggin' you."

Anne reached up to caress the soft cheek. "You have it, Branna. You have it all, everything in my power to give you—everything your gods will allow. Take it all." She pulled Branna down for a soulful kiss.

Their lovemaking was all-consuming that night—time after time reassuring each other of their love everlasting.

Long into the night, Anne welcomed Branna to love her any way she needed, taking her very soul into battle with her.

Anne woke alone. She scrambled out of bed in the darkness, feeling for her robe. The sun was not yet up as she frantically looked for Branna.

As she walked down the long hall, she saw Branna kneeling beneath a crucifix that hung on the wall at the far end of the great room. Anne did not move, nor did she try to go to her. She watched in silence.

Branna was dressed in a short white tunic, gathered at the waist. Short sleeved, it nearly looked like a dressing gown. Her hair was flowing down her back as she knelt there. Anne instinctively knew she was praying. There was a lone candle at her side and Anne smelled some type of incense in the air, a pungent aroma that was not from the roaring peat fire.

Feeling as though she was intruding, Anne quietly made her own prayer and walked back to their room and slipped into bed. A few moments later, she heard Branna move about the room. "I'm awake," she said and sat up.

Branna walked over to the bed and sat next to her. She lit a few candles. "It'll be daybreak soon and I must go, luv," she said and took the hand in her strong one.

"*Tá mo chroí istigh ionat,*" she whispered and grinned at the confused look on her lover's face. "My heart is within you, Annie," she said. "I want you to know how much I love you and will never love any other."

"You best not. Not after what we have gone through to be together."

Suddenly, an overwhelming feeling of contentment pulled at Anne's heart and she smiled warmly.

Branna saw the look and smiled, as well. "What is it, luv?" she asked curiously.

"A feeling of complete happiness just swept through me,

Branna. I-I saw us old and together, with children all around us."

Branna chuckled. "I can see us old and together, darlin', but the children? I love you, Anne, but even the gods don't favor me that much."

Both women laughed, breaking the tension of the morning.

"It's time you readied yourself," Anne said as the thought of what may happen on that morning tore through her heart. "Come, I'll help you dress."

In the pre-dawn hours, they stood together in the great hall. Anne had braided Branna's long thick hair and tethered it with the leather strap. Branna wore the kilt and sat as Anne laced up the deerskin boots. Branna stood and picked up the leather pleated armored skirt. She lifted her arms as she instructed Anne on how to secure it in the back.

"It's heavy," Anne said in awe, wondering how this woman would be agile while wearing it.

"'Tis good," Branna said with a wink. "The Romans wore this many, many years ago. Uncle Brian, um, borrowed it when we were in Scotland. They don't wear 'em anymore, but it serves the purpose. Besides, it brought me great luck many times."

"Then don't you dare take it off."

Eamon and Connal came down the hall dressed and ready. Elizabeth soon followed. Connal and Eamon helped her into the leather armored chest plate.

Anne assisted her with the leather gauntlets. "This is how I first saw you standing right over there," she whispered and kissed her deeply. "I think I loved you even then."

"You thought I was a man," Branna reminded her.

"You would bring that up now," she retorted, and Branna laughed.

Anne was amazed at how calm and sure Branna was as she talked with her brothers. She watched Eamon strap the sword around her lover's chest. With the sheath attached to Branna's back, he slid the sword into it.

"Honed it myself. Now run him through quickly and come home."

Branna nodded with a wink. Connal took the leather headgear, but before he put it on her head, Branna held up her hands. "Give us a moment?"

Both men and Elizabeth walked out of the room. Branna turned to Anne, who was taking deep calming breaths.

Branna took both cold hands in her strong steady ones. "I love you," she said simply and grinned. "Thank you for being strong. You'll make a good Irishwoman yet."

"I love you more than I thought possible. Come back to me," Anne said in a quivering voice and kissed her.

She then slipped an object into Branna's right gauntlet. Branna looked down and pulled it out. It was a wooden crucifix.

"When I first came here and slept in your room, I-I looked in the drawer and saw this. I thought it was so simple..."

"I carved this when I was a young girl," Branna said in awe. "Da showed me how and Mam got so angry. I was usin' a dagger to carve it."

She looked down into the violet eyes. "God Bless you, Anne," she said with such tenderness, tears caught in the back of her throat. She took a deep breath and roughly cleared her throat. "When I come home, I'm having my way with you, lass," she said with a roguish grin.

"You are a barbarian," Anne said, kissing her again. "Go now before I stop you."

Branna pulled back and called for Eamon and Connal. Elizabeth walked into the room and up to Branna, pulled her tall frame down, and kissed her on the lips. "Come back to us, child," she said through her tears.

Branna smiled and kissed her forehead, then turned to Eamon. "Eamon, you stay here. If he sees you, we're finished, right?"

Eamon ran his fingers through his hair. "I can't, Branna. I can't let you do this," he said and pulled at her sword.

"Eamon, you damned idiot, don't make me—" she warned, and Eamon struggled. Branna sighed deeply. "I warned you," she said and punched him dead in the face.

Poor Eamon flew across the table and landed in an unconscious heap.

Anne and Elizabeth stood there gawking. Branna shook her hand and flexed it. "Keep him here. I don't care if you have to tie him up," she said angrily.

Connal walked into the room and sighed. "Oh, you two." He stepped over the laid-out figure of his brother. "What happened?"

"He tried to stop me. I had a feelin' he might. He's fine. Give me the head gear now," she said impatiently.

Connal placed the leather headgear on as Anne held up the braid. He slipped it on her head, the metal nose guard hiding her upper face.

"You can't tell. It'll work. Just don't let him get under your kilt," Connal said, wiggling his eyebrows. Branna laughed and pushed him toward the door.

Branna turned one last time to Anne. Their eyes met as Branna placed a hand over her heart.

Anne smiled and put her fingertips to her lips and Branna strode out of the great hall and into the cold foggy morning.

Chapter 15

Anne and Elizabeth got Eamon to his room. Anne took the key and locked him in while Elizabeth watched curiously. "What are you doing, child?"

"I'm going to Branna. She'd worry if I was there, but I can't let her do this alone. I have to be there, Aunt Elizabeth. Please understand."

"I do. Go, I will wait here. I love you and that Irish barbarian," she said and sniffed.

Anne never ran so fast in all her life. As she got to the clearing, she hid behind a mass of shrubs and trees.

Henry Sussex was already there. He was in the same type of battle dress as Branna, only he had a skirt of maile. His gauntlets were also made of shiny mesh, and Anne bit at her bottom lip thinking of Branna protected by only a layer of thick leather.

Charles Wolfingham was standing next to him examining his sword. She gave them both a hateful look as she heard riders approaching. She ducked down and saw a magnificent sight.

It was Branna O'Malley riding up on Morrighan with Connal next to her on a black steed. They stopped and Connal rode alone the rest of the way. He and Charles Wolfingham spoke briefly and nodded in agreement. Henry nodded impatiently and wielded his sword in practice swipes.

Branna sat tall on Morrighan, who was snorting and bobbing her head. Connal waved to Branna, who held up her hand in agreement. She dismounted and Anne noticed she took the crucifix out of her gauntlet, kissed it, and replaced it. She slapped Morrighan on the flank and sent the horse galloping away from the clearing.

It was eerily quiet as the gray dawn broke and the low fog swirled around their feet. Anne held her breath, if she was breathing at all.

Charles Wolfingham finally spoke. "It is agreed, the victor will have full ownership of the O'Malley land and all its boundaries." He shook hands with Connal as both men walked back to their respective participants.

Connal said one last thing to Branna and patted her on the back. He made final adjustments to her armor and Branna unsheathed her sword, making a metallic scraping noise that echoed throughout the clearing. She made her way toward Henry Sussex, who flexed his neck in what Anne thought was a nervous gesture. Charles handed him his sword, and he too made his way to middle ground.

"I will have your property when this is done, Eamon O'Malley. Your property and your wife."

Branna took a deep breath, said her last prayer to God and the gods of old, and let her breath out in a long steady stream. "You will not have my property, and more important, you will not have my wife. You English love to own things. Why must you muck up everything you touch?" she bellowed, and Anne winced at her sarcasm.

"You Irish are a backward people. Your time is done."

Branna let out a hearty laugh. "Stop your prattlin', Sussex, and fight!" Branna challenged, and the bait worked.

Sussex flew toward her with a cry, and Anne held her breath. Branna readied herself and raised her sword in defense. He swung and Branna fended off the blow as the swords clanged together. Blow after blow, each combatant returned and rejected. In a close struggle, Sussex raised his leg and viciously kicked Branna in the midsection, lifting her off her feet, driving her to her knees.

Seeing the opening, Sussex raised his sword overhead and swung at Branna's head. She rolled out of the way, narrowly missing the hissing blade. It grazed her shoulder and she cried out as she quickly got to her feet, blood seeping down her arm.

Connal was hiding his face. Anne was biting her lip so hard

she drew blood.

"You're mine, O'Malley."

"Hardly, Sussex," she spat and charged ahead. Swipe after swipe, she backed him up and danced him all over the clearing. Branna raised the sword and in a swiping motion, cleanly sliced through his skirt, cutting his thigh. He cried out and stumbled and Branna took to the offensive. She let out an unearthly growl and kept coming, swinging her sword in masterful strokes. Anne was riveted to the spot. She could not take her eyes of this woman-warrior.

Branna was relentless as she drove Sussex to his knees. He raised his sword in defense, and as Branna raised her sword, he fell to his back, then swept his foot out and kicked her feet out from under her.

Anne stifled a scream as both struggled for control, rolling around in the fog-covered meadow. Grunting and growling, Sussex broke free and took a wild swipe. Branna leapt, but the tip of the sword pierced the back of her thigh, sending blood streaming down her leg. She buckled and fell to her knees.

She was exhausted, but Sussex did not pay attention. He was greedy, hungry for the kill. He came up behind her and raised his sword overhead, and as he brought it down, Branna rolled out of the way, and in one movement, that Anne could not believe, she bolted up and drove the sword through his lower abdomen, below his armor. He let out a strangled cry as the blood sprang from the mortal wound. Branna leaned forward and drove the sword home, impaling her opponent. Anne winced at the vicious growl that came from the woman she loved.

"I'm sendin' you straight to hell, Sussex! Anne Warrington is my wife." She emphasized her point by violently thrusting the sword farther into the Englishman's blood-soaked body. "This is, and will always be, *O'Malley* soil," she yelled as she yanked the bloodied sword out of Sussex, who was kneeling now with an incredulous look of death. "Anne is an O'Malley!" She then kicked his lifeless body over.

She swayed back and forth, covered in blood, then she stumbled and fell over, lying on her back. Connal ran to her, as did Anne. Charles ran to Sussex and examined the body.

"Leave Ireland, Wolfingham. Don't ever come back or I'll kill you myself," Connal said as he knelt by his sister, making sure the headgear stayed in place.

Wolfingham ran the back of his hand over his mouth, looking at the bloodied corpse.

"If he doesn't, Charles, I will. I swear by the blood of my spouse, I will kill you if I ever see you, or anyone else, on O'Malley soil again," Anne said.

Branna smiled weakly and reached a bloody hand up to Connal. "She'll make a fine O'Malley, Connie," she whispered and winced painfully.

Charles walked away and got the wagon. Connal helped lift the lifeless body of Henry Sussex into the wagon, and Charles drove it down the road and out of sight.

Anne knelt beside Branna to examine her wounds. "I don't know where to start," she said, and frantically ran her hand through her long brown hair.

"You can start by kissing me, wife," Branna said with a wink.

"Yes, my spouse." She slipped the headgear off and kissed her.

"Ladies, he's gone. You don't have to pretend, Branna. Anne," he said helplessly.

"Keep still, Connie," Branna said and kissed Anne deeply.

Between them, they got Branna up on her horse, despite Anne's protests.

"I can ride," Branna grumbled down at Anne, who had her hands on her hips.

"You're bleeding all over the place. Why won't you wait and let Connal get the wagon?"

Branna gave Connal a smirking look. He nodded and threw Anne on his black steed and slapped his flank. The horse took off with Anne screaming.

Branna laughed and winced as she watched. "You're a good brother, Connie." She pulled the reins of Morrighan and galloped after the screaming woman on the black steed.

Eamon was sitting at the long table with a cold cloth on his face when Branna staggered in. He and Elizabeth dashed over and helped her out of the leather armor, then into her room.

"Hot water, Aunt Elizabeth," Anne ordered as she stripped the bloodied tunic off Branna.

"I already have it on the hearth, dear," she said and patted her shoulder.

"I'll get the bandages," Eamon said, remembering his orders.

"I'm all right, luv. You should've seen the battle in Edinburgh. Much worse than that English bastard."

Anne took a deep quivering breath as she wiped the blood away. The wounds were small, however…"Your beautiful body, Branna." She shook her head.

Elizabeth brought in the bowl of hot water and Eamon was right behind her with the bandages.

Connal came running into the room. "Eamon, you should've seen her!"

"I would've liked to," he said dryly and rubbed his face.

Eamon and Elizabeth listened in awe as Connal, holding Branna's sword like a relic, retold the story. Anne ushered them all out and closed the door.

Branna was smiling affectionately as Anne returned to her nursing. "You were magnificent, Branna," she agreed as she bathed her arms and legs.

Branna watched her. "What were you doin' there?"

Anne shrugged as she finished placing a bandage on her arm and thigh. "There, you need to rest now. Sleep, I'll come back—"

"Why did you come?" Branna asked again.

"I-I couldn't stay away. I had to be there. I couldn't bear it if you…" She stopped.

Branna pulled her down, holding her as she protested. She kissed her deeply and pushed her away. "Get out of those clothes and into this bed. I told you I'd have my way with you," Branna ordered with a cocky grin. She reached up and cupped her full

breast, sending shivers down Anne's spine.
Anne quickly complied with her wishes.

Later in the day, Anne woke slowly. She looked over at her warrior, who was sleeping so soundly she had to check to see if she was breathing. Anne lay on her side, watching the peaceful slumber.

In her sleep, Branna looked so young that, for the first time, Anne wondered how old this woman was. Her black hair covered the pillow and Anne pulled back the blanket to gaze at the magnificent body. She reached up and traced her fingers along Branna's strong jaw line; Branna stirred, her eyes fluttering open. Anne smiled and gazed into the green pools. "By your gods, Branna O'Malley, you are beautiful."

Branna stretched. "After this morning, I don't feel very beautiful, luv, but I thank you just the same," she replied in a sleepy voice and rolled Anne onto her back. Branna now gazed down into the violet eyes she adored.

"I've been in many battles, Anne, and I've killed many men. I won't deny it."

Anne opened her mouth and Branna shook her head and placed her fingertips against the warm trembling lips. "Shh now, luv, and let me finish. This morning as I knelt in prayer, I prayed as I have always done before battle. I prayed for strength and courage." She stopped for a moment. She smiled down at the pretty face she loved and caressed the lips with her fingertips.

"I have always wondered why God had seen fit to make me the way I am. After this mornin', I'll wonder no more. It's as if all my life I've been preparin' for this moment. I've never been scared in my life, but the thought of that man takin' you from me—it scares me that I love you so much."

Anne stopped her now. She reached up and pulled her down for a long tender kiss. Branna pulled back and Anne was shocked to see tears welling in her eyes.

"Tell me, Anne. Tell me you love me," she begged.

Anne reached up to cup the tired face. "I love you, Branna, my warrior, my only love," she said fervently as she raked her fingers through long raven hair and pulled Branna to her breast. Branna wrapped her arms around Anne in a crushing embrace, kissing her breasts, her neck, needing to possess every inch of her. She trembled and shook. "My prayer, Annie. You're my prayer. God, I love you so." She nearly sobbed as she kissed her, her passion surging through her veins.

Anne felt the urgency in Branna's strong, trembling body. She parted her legs, welcoming her lover's touch. She needed Branna as badly. "I'm yours," she said in a confident low voice.

Branna whimpered with need as she kissed Anne deeply. "I need you like the air I breathe. Don't ever leave me," Branna murmured against her lips as she moved over her.

"Love me now, Branna. Love me as if you will never have me again," Anne said urgently, and Branna moaned deeply and pulled back.

"I will. We'll have each other, now and till the day we die," Branna promised in strong steady voice.

Green eyes filled with passion gazed into violet wanting eyes as she fulfilled her promise.

One afternoon, Anne and Branna sat in the great hall smiling and watching the mayhem.

"Cousin Branna, show me again?" the little girl asked.

The other redheaded child agreed. "Please, Aunt Branna. Show us one more time," she pleaded, as well.

Branna laughed heartily. "All right then, now watch. You have to be quick. What is the first rule?"

The girls thought for a moment. "Choose your battles wisely. If you can't, then battle them wisely," they repeated in unison.

Branna nodded and looked over at Anne, who was feeding yet another nephew. She gave Branna a glare and the woman-warrior shrugged helplessly. "Can I help it if the lasses are inquisitive?" she asked innocently.

"Branna, please," the girl said. "After this, can Cousin Connal take me to see the ships?"

"All right then. By the goddess Aine, you're an impatient one, Gráinne O'Malley. Why do you want to see a ship?" Branna asked as the parents, who were the better-known sea-faring O'Malley, came out to claim their children. Gráinne and her brothers waved goodbye as they rode off.

Eamon announced to his family that it was time for them to leave, as well. Branna was grateful for the rest. Mairéad turned and waved happily to her aunt as her father playfully whisked her into his arms and carried her off.

Branna laughed openly at the smiling child and waved back. Anne put her arm around the lean waist and held her tight as she balanced the baby on her hip. "They love you, Branna."

Branna slipped an arm around her shoulders. "They love both of us, Annie," she corrected her with a kiss on the head. She kissed her nephew's head.

Moiré rescued Anne by taking her wailing son. She kissed each woman and headed off.

"Well, they're gone and I am exhausted," Branna said. "Mairéad is a darlin' and Gráinne is a cute little lass. Why she wants to be bothered with ships—"

"When she can play with a sword like her cousin?"

Branna laughed openly and lifted Anne out of the chair; she sat down and pulled Anne back onto her lap.

Anne laughed, as well, as she ran her fingers through the dark mane, now speckled with gray. The green eyes, however, still sparkled wildly as they did all those years before when they first met. Anne smiled as she thought of her family.

Eamon had married Moiré as planned. The O'Malley clan was proud as the couple promptly had two sets of twins.

Connal was still at home, working the cattle and helping Branna with the land, though he had an eye for the O'Brien lass in the next village. Elizabeth still took care of all of them.

"Still love me?" Branna asked as she nibbled at her neck.

"I suppose it's too late to got back to England," Anne said thoughtfully, and Branna held her tighter. "I suppose I must love you," she said against her lips. She pulled back and playfully slid her hand along the smooth muscular thigh. Coming to a familiar scar, she traced it with her fingers.

"I love it that you wear a kilt," she whispered and ran her

fingers farther.

Branna, as always, took a deep calming breath to stop her racing heart. "And why is that, luv?"

"I can love you like this and nobody will know," she whispered the old game. *How many times have we played it over the years?* Branna ran her fingers up her lover's thigh, as well. "I'm happy you've taken to wearin' a kilt on occasion, as well, luv."

Anne's fingers were dangerously close to their destination. She felt the heat emanating from Branna and saw her nostrils flare.

Branna saw the rakish grin. "Annie," she said with a low loving growl, "I'm warnin' you, woman."

Anne did not heed the warning from her lover, who groaned openly as she felt her lover's touch.

"I warned you..." Branna said, catching her breath. She jumped up, tossed the laughing woman over her shoulder, and marched down the long hall.

"Who's the barbarian now?" Branna asked as she gave the bare bottom a hard slap.

"I am," Anne obediently answered and let out a shriek of laughter as the door closed behind them.

They lay in sated contentment in the darkness. "Branna, can we talk for a moment?" Anne said as she lazily lay across her lover's body.

"If we must," Branna groaned tiredly.

"I've been thinking about your mother's brooch," she said.

Branna raised a curious eyebrow and placed her hands behind her head. "It's yours, Annie."

"I know, but I keep harkening back to what your mother said. She wanted your daughter to have it and give it to her daughter and so on," she said and sat up. "When the time comes, I think we should give it to one of your nieces."

"I've thought of that, as well." She smiled and tossed the squealing woman on her back. "When the time comes, we'll decide together, but we have a long life ahead of us, luv. I intend to spend that time loving you."

Anne slept peacefully as Branna eased out of bed. She slipped into the fur-lined robe, cuddled it close, and stood by the window. A restless feeling wafted through her. She shivered as the cold wind whistled through the thin panes.

"You are the O'Malley," she heard her mother's voice whisper, mingled with the howling of the wind. Branna looked around the dark bedroom. The embers of the dying fire were the only illumination. *Was that my mother's voice or was it the wind?*

Branna thought of her mother and hoped she had done what her mother asked: Keep the family together, safe, and away from harm.

She and Anne would be there for them, watching the little ones grow into the fine strong O'Malley they were destined to be. A sudden feeling of loss tore through her as she thought how neither she nor Anne would ever bear children.

She looked down at her slumbering Englishwoman and smiled. Anne was right. Together they would help raise her brother's children. This was enough. To have Anne and her family beside her filled her heart and lifted her soul.

"I'm doin' the best I can, Mam," she said into the darkness.

An inexplicable surge of contentment came over her.

In the cool moonlit night, Branna stood by the window and gazed out at the endless sea.

Kathleen watched young Branna as she gazed at the grassy hill. Reagan had long since disappeared, yet she still watched as if she were waiting for her to ride back. She couldn't help but notice the sad, pensive look on Branna's face.

"What are you thinking?" she asked in a soft tired voice.

Branna took a deep breath and looked at her. "I'm thinking you should be inside. You look very tired. I need to make supper for Rose, as well. All this story tellin' and Reagan Shaunessy..." Her voice trailed off as the three of them walked back into the cottage.

Kathleen sat in her chair by the fire and groaned. "I am tired," she conceded.

"I'll put the kettle on to boil and get supper ready," Branna said, and disappeared into the kitchen.

Kathleen stared at the dancing flames and recalled the intimate private times between she and Seana. All the years of lovemaking, holding each other in the dark night. Kathleen would listen to Seana's heart beating, knowing it beat for her and only her. She closed her eyes and put her head back.

"You love me, right?" Seana asked as she held Kathleen.

"Yes, Shawneen, I love you more than you know," she said and kissed the top of her breast.

Seana sighed and gently rolled Kathleen onto her back. "I need you, Kath, I can't live without you." She ran her fingertips up and down her arm, then across her breasts. "I love the feel of you. I'll always love these quiet times we share." She kissed her once more, tenderly and slowly. "Promise me..."

Kathleen sighed and closed her eyes as Seana's soft lips nibbled at her earlobe. *"Anything," she said in return.*

"Don't ever leave me in this world alone."

Kathleen opened her eyes. She reached up and caressed Seana's cheek. She saw the pleading look and her heart broke. *"Never, Seana. I'll never leave you alone."*

"Kathleen?"

She opened her eyes to see Branna standing there with a teacup. "Would you rather go lie down?"

Kathleen shook her head and reached for the teacup. "No, I was just remembering. Seems to be the day for it."

"Well, Rose is fed, let me get her to bed," Branna said. "Say good night, darlin'."

Rose waddled up to Kathleen, who grinned and sat forward. "Night," the tired girl said.

"Good night, Rose. Sleep sweet, baby." Kathleen kissed her on the lips. "My little O'Malley," she said and chucked her under the chin.

Branna returned a few minutes later and rekindled the peat fire, then dusted off her hands and took her place back on the hearth. She blew at the steamy teacup and said nothing.

"What are you afraid of, Branna?" Kathleen asked as she set

her teacup on the table.

Branna's head shot up at the question, and she frowned. "I-I'm not afraid of anything. If you're talkin' about Reagan, I'm not afraid of her, either."

"I know you're not afraid of Reagan. It's yourself that's got you terrified."

"What does that mean?"

Kathleen heard the angry voice but continued. "It's how I felt when I first knew I was in love with Seana. I was terrified. I didn't know what to do. I had never been with another woman, never thought of it. However, something about Seana just pulled at my heart." She stopped and picked up her teacup again. "I never thought I could love Seana the way she needed. So I denied it until she was gone. I was very lucky to find her and tell her." She looked at Branna, who was staring at her cup.

"I'd hate like the devil for that to happen to you and not be so lucky as to find Reagan again. She loves you," Kathleen said, willing her to understand.

When Branna said nothing, she took a deep breath. "You're like your great-great-great aunt—Quinlan Stoddard," Kathleen said and drank her tea.

Branna narrowed her eyes at Kathleen. "Why do I have a feelin' there's another story comin' on?"

Kathleen laughed tiredly. "Quinlan Stoddard sailed the Jamaica winds right into the heart of a young Frenchwoman…"

"Quinlan Rose, stop gazing out the window. The ocean isn't goin' anywhere," her mother said in her soft Irish brogue.

The young dark-haired girl with violet eyes pulled a disgruntled face and flounced in a chair at the table by the fire.

Her mother gave her an indulgent grin. "Help me peel these potatoes. I have to get this on the hearth or we'll never have dinner."

Quinlan sighed as she picked up the knife and got to work. "When will father be home?" she asked absently. "I wonder what he'll bring back from his voyage."

"Probably something of absolutely no use at all, and he'll be back in two weeks time, darlin'."

"Why can't Joshua help, as well?" the young girl grumbled.

"Because your brother is only five. When you're done, you can go gaze at your ocean. Now peel," her mother said and tickled her daughter's side.

Quinlan shrieked with laughter and wriggled out of the way. Rose Quinlan O'Malley-Stoddard knew her daughter's love of the sea. They shared that love, as they shared many things. Rose was a tall woman with coal black hair and green eyes. She loved her only daughter completely and knew no one could stop her adventurous spirit. She was an O'Malley, as well as a Stoddard, and she knew Quinlan was destined for something great. Her heart swelled at the vision of Quinlan as a grown woman, finding her place in the world like all the O'Malley women before her in Ireland.

She remembered how she felt when she left Ireland in the mid-1780's to come to America. Rose was only nineteen and scared to death. However, she needed to know what was beyond the vast ocean she gazed upon in her youth. Her grandmother would tell her time and again not to allow the fear of the unknown to stop her. Therefore, all alone, she booked passage and came across an ocean to this new land.

When she landed in the port of Charleston in the Carolinas, she met Robert Stoddard. Time stood still, and Rose O'Malley fell in love. They married, and Quinlan Rose was their firstborn. She came into the world screaming and kicking, her fiery independence bursting forth with her first breath. She felt her daughter was destined for...

"Mother, look," she said urgently.

Rose looked down at her daughter, who was balancing a spoon on her nose, deep in concentration. "Bet Joshua can't do this," she said proudly, intent upon her task.

Her mother gave the young girl a disturbed, albeit affectionate look. Her only daughter, Quinlan Rose Branna Stoddard, destined for greatness—balancing a spoon on her nose.

Chapter 16

The young woman looked around the seaport in the Carolinas. She had the look of an aristocrat about her. She was dressed in expensive silks, and her dress ruffled and billowed as she made her way through town. Completely lost, she frantically tried to find her party.

"Mon Dieu," she said, angry with herself and her guardian for being separated at the dock. "I should have stayed in Paris," she said, her accent obvious. "This backward country," she continued as she looked down every street.

It was 1820, and the seaport town of Charleston teemed with traders, sailors, and businessmen. Many watched with an interested eye as the young, flaxen-haired, woman looked about in confusion. Her dress of pure green silk rustled as she whirled around, then walked down another unknown street and headed toward a dark alley.

The two men sat in the tavern drinking their rum from pewter tankards. The young one, a redheaded Irishman, took a deep reflective breath.

"The capt'n will never let us back aboard." He sighed and took a healthy drink. "The *Pride of Charleston* sails tonight."

The older, a short, educated man from Charleston, sported a more hopeful demeanor. "Oh, I don't know, Thomas."

"Are you crazy, Will? If we hadn't gotten drunk, the capt'n would be halfway 'round the Cape by now. We're doomed." He buried his head.

Will looked fondly at the youngster. "Don't be so hard on

yourself," he said with a grin.

Thomas shot his head up and glared at his old friend. "Myself? I believe you were the one who said, 'One more, Thomas, won't hurt us,'" he said, and Will laughed.

"It's not as bad as you think. Now let's put our heads together and think of a solution. What would make the capt'n happy?"

Thomas thought for a moment and grinned evilly. "A wench. God, William, you're a genius. Of course," he agreed, seeing light at the end of the tunnel for the first time. He leaned back in a dejected heap. "Where are we gonna find a woman this late in the day?"

"Well, you never know, my boy. Something—"

Both men looked up as the heavy wooden door opened and in walked the answer to their prayer.

"Mother of God," Thomas exclaimed and took a healthy swig.

William watched her; she was dressed in silk, nervously looking around the dingy tavern.

"Excusez-moi?" she said and shook her head. "Pardon, me?" she corrected herself, knowing her French confused the tavern owner.

Suddenly, William was on his feet as he made his way to her. "May I offer some assistance, mademoiselle?"

"You speak French, oui?" she asked hopefully.

For the next minute or two, Thomas sat mesmerized as William and the woman conversed in French.

William tried to keep up with the rambling. He nodded in understanding, put a hand on the woman's arm, and guided her to their table.

Thomas immediately stood and pulled off his cap. He gave William a curious look.

"This young lady is lost," he said and winked at Thomas. "She believes the party she was with is searching for her, but she doesn't know where to start."

She nodded and smiled at both men. William saw the hesitant look, knowing this woman was not sure if she should trust them or not. He knew she had little choice.

"I believe we should start at the dock," William said evenly.

Thomas nodded in agreement and winked. He bowed, as well. "Miss, we'd be only too happy to help you."

As they escorted the young Frenchwoman out, Thomas leaned into his old shipmate. "You're a genius, William. A pure genius."

"Now, this is where you last saw them, n'est-ce pas?" Will asked as they stood on the dock.

"Oui. Je..." She stopped and collected her thoughts. "Yes. I stand over there waiting and next minute, they are gone," she said sadly. "We were on our voyage back to France. Now..."

Thomas looked at the dock and noticed the *Pride of Charleston* at the end. The three-mast schooner sat low in the water. That meant she was loaded and ready to set sail. He nervously motioned to William, who merely nodded.

William patted her hand. "Now, now. Let's take you aboard our vessel. Our capt'n I'm sure will be able to help you find which ship is sailing to France. At the very least perhaps, help you find your party."

The young blond woman smiled. "Merci, monsieur. Thank you."

They walked toward the tall ship ready to set sail. "Um, give me a moment, please. I'll make sure the capt'n is aboard. Thomas, please stay here with... Oh, my dear, I am sorry, what is your name?"

"Celeste Marchand," she said and shook hands with both saviors.

William walked up the gangplank, and a young man immediately stopped him. "Hold on, William, are you crazy? The capt'n will skin you alive..."

William grinned at the first mate and looked back at Thomas and the Frenchwoman. "Not when the capt'n sees what I have."

The other man, holding his chart, looked and raised a dubious eyebrow. "And where did you find her?"

"She's lost and needs to get back to France—"

"We're not going to France."

"I think the capt'n could use a little company on the voyage.

She has nowhere to go and doesn't know a soul, Jack."

Jack scratched his head. "William, this is not a good idea. The capt'n will be furious."

"For a second, if that long," William assured him. "What happened the last time the capt'n was…twitchy?"

Jack thought and winced. "We scoured the quarterdeck the entire day. You're right, get her aboard. We sail in an hour. You are one lucky old sailor, William Drury."

Will laughed and slapped the first mate on the back.

They settled Celeste in the captain's quarters. "If you please, Ma'amselle Marchand, make yourself at home. The capt'n will be here soon."

"Merci," she said.

William felt a pang of guilt as he walked out. She looked young and innocent. Well, she'd get back to France, just not across the Atlantic and not for three months or so.

Celeste took off her silk hat and idly looked around the captain's quarters. Off in the far corner, a bunk built into the wall looked cozy and warm. By the big window, a desk found a happy home. She absently looked around, seeing a charted map and the utensils one would imagine a sea captain needing.

She sniffed the air, expecting the aroma of pipe tobacco but found none. As she looked around the room, she saw an eating area under yet another window. Looking out, she realized that the captain's quarters were at the stern of the ship. It was big and roomy and the dark mahogany wood gave it a lived-in and comfortable atmosphere.

All at once, she was exhausted as she sat on the bunk and looked out the window at the bay that led to the Atlantic, which led to France. She did want to go back, did she not? Breathing in deeply, she fought the wave of sleep.

She must have dozed, for she felt someone watching her. Her eyes fluttered open to see a tall man standing by the bed, hands on his hips and frowning. Feeling like a fool, she quickly sat up and straightened her hair.

"Pardon, monsieur…" she started and rambled in her native tongue. She then stood and stopped abruptly at the smirk on the

… woman's face. Mon Dieu, she thought.

The woman stood very tall. She was trim and fit, but Celeste noticed the subtle curve of her hip and the swell of her breasts beneath the billowy white shirt opened at the neck. She looked up into the deepest darkest eyes she'd ever seen. They may have been blue, but in the dimly lit quarters, she could not be sure. Her brown hair lay in a mass of thick waves around the nape of her neck, touching the wide collar of her shirt; she wore men's breeches and high leather boots.

"Who the devil are you?" the woman asked with a grin. Her eyes raked over Celeste's body.

The Frenchwoman bristled under the scrutiny. "Who are you? I am waiting for le capitaine of this vessel," she said in an indignant voice.

Quinn raised an elegantly arched eyebrow, folded her arms across her chest, and leaned against the desk. "I am le capitaine of this vessel," she responded with a smug grin.

Celeste looked at her in confusion. "Non."

"Oui," Quinn countered sarcastically. "Now suppose you tell me why you're sleeping in my quarters. Not that I mind at all, believe me. You're quite fetching."

Celeste was dumbfounded as she shook her head. This was too bizarre for her brain to accommodate. *Fetching? Another woman is speaking to me like this?* Her heart pounded in her chest. She looked past this tall smirking woman to the door.

"Ma'amselle?" she asked sweetly.

Celeste took a deep breath and explained.

Quinn listened and frowned as Celeste brought up Will and Thomas's names. She shook her head and rubbed her face. Celeste noticed she took a deep angry breath; her right eye twitched as she marched to the door and threw it open. Looking up to the deck, she bellowed, "Jack! Get your ass down here now!"

Celeste backed up in fear and stood against the wall.

Jack quickly entered her cabin. "Yes, ma'am."

Quinn tried to control her anger. "Did you know about this?" she asked as her jaw tightened.

The young mate swallowed. "Can I speak to you alone, sir,

er, capt'n?" he corrected himself. Quinn glared at him. "If you please," he pleaded.

She narrowed her eyes at him and marched out of her quarters, slamming the heavy door.

Celeste started breathing again and stopped when she heard the angry woman's voice.

"What? Are they crazy? Of all the stupid goddamned things. I'll have them both flogged!"

She heard the muffled sound from the gentleman.

"I don't care if it's against maritime law, Jack! Then I'll have them both shot!"

After a moment, of what Celeste thought was the gentleman trying to calm her down, Quinn re-entered her chambers. Her face was beet red as she took a deep breath.

"What is your name, miss?" she asked.

Celeste watched her with a careful eye. "Celeste Marchand. And you are?" she asked, standing straight.

She grinned and offered a sweeping bow. "Quinlan Stoddard at your service. The 'captain' is optional," she said, still grinning. "And I'm afraid you'll be with us for a while, ma'amselle. I'm sorry, but this ship is not sailing for France. We're headed for the Caribbean."

Celeste's eyes grew wide as she looked out the portal. The schooner had left the dock. "*Non!*" she shouted and rambled off in French.

Quinn watched her rant and took a deep breath. "Miss Marchand," she said calmly, but Celeste ignored her as she spoke, pointed out the window, and ranted. "If you would—"

Still Celeste continued, until Quinn painfully pinched the bridge of her nose.

"Enough!" Celeste stopped immediately. Quinn took a deep breath and started more calmly. "Now I'm sorry, uh… *Je regrette, mais* … Oh, bloody hell. I'm sorry, but I have no choice. Had I known you were here, I'd have sent you ashore. Unfortunately, I can do nothing about it. We're bound for Jamaica, and we won't be back in Charleston for at least two months. Now I'm sorry, but—"

"You turn this ship around immediately," Celeste insisted.

Quinn chuckled at the suggestion. Celeste seethed with anger.

"Do not laugh at me, Capitaine. Take me back to Charleston."

"I cannot take you back to *Sharleston*," Quinn answered sarcastically. "The best I can do is to get you on a ship to France, but I can't do that until I get to Jamaica."

She smiled broadly and stepped closer to Celeste. "Now let's make the best of this situation. I'll leave you to gather yourself. We'll dine together here in my quarters and get acquainted."

Celeste felt her face redden with anger as Quinn laughed and walked out, closing the door.

Quinn walked out on deck and eyed the two troublemakers. "Will, Thomas!" she barked, and both men immediately dropped their duties and were standing in front of her. Quinn took a deep breath. "You have two minutes before I toss you overboard," she said in a dark voice.

Thomas looked as though he might faint. William stepped up.

Quinn regarded the older man warily. She liked Will Drury. He was a seasoned sailor and knew his way around a ship, that was certain. Unfortunately, he had a weakness for rum, and for that, no other ship would have him. He had a wife and four children. His little escapade with Thomas, and getting them out of jail, cost her the more lucrative voyage around the Cape. Cursing herself for her sentimentality, she watched him.

"Well, Capt'n, Thomas and I, well, quite honestly, we were trying to get back into your good graces. We know how you fancy—" He stopped as Quinn folded her arms across her chest and glared at him. He continued quickly. "Yes, well. We were only looking out for your best interest. You seem a little tense lately," he said, and tried not to smile. He glanced at Thomas, who didn't move. Quinn wondered if the poor lad was breathing.

"My best interest, was it? Or a way back on the *Pride of Charleston*?" Quinn leaned into them. "I thank you for your concern, but did you happen to notice how she's dressed?"

Neither man said a word. Quinn's right eye twitched. "She's

probably an aristocrat," she said, her voice rising with each word. "More than likely, she's related to royalty!" Will and Thomas winced. "And I, for one, will not be hanged for kidnapping! You idiots!" she finished with a roar. "The quarterdeck needs cleaning." She turned and marched up to the helm.

Jack busied himself with the other shipmates, instructing them as they worked. The helmsman looked straight ahead, as he steered the ship.

"I'll take over," she said angrily.

"Yes, ma'am," he said and quickly stepped aside.

Quinn took the helm as she watched the sun fading in the horizon. It was a calm night. It would be smooth sailing until daybreak. She gazed at the ocean stretched out before her. The endless sea calmed her immediately.

Quinn closed her eyes and took a deep breath of sea air. How she loved to be on the ocean with only the ship's deck beneath her. Her father, Robert, was a captain in the newly formed Navy when America won its freedom. He served all his life, but he was barely home. However, when he was, she loved the way he talked of the sea. He took Quinn aboard ship whenever he had the chance. Her mother, Rose, also had a love of the sea. Coming from a long line of Irish fishermen, Rose never quelled her only daughter's love for her father and the ocean. She let the young Quinn go many times against her better judgment. For weeks at a time, she'd be gone with her father. It was in their blood.

When her father retired from the Navy, he started his own sailing line—the Stoddard Line. His dream was to have a fleet of ships. However, that was not to be. He had only two ships, the *Pride of the Carolinas* and the *Pride of Charleston*. It cost him every cent he had. His idea was to sail the Caribbean where the islands were rich with sugarcane and molasses.

Quinn now shook her head as she thought about molasses: the main ingredient for rum. Her father had a weakness for that, as well. Perhaps that's why she had a soft spot in her heart for Will Drury. Now that he took young Thomas Maloney under his wing, they had become a matched set. She glanced down at both of them scrubbing the quarterdeck and hid her grin.

When her father approached Quinn with the idea, she was excited and had ideas of her own. However, being a woman in 1820 meant very little besides taking care of home and hearth. That was not for Quinlan Stoddard. She knew she was different—knew at a very early age.

She remembered her discussion with her parents about captaining a ship on the Stoddard Line. Her brother, Joshua, was younger and had set out on his own a few years earlier. He did not share his family's love of the sea. He needed to explore this new land and traveled westward. Quinn understood her brother's desire to explore, but on land? She knew her father was disappointed that Joshua did not share their love of the sea, but her father could not deny him his spirit.

When he saw the passion and spirit in his only daughter's eyes, he grinned at the idea, and her mother shook her head. However, both tried to discourage her.

"Quinn, darlin', you're a woman," her mother challenged, *gauging her reaction.*

Quinn frowned. "What has that to do with it?"

Inwardly, Rose's heart swelled with pride for her daughter. Yes, she thought, she has O'Malley blood flowing through her veins. Generations of O'Malley women, struggling to find their way in this world, determined not to be passed over for any reason. She watched her only daughter on her quest for her place in life.

Quinn turned to her father. He was sitting by the fire, puffing away on his pipe. He looked up and sighed. "Quinn, your mother is right. No man will allow a woman..."

Broken from her reverie, Rose stood and faced her husband. "Our daughter is as good a captain as any man you know, Robert. Is there one other person you trust more than Quinn?"

Her husband struck a thoughtful pose. "No, there isn't."

Quinn rushed to him and knelt in front of him. "Father, I know all the men, and I know they'll listen to you and me. Let me pick my crew. I know we can do this. You've taught me all you know about seamanship. I've studied every map you've given me. I swear I could sail the Jamaica winds blindfolded. Please, let me do this. You, me, and the sea."

Robert looked into the passionate eyes so much like her mother's. He glanced up at his wife, who stood proud and challenging, although she had tears in her green eyes. Oh, these Irishwomen, he thought and laughed openly.

Quinn stood and looked back and forth from father to mother as they laughed.

Her father stood and walked up to his wife and put his strong hands on her shoulders. "God bless the day I met you."

"I fell in love with you right there on that dock in Charleston. The sea is in our soul, darlin'. It's in our daughter's, as well. Don't be askin' her to deny her soul. You can't do that." She touched his weathered face.

He kissed the palm of her hand and turned to his daughter. "Pick your crew, Quinlan. You're the captain of the Pride of Charleston *now. Command with a strong hand but with a compassionate heart. Your word must be law and final. Trust your heart and your soul. This is what I had planned to tell Joshua when it came time for him to captain a ship on the Stoddard Line. It's what I tell you now." Tears filled his blue eyes.*

Quinn ran into his arms and hugged him fiercely. "I will, Father. I swear I'll make the Stoddard Line the best in all the Carolinas."

That was six years earlier, and Quinn had sailed this route many times. She could indeed do it blindfolded. No longer able to sail due to his failing health, Robert took care of the business end of the Stoddard Line. The *Pride of Carolina* would be halfway around the Cape by now, Quinn thought with a pang of envy. She wanted the *Pride of Charleston* to make that voyage. Quinn took a deep breath as she stood at the helm of the three-mast schooner. The wind picked up quickly as Quinn barked her commands and pointed to the rigging. With practiced precision, the men trimmed the mainsail quickly.

"Jack, get that aft sail trimmed," she called out. Jack nodded and yelled his commands.

"Samuel, take the helm," she said, and Samuel came back to his post. She smiled and slapped him on the back. "With this wind, we'll be in Jamaica in no time."

"Yes, ma'am," Samuel agreed heartily.

"Jack, I'll be in my quarters. Have Henry bring my dinner and Ma'amselle Marchand's," she added with a haughty air.

Jack sighed in relief. "This is an awkward situation, Quinn. I'm sorry for this. I wasn't thinking. I saw Will and I know how much we need him. And you—" He stopped short and blushed horribly.

Quinn cleared her throat. "You're a good first mate, Jack. I don't blame you, but it is a damnable situation. We have no idea who this woman is. Damnable…" she muttered.

"I'll have Henry bring a bottle of claret, as well," Jack said and walked away.

"Have him bring two," Quinn said.

This was going to be one outrageous voyage.

Chapter 17

Celeste poured the water into the basin, slipped off her dress, and unbuttoned her chemise. Lathering the cloth with the lavender soap, she lightly washed her face and hands. Concentrating on her task, she did not hear the door open. She dried her face on the towel and turned around to see Quinn standing there, smirking again.

She stood there holding the towel up to her chest. "Do you not know how to knock?" she asked angrily.

Quinn smiled slightly as she walked into the room. "These are my quarters, Ma'amselle Marchand. I do not have to knock." She sat at the large desk in the corner. She put her booted feet on the desk and put her hands behind her head. "Continue bathing, don't mind me."

Celeste felt the color rise to her face as the arrogant woman sat there, watching her. She turned on her heels and slipped into her dress once again. She could feel the eyes of Quinn on her as she dressed.

Behind her, Quinn's mouth went dry noticing the milky white skin. It was quite the contrast to hers, which had been darkened by the sun and wind. The towel covered all the vital areas, but Quinn noticed the top of the larger heaving breasts that seemed to beg their release from the constraints. Her groin ached, and she knew she should have taken the time in Charleston to pay her usual visit to—

The knock at her door broke her from her bawdy musings. Celeste quickly buttoned her dress as Quinn barked, "Come."

Celeste whirled around to see Quinn grinning widely. "I

152

meant the door, Ma'amselle Marchand."

Celeste glared at her as an old man walked in with a large tray. "Capt'n Stoddard, Ma'amselle Marchand, dinner is served," he said with a wink.

Quinn's lips twitched as she bowed. "You're right on time, Henry. Ma'amselle Marchand, this is Henry Paxton. He's our cook, doctor, and clergyman while we're at sea," she said with a wicked grin. "So if you have any sins you'd like to confess, he's your man."

Henry shook his head as he set up the table under the portal. He turned and extended his old weathered hand. "A pleasure, Ma'amselle Marchand. And might I say you are a beautiful young lady."

Celeste gratefully took his hand, giving a side-glance to the arrogant woman. "Merci, Monsieur Paxton. It is nice to see a bit of culture on this ship. You are indeed a gentleman." She curtsied.

Henry bowed and kissed the back of her hand.

Quinn rolled her eyes and stood quickly. "Thank you, Henry. Ma'amselle Marchand is properly impressed."

Henry gave his young friend a stern look. "You could do with a little culture, yourself, Quinlan," he whispered as he passed.

Quinn opened the door, bowing dramatically. "I am sufficiently rebuked." Henry sighed and walked out with the tray.

As Celeste walked up to the table, Quinn stood beside her and pulled out the chair. "Allow me."

The young blonde took the offered chair. "Merci," she murmured, and the soft voice sent a jolt right between Quinn's legs.

Quinn walked over to the basin, poured more water into it, and began to take off her shirt.

Celeste tried to look away from Quinn, who stripped off her shirt, grateful she was wearing a white chemise, as well. She stared at Quinn's back as she washed her face and neck. She noticed the strong back and narrow waist. She swallowed as she watched the firm muscles in her buttocks, encased in the tight breeches. *Mon Dieu, what am I doing?* she chastised herself. Her mind instantly went back to Paris, where the previous year she had the same feeling for her tutor, an older Frenchwoman who smelled wonderfully of perfume and roses. She remembered the feelings she had for Marie Boucher. Celeste took the napkin and dabbed her forehead, feeling a little perspiration beading.

She nearly fainted when the captain turned, toweling her face and arms. She had well-defined muscles for a woman, though she was distinctly feminine. Quinn's breasts were not as large as her own, and Celeste was shocked to see that she wore nothing to confine them. Though they were small, Celeste noticed their firmness... *Oh, please, stop!* She shook her head rapidly.

Quinn pulled on another shirt. "I hope you're hungry. Henry is very good in the galley." She sat opposite Celeste and poured wine into her goblet. "So tell me about yourself, ma'amselle. How did you get separated from your party?"

Celeste picked up her goblet. Quinn followed suit and held it across the table. Celeste smiled so slightly that Quinn almost missed it—almost.

For a moment, crystal blue eyes met the dark sapphires. "I'm sorry for this inconvenience. I promise it won't be too upsetting for you." Her eyes traveled down to the heaving breasts, then back to her face.

Celeste pulled her glass back and took a drink. "Thank you, Captain Stoddard," she said coolly and concentrated on her dinner.

"So now tell me about yourself," Quinn repeated as she ate and drank heartily. She opened yet another bottle of claret and sat down, wiping her hand across her mouth as she poured two glasses.

Celeste was intrigued and slightly disgusted by this woman. In France, a woman would never wear men's breeches, much less walk around improperly dressed. Celeste decided then, Quinlan Stoddard was uncouth and base.

"I am from Paris. I was in America visiting family friends in the Carolinas. We were on our way back when I was separated from my party. I am sure they think I am dead," she said sadly.

Quinn listened as she drank her wine. As she ate the beef, she grabbed for the bread, ripping a chunk off, and dunked it into the gravy; she washed it down with a healthy drink of wine. "Again, I'm sorry. It's an unfortunate situation." Quinn sat back. "My, that was good." She glanced at her dinner companion. "You haven't eaten much."

"I am not very hungry."

Quinn grinned slightly as she put her wineglass to her lips. The French accent was appealing; so was the woman. Her heartbeat quickened as she studied Celeste, who could be no more than eighteen, if that. Her skin was flawless, milky white as if it had never seen the sun's rays. She wore no powder or rouge on her face, though Quinn was sure she had a natural pink glow. Perhaps it was the wine.

As the lantern swayed slowly beside them, Quinn saw Celeste's golden hair shimmering in its light. Her crystal blue eyes captivated Quinn as Celeste gazed into the wineglass. She thought of Celeste in her chemise as she bathed earlier. Now in her satiny dress, Quinn swallowed convulsively as she peered at the copious amount of cleavage; the larger firm breasts heaved in rhythm with every breath.

The ache between her legs grew with each passing moment. Will Drury did indeed know what he was doing with this little wench. However, she was not the typical companion with whom she usually found herself.

"How old are you?" Quinn asked.

Celeste felt color rise to her face for some reason. "I am twenty," she answered almost shyly and looked up. "I will be twenty-one in this month. How old are you?"

Quinn raised an amused eyebrow. "Old enough," she assured her. "You're not married?"

Again, Celeste looked down at her glass. "No, I am not."

"I'm not familiar with the customs of your country. I only know that you helped us during our war with the British, but I thought marriages were arranged. How did a lovely girl as you manage to avoid that?"

Celeste shrugged but said nothing. How could she tell a stranger she wanted no man? That every time a marriage was arranged, Celeste ran away, only to be brought back. Her father was in great debt, her mother died when she was a girl. Marrying her into money was his only choice.

Quinn saw the pain in her eyes. "Well, I usually take a walk on deck after a meal like this. Join me," she said and finished her wine.

Quinn and Celeste strolled along the top deck of the sleek schooner. The warm breeze was light as they sailed southward. Quinn stopped and leaned on the gunwale, gazing at the starry night.

Celeste looked out at the vast sea before her. "*C'est beau de mar.*" She took a deep breath of the night air.

Quinn smiled and turned to her, her elbow leaning on the side.

Celeste looked straight ahead in the dark night, aware of Quinn as the ship rocked back and forth.

"What did you say? It sounded so beautiful," Quinn asked.

Celeste thought for a moment. "The ocean, it is beautiful."

Quinn gazed at the pretty profile. "Yes, very beautiful." When she noticed Celeste shiver in the night air, she fought the urge to take Celeste in her arms. "Come, it's turning a bit chilly."

Once back in Quinn's room, Celeste nervously looked around.

Quinn grinned slightly. "You'll sleep in my bunk. There's nowhere else for you, and I don't want you wandering the ship alone. I trust my men. However, you're a fetching young woman."

"I cannot sleep in your bed. This is highly inappropriate. I will sleep in the galley before I sleep in your bed," Celeste said, her French accent accentuating her point.

"You don't have to sleep in my bed, but you will not sleep anywhere but this room. You can sleep on the floor for all I care, but I won't have you wandering this ship. It will be a long two months. You will do as I say."

Celeste turned around and walked over to the window.

"Now you will get into bed. I'm exhausted and need my sleep," Quinn said. "I'll be back in ten minutes." She picked up the bottle of wine and marched out, slamming the door and locking it.

Celeste sat there for nearly the entire ten minutes, looking at the soft bunk. She too was exhausted. Realizing that fighting was futile, she undressed and slid under the quilt wearing her chemise. She pulled the quilt up to her chest.

Quinn Stoddard was an awful woman, she thought. She was crude and disgusting, treating her this way. Why then, did her heart start pounding when she told her to get into her bed?

Well, she didn't really want to go back to France to face a loveless marriage. Now she had her wish, but she was at Quinn's mercy. She felt her eyes get heavy, and finally, she fell asleep.

Suddenly, she felt the bed move. She was shocked and let out a screech as Quinn slipped under the quilt.

Quinn put her hand over her mouth. "Keep still, you silly woman. I mean you no harm."

She loomed over the wild-eyed woman. "Now I'm taking my hand away," she said and looked into the crystal blue eyes. "No screeching."

Celeste scooted to the far end of the bunk, which wasn't very far, and turned her back to Quinn.

Quinn lay back, putting her hands behind her head. "Good night, ma'amselle. Sweet dreams." Quinn yawned and fell instantly asleep.

Celeste would not fall so quickly. However, she soon followed Quinn into a peaceful sleep.

She woke slowly, feeling something pressing against her back, and a warmth around her chest. Blinking to adjust to the darkness of the cabin, Celeste felt the warm breath tickling the back of her neck. She was shocked when she felt a hand engulfing her breast. She didn't want to move lest she wake the slumbering woman. God knows what to expect then. *How improper of her to hold me this way!* She tried to avoid the comfortable sensation and the aching between her legs.

Never having been with a man like this, much less another woman, Celeste was light-headed with the sensations. Her body trembled as she felt the captain move, pulling her closer. She lay perfectly still for some time.

"You're awake?" Quinn asked in a sleepy voice.

Celeste took a deep quivering breath and merely nodded.

Quinn shifted and moved closer behind, sensually moving her hips.

Celeste caught her breath, and cried weakly as the hand squeezed her full breast.

"You're very warm and inviting, Celeste," Quinn whispered into her ear.

Suddenly, she was on her back with Quinn looming over her. She let out a cry as she noticed Quinn wore a chemise as her own. However, hers was completely opened, her breasts in plain view. Quinn quieted her again, this time with a kiss.

Completely astounded, Celeste struggled against her, trying to get her hands between them. The lips that tasted of wine felt warm and soft. *"Non!"* Quinn pulled back slightly. She put her hands up to Quinn's chest to push her away and got a handful of soft flesh.

Quinn moaned as the innocent hands palmed her breasts.

Celeste whimpered, and Quinn felt her body tremble beneath her. Quinn realized what she was doing and released her.

Celeste's hands were still on her breasts, moving lightly across the firm mounds. She removed her hands as if they had been scalded and stared up into the dark violet eyes. Celeste had no idea what lust was, but she was sure she saw it in Quinn's eyes.

Quinn swallowed through her labored breathing. "I- I apologize. I had no right to treat you this way," she said in a coarse voice.

Celeste gazed up in confusion.

Quinn moved away from her and pulled the quilt around the trembling woman. She saw the innocence in her eyes once again. "Go to sleep," she said and lay on her back.

Out of the darkness, Celeste could hear her heart hammering away. She was sure Quinn could hear it, as well. Soon, with the gentle rocking of the ship, she fell back into a deep sleep.

Chapter 18

When Celeste woke in the morning, she was alone. She sat up, looked around the cabin, and noticed a chest lying by the desk. She slipped out of bed and knelt by the chest. A note lay on top of it.

Celeste,

Please accept my apology for last night. The garments in this chest might be to your liking. I fancy the blue one… However, please, take whatever you like.

I trust you slept as well as possible. I can give you a tour of the ship today if that would please you. Come topside whenever you like.

I won't disturb you.

Quinn Stoddard

Celeste grinned slightly and opened the chest. There were several dresses of beautiful colors and undergarments. Celeste wondered where Quinn would get such beautiful clothes. She held them up to her; only two would need adjustments. The others were perfect. She noticed the cloth package, gently opened it, and found a pin, perhaps, a brooch. It was made of gold and was circular with a long gold piece placed through the center. Little green and blue gemstones circled the outer part of the brooch. It was elegant, Celeste thought. She carefully placed it back in the cloth.

She bathed and slipped into the blue dress. American fashion was quite mundane, she thought. However, this dress fit well, and when she twirled around, she was satisfied with the quiet rustling of the material.

Celeste heard a gentle knock at the door. Quinn, she thought, and didn't know why she was grinning. She opened the door to see Henry standing there with a breakfast tray.

"Good morning, miss. My, don't you look lovely. Quinn wanted me to bring you breakfast," he said and set up the table.

"She will not be joining me?"

Henry glanced up to see the disappointment in her face. "No, no. She's eaten long ago. However, she told me to tell you to come on deck whenever you like. It's a glorious day, miss," he said and winked as he walked out.

Celeste sat in a dejected heap at the little table. She drank her coffee and picked at her breakfast. Why should she care if the captain ate with her? She was a crude woman, taking advantage of her the night before.

At once, Celeste was sick to her stomach. Her body trembled at the memory of Quinn's warm lips against hers. She instinctively felt her palms perspire, remembering how she touched the soft breasts. "Mon Dieu," she moaned and finished her breakfast.

Later in the morning, as Celeste walked out onto the deck, she noticed the men washing the deck, hoisting the riggings, and attending to the everyday routine. She looked around and saw her.

Quinn stood at the helm, her hands on her hips, her white blouse billowing in the wind. "The wind is changing, Jack. Tighten that staysail and jib or we'll lose it," she called and Jack nodded and barked his order.

Celeste made her way up to the helm and was about to say good morning, when a gust of wind swept across the bow of the schooner.

"Damn it, man, move!" Quinn yelled and took the helm, steering the ship. The wheel swirled out of control until she stopped it. Four sailors pulled at the jib sheets to trim the three sails. Quinn turned to examine the aft sail.

"Thomas! Get aft and trim that sail, quickly before—" She stopped dead when she saw Celeste standing there, wild-eyed with her blond hair blowing in the wind. She smiled slightly, as another gust of wind blew portside.

The schooner went with the wind and so did Celeste. Quinn dove for her and wrapped her arm around Celeste's waist.

"Steady on," she said, looking down into the blue eyes. She held her tight as the fragrance of Celeste's perfume wafted over her.

In a moment, the ship was flying through the water. All hands accomplished their duties, and the schooner was trimmed and sailing strong.

Quinn let her go and stepped back. "You must be careful when you are topside, Celes...Ma'amselle Marchand," she said sternly.

Jack leaned in as he walked by. "Yes, miss. Many a shipmate's been swept overboard," he said seriously.

Celeste's eyes widened in horror as Quinn glared at her grinning first mate. "Mr. Fenton, you've work to do, I'm sure," she said, and Jack laughed as he walked away.

The uneventful day aboard ship turned into a warm quiet night as Quinn walked into her quarters; she found Celeste sound asleep. She stood by the bunk for a moment, gazing at the woman lying in her bed. Her body ached as she thought of how she kissed those sweet rose-tinted lips. She raised an eyebrow. *Fine, Quinlan, you finally have a woman who grabs you by the heart and she's an innocent. You'll ruin her life, that's what you'll do. So put it out of your mind.*

Only twenty, though Quinn was younger than that when she first tasted the joys of another woman. However, Quinn was not the same as this cultured Frenchwoman. Quinn was raucous to begin with as she spent her young life by the docks of Charleston. She knew little else.

It'll be a long voyage, but once they got to Kingston, Quinn was sure there would be a ship ready for France. Quinn reached over and brushed the flaxen hair off Celeste's forehead.

She opened the bottom drawer of the bunk and took out the hammock. Hanging the ends in place, she slipped off her boots and breeches, grabbed a pillow and blanket, and hoisted herself into the swaying bed. She lay there for a time, listening to Celeste's deep breathing, lulling her to sleep.

For the next week, Celeste and Quinn eased into a nice, but somewhat distant, friendship. Neither spoke of that first night and the kiss.

One morning, Celeste woke and frowned as she saw the hammock lying by the chest. She knew it could not be comfortable for Quinn to be sleeping in the makeshift bed. However, she grinned at the kind gesture.

After breakfast, she hurried to the deck. She shielded her eyes against the blinding rays of the hot sun on the beautiful calm morning. Looking around, she spotted Quinn, standing by the helm with Jack.

She walked up to them and Jack grinned. "Good morning, Ma'amselle Marchand. You look lovely this morning." He bowed slightly.

Celeste smiled and glanced at Quinn, who concentrated on her maps. "Bonjour, Monsieur Fenton. It is a magnificent morning," she said happily.

"I trust you slept well?" Jack asked with a side-glance at his captain.

"Oui, I sleep like a baby, merci," she said and looked at Quinn. "Bonjour, Captain Stoddard."

Quinn looked up and smiled slightly. "Good morning. I'm glad you slept well," she said with a smirk.

Celeste felt the color rising in her cheeks. *Must she always be with the smirk?*

Jack watched Celeste watching Quinn. "Well, I have to check below. Excuse me, if you please, Ma'amselle Marchand," he said with a smile and walked away.

"Monsieur Fenton is a gentleman," Celeste said absently.

Quinn grunted and continued with her logs.

Celeste leaned on the wheel box and watched. "What are you doing?"

Quinn hid her grin as she glanced up. Celeste had her arms across her chest as she leaned. Quinn raised an eyebrow at the copious amount of cleavage before her. She swallowed and cleared her throat. "Charting our course and speed."

"Hmm," Celeste said and picked up an instrument, turning it around in her little hands. "Do you use this?"

Quinn cringed and reached for the navigational guide. "Oui, ma'amselle. I use theeze."

"What is it for?"

Quinn took a deep patient breath. "It's called a sextant, and it's used to measure distance and angles. When you're at sea and have no landmarks, you have to rely on the sun and moon and the stars. This instrument helps you."

"Show me."

Quinn looked down at the enthusiastic face and laughed. "All right, here," she said and turned Celeste toward the horizon. "Please don't drop this," she begged as Celeste giggled. Quinn stood behind her and put both arms around her, holding the sextant.

"I'd best hold it, as well," she said. "It's a sensitive, not to mention expensive, instrument. You look through this piece here, finding a celestial body. There are two mirrors. They steady the sextant when the ship rolls. When the edge of the image touches the horizon, you mark the angle on the scale below," she continued as the fragrance of lavender invaded her senses. She closed her eyes for a moment and took a deep breath.

Celeste shivered as she felt the warm breath close to her ear. She swallowed as she looked through the eyepiece. She had no idea what she was looking at, nor did she care. She was only aware of the warm fingers over hers as they held the heavy metal instrument.

For several moments, neither woman spoke, each trying to control her racing heart.

Celeste swallowed hard before she could talk. "Like this?" She leaned back into Quinn as she raised the instrument to her eye once again. She felt Quinn's hand move to her shoulder, the fingers caressing her bare skin.

"Exactly like that," Quinn murmured against her ear.

Celeste turned her head to look up into Quinn's deep blue eyes. "Then what?"

Quinn looked down into the ocean of blue and realized she was not breathing. She took a gulp of air and moved away, taking the delicate instrument with her.

"Then we use the chronometer and measure the time. That coupled with the sextant's measurements of the angles, we have our course and—" She stopped and had no idea what to say next.

"Why do they call it a *sex*tant?" Celeste hid her grin as Quinn stammered.

Quinn gave her an incredulous look. "I-I don't know. I believe it has to do with the degrees of the scale." She showed Celeste the arched scale. "It's one-sixteenth of a full circle that's sixty degrees h-hence the name," she said, trying to regain her calm. She looked to see Celeste sporting an innocent gaze. "I believe it's Latin for—bloody hell, I don't know," she finished with an irritated wave of her hand.

"Capt'n?" Thomas's voice called.

Quinn whirled around. "What!" she said angrily.

Thomas took a protective step back.

Celeste bit her lip, trying not to laugh openly. "*Excusez-moi*," she mumbled and skirted away.

That night as they ate dinner, Celeste stole a glance every now and then at Quinn, who was quiet and picking at her food. "Thank you for showing me the sex today."

Quinn's head shot up and gave her an incredulous look. The next moment, she laughed openly.

Celeste glared at her and threw down her napkin. "Why must you always laugh at me?" she said angrily. She stood, walked over to the portal, and opened it.

The salty sea air rushed in and Celeste closed her eyes. She felt Quinn standing behind her as she shivered uncontrollably.

"I was not laughing at you, ma'amselle. I would never laugh at you."

Celeste took a deep breath, and as she turned, the door closed and she was alone. She turned back and looked out the portal, remembering how close Quinn was to her that morning. She laughed as she recalled Quinn's frustration. She secretly wanted

Quinn to take her into her arms. She wondered if Quinn felt the same.

Quinn walked to the bow of the sleek schooner and closed her eyes against the warm Caribbean breeze. She desperately wanted to take Celeste into her arms. The need for Celeste was overpowering. She fought the urge, which was something Quinn rarely did. She was getting twitchy…

She returned to her quarters to find Celeste asleep in the bunk. Smiling slightly, she slipped out of her clothes and jumped into her hammock. Groaning, she settled herself, perched in her swaying bed.

"Good night, Quinn," Celeste whispered into the darkness.

Quinn looked down and smiled slightly. "Good night."

In the days to follow, Quinn truly came to like Celeste. She was feisty and incredibly independent, while at the same time almost childlike in her innocence. Quinn had no idea how truly in love she was becoming with Celeste.

Celeste became more and more attracted to the confident arrogance of the captain. That confused her completely. The feelings she felt for her tutor in Paris were passed off as a childish infatuation. However, she was having the same feeling for Quinn, who boldly lived in a man's world. Quinlan Stoddard was as kind as she was arrogant, as gentle as she was crude.

The combinations enticed Celeste. The ache for her homeland dissipated as the Jamaica winds took her deeper into Quinn's heart.

Chapter 19

"We should be sailing into Kingston harbor in a few days time," Quinn said as they ate dinner. She glanced at her lovely companion, who frowned. "I know many people in Kingston. I should be able to find you safe passage back to France. I know it's been a disheartening experience. I only hope it has not been too distressful."

For some reason, Celeste felt tears welling in her blue eyes. She looked down at her food. "It has not been distressing at all," she said in a trembling voice. "I-I have enjoyed my time with you."

Quinn took a healthy drink of wine and calmed her racing heart. She was astonished to see tears and Celeste's bottom lip quiver. "As have I, Ma'amselle Marchand."

For a long moment, neither spoke as they looked into each other's eyes. Then, as if drawn like moths to a flame, they were in each other's arms.

Quinn kissed her deeply. Celeste clung to her, her head spinning as her heart raced.

"Celeste," Quinn whispered against her lips.

"Oui, Quinn." Celeste whimpered and raked her fingers through the rich brown waves.

Just then, they felt the ship roll. Celeste let out a cry as Quinn steadied and looked out the portal. "Jamaica winds," she muttered.

Celeste looked frantically at Quinn.

"Stay below," she ordered and ran out the door, bounding up to the deck.

The weather turned quickly as the wind changed. Gusting across the bow, the ship listed as Quinn ran to the helm.

"Clew up that mainsail and trim the topsail on the mizzen!"

Suddenly, men were everywhere, scurrying as Jack and Quinn barked their orders. The clouds moved in quickly, the lightning started when the thunder rolled. The winds angrily blew the schooner toward the Caribbean and the West Indies.

The rain came in torrents. Quinn wiped the pelting rain from her face as she took the helm. Studying the wind and the sails, she guided the sleek schooner as best she could through the darkness. The wheel slipped from her hands, and she and Jack struggled to keep the schooner on an even keel.

"We'll ride it out, Jack!" she called in his ear.

"Aye, Quinn!" he shouted.

As the storm raged, Celeste sat huddled in the bunk. Henry came in, soaked with rain. "Quinn sent me, miss, to see how you are faring," he said kindly.

The ship rocked precariously as she stood. "*Je suis très …* petrified!"

Henry chuckled as he wiped his brow. "Well, so am I, but Capt'n Stoddard knows these waters and these winds better than any man. We'll weather this storm, don't you worry. Now you stay below. Don't worry, lass," he said and left.

Celeste sat back on the bunk, her heart pounding with each crack of thunder and flash of lightning.

Quinn shook the rain from her face as she struggled at the helm. Then a blinding flash of lightning streaked across the topsail of the mizzenmast. Every man ducked when he heard the horrendous crack as the mast split at the top. The topsail gave way as it came crashing down.

All hands scurried out of the way of the falling mast as Quinn barked her orders. She saw Thomas tangled in the rigging and looked up to see the shattered mizzenmast falling directly above him.

"Jack, take the helm!"

As Jack flew to the whirling wheel, Quinn dove for

Thomas, whisking him out of the way before the mast crashed to the quarterdeck. Both now tangled in the rigging, Quinn felt something pierce her side and she cried out. Thomas struggled with the heavy ropes as Quinn lay in a painful heap.

"Capt'n!" Thomas called to her.

Quinn moved, wincing as they untangled themselves.

Will and several men helped Quinn to her feet. Thomas pulled his hand away from Quinn's side; it was covered with blood. "Capt'n you're bleeding," he yelled.

Will helped him, as Quinn faltered. "Get back and trim those sails. Go on," Quinn ordered and pushed the men back to their duties. "Get that rigging over the side!" She stumbled to the helm where Jack still struggled with the heavy wheel.

"Are you all right?" he yelled in her ear.

She only nodded as both of them continued at the helm.

For the next hour, the storm raged until finally, it quieted. The winds continued, but the rain mercifully stopped.

Celeste heard another knock at the door, and this time, a young redhead poked his head in.

"Are you faring all right, miss?" he asked.

Celeste came to the door when she noticed the cut above his brow. "You are bleeding, monsieur."

Thomas put a hand to his forehead. "It's nothing, miss. You should see the capt'n."

Celeste's eyes widened. "She is hurt?"

"Yes, but she won't let up. We tried to get her to come below, but she nearly bit our heads off," Thomas said with admiration. In his young eyes, Quinn Stoddard was a goddess. "No one can make her—" He didn't get a chance to finish.

Celeste pushed him aside and stormed topside. She angrily looked around and found Quinn, soaked with rain, leaning against the wheel block, yelling orders. Even in the darkness, Celeste could see her blouse stained with blood.

All hands noticed Celeste as she marched up to their captain.

"Thomas, get that goddamned rigging off the quarterdeck and over the side. I cannot assess the damage to the deck with—" Quinn stopped when she saw Celeste. "What are you doing up here? Get below. This wind will carry you right over."

Celeste put her hand on her hips. "*Tu es malade, mon capitaine*," she said and started a tirade in her native tongue.

Quinn raised her eyebrows in surprise as she listened to the angry words. She had no clue what Celeste was saying, but any fool could hear the anger in her voice. She grinned slightly as she listened, amused by the sputtering and hand waving. She heard the men stifling their laughs as they continued with their duties.

"*Tu es malade à la tête!*" Celeste yelled as she touched her temple.

Quinn laughed openly. She looked around to see Will, who was also laughing. "Will? What the devil is she saying?" Quinn asked as she winced.

"She said you're a crazy and arrogant woman."

Quinn immediately stopped laughing, as did the interpreter, who suddenly found the quarterdeck fascinating. Quinn looked down at Celeste, who was breathing heavily.

"Go to your cabin," Celeste ordered.

Quinn gaped in astonishment. She avoided Jack, who was staring straight ahead, as he took the helm. The storm had calmed, but not in Celeste's crystal blue eyes. She stood defiantly and waited.

"Ma'amselle Marchand, I have work to do—"

"You are bleeding," Celeste said angrily. "Will!" she called out, and the old sailor scurried over to her.

Quinn's eyes flew open. Will Drury had never moved that fast for her.

Celeste spoke in French, and Will listened and glanced at his captain every so often. When she finished, she pushed him. "*Vit! Vit!*" she exclaimed as he shooed him away.

Quinn stood there, leaning against the side, staring in amazement.

Celeste stood in front of the dumbfounded captain. "Quinn, *s'il vous plaît*...Please go below and let Henri look at you," she said in a soft voice that made Quinn weak in the knees. She put a gentle hand on her forearm. "*Pour moi*," she said. "For me."

Quinn frowned and looked around. All hands were busy with

their work and seemingly not paying attention.

"I'll go to keep you quiet, ma'amselle," she grumbled as she painfully stood. "But as soon as Henry takes a look, I'm coming back on deck," she finished loudly, so every man could hear her. Celeste nodded. *"Oui, merci beaucoup,"* Celeste said, knowing now how to handle this woman.

As Quinn started below, she suddenly felt light-headed. The pain ripped through her side as she stumbled. Celeste put an arm around her waist, but Quinn stood tall and pulled away. "Don't coddle me, woman," she grumbled childishly.

Celeste raised an eyebrow as she let go, allowing the stubborn woman to stagger to her cabin unassisted. Celeste followed, shaking her head. *"Malade à la tête."* She sighed.

"Sit down," Celeste ordered.

Henry poked his head into the cabin. Quinn's face was damp with perspiration as she sat at her desk.

Celeste turned to see Henry standing at the door with bag in hand. "Come in, Henri."

Henry knelt at Quinn's side to assess her injury. Quinn said nothing as he lifted the bloody shirt. "Hmm. Looks like you have part of the mizzenmast in your ribs, Quinn."

Quinn painfully let out a short laugh. "Well, get it out, Henri," Quinn said in a horrible French accent, which caused a scowl from Celeste and a laugh from Henry.

For the next twenty minutes, Henry worked his doctoring skills on a silent patient who winced and flinched only once. When he had the bandage applied to her side, he wrapped it once around her ribs to hold it in place. He sat back on his heels, admiring his work. "That should do it. It really isn't too bad, but you'd best get into bed and rest. Jack can handle things till morning."

There was a knock at the door and Jack walked in. "How are you, Quinn?"

Quinn nodded. "I'm fine. Did you get that rigging over the side? Was any of it salvageable?" Quinn asked as she stood, testing her mobility.

Celeste made a move toward her and Quinn put her hand up. "Ma'amselle Marchand, I have a ship to run," she said in a curt, dismissive tone.

Celeste stood tall and Quinn swallowed when she saw the tears in the blue eyes.

Henry gave his captain a scathing look as he cleaned up. Celeste ran past Jack and out of the cabin.

"Damn it," Quinn said and took a deep painful breath.

"She was worried about you, Quinlan," Henry scolded. "Came up on deck in a storm, could've been easily washed overboard, just to help you." He picked up his bag. "Well, I've got a few men to see to. You do as you like."

Jack watched his friend and captain as she struggled with her emotions. He'd known Quinn for eight years. His father was in the Navy with Robert Stoddard, where they served side by side during the war with the English in 1812. In all the time he'd known Quinlan Stoddard, he had never seen her back down from anything or anybody. He had known about her way for quite a while. The men respected Quinn because she was fair and determined—kind, but stern. They didn't look at her like a woman, probably because she didn't act like one.

Jack was not prepared to understand Quinlan Stoddard. He only knew that when every other ship refused him, Quinn did not. Without question, she took him on as her first mate. He would never forget her faith in him, and he would never betray her.

Over the years, they shared their secrets and their shortcomings. When Jack had the nerve, after a few tankards of rum, to tell Quinn why no other ship wanted him, he knew he was taking a chance. He remembered the conversation clearly.

Quinn watched her friend as he struggled with his past. He gulped the rum from the pewter tankard and wiped his hand across his mouth. "You can tell me, Jack."

He nodded and avoided her eyes. He liked Quinn and didn't want her to think badly of him, but she had taken such a chance with him when she hired him as first mate on the Pride of Charleston. *He owed her this.*

"When I was younger, I sailed with a clipper up the coast in Boston. There was a storm and I was young. I was aloft on the mainmast, the rigging was all tangled, and I and another mate

were trying to get it free when he slipped. He held on and cried out for me to help him. I-I froze. I didn't help him. I was too scared I'd fall with him. He slipped farther, and I just held on. When I realized what I was doing, I reached for him too late. Just before he fell, he gave me such an odd look," he said in a quiet voice, then buried his face in his hands. "I let that man die. He had a wife and children."

Quinn watched her friend as he tried desperately not to break down. She said nothing for a moment or two.

"The whole ship saw what happened. They put me ashore when the ship docked back in Boston. You know the life. It followed me here and..."

Quinn hailed the barmaid for another round. She reached over and put her warm hand on Jack's arm. He looked up with sad, shameful eyes.

"We all have things in our lives that others will never understand. Look at me. I live in a man's world doing a man's job. How many people do you think understand that or accept it? Not many, I'm thinking. You're an honest, good man who made a mistake. There's no shame in being scared. I won't judge you. That's not my place, but if you think by your admission that it changes anything, you're wrong. You're my first mate because you're a good sailor and I trust you," Quinn said firmly and smiled. "I too know what it's like to be an outcast."

Jack knew to what she was referring. She avoided his eyes. He smiled and reached over and put his strong hand on her arm. "I won't judge you. That's not my place, and if you think by your admission, it changes anything, you're wrong. I'm your first mate and I am loyal to you, your father, and the Pride of Charleston, *Captain Quinlan Stoddard."*

Tears leapt to Quinn's eyes as she swallowed and raised her tankard. Jack followed suit. "Seems we have something in common other than the love of the sea... Capt'n," he said as he raised his tankard to his lips. Quinn laughed heartily and agreed.

Jack watched his friend now, as she struggled. This was foreign territory for Quinn. Her usual liaisons were fleeting and raucous. Quinn was very much like a man in that regard. Jack smiled inwardly as he thought of how the feisty Frenchwoman stormed up to Quinn, demanding she get below. When Quinn obeyed, all hands were shocked.

"Quinn, the rigging is off the quarterdeck. I don't think there's too much damage. We can get the mizzen repaired in Kingston," he said.

Quinn nodded and took a deep breath. "The men?"

"Thomas has a bump on the head. It'll probably do him good," he said, and both laughed. "Minor injuries. The men did well."

"They always do. We'll be in Jamaica in two days, and we'll be stuck there for a time while the ship is repaired. That will give them time to relax for a few more days. They've earned it. Break out the rum, but not too much," she said with a grin. "Watch Will, for heaven's sake."

Jack laughed heartily and agreed. As he opened the door, he looked back at his captain. "And… Ma'amselle Marchand?"

Quinn's head shot up, and she knew she was blushing horribly. "Get back to work," she said in a gruff voice.

"Aye, Capt'n," he said and closed the door.

Quinn stood for a moment in confusion. She knew she was wrong to snap at Celeste like that. Henry was right, she was only trying to help and she could have been swept overboard with little trouble. The idea pulled at Quinn's heart as she tried to erase that image of Celeste. These feelings were so foreign to her. There was never love, never intimacy. How could any woman want that with her? She had always felt alone in that regard.

Now Celeste stumbled into her life and Quinn had no idea what to do. She took a deep breath and walked to her fate.

Chapter 20

Quinn found Celeste leaning against the wheel box. Behind her, Thomas was at the helm. The night had calmed considerably as the men tended to the task of cleaning debris off the deck.

Quinn nodded and thanked each man as she passed by him. Each man offered his hand. Thomas walked up to her and stuck out his hand. With his red hair tousled from the wind, it struck Quinn how young he was. No more than Celeste, she was sure. She took the offered hand.

"Thank you, Capt'n Stoddard. That mast would've surely—"

Quinn put a strong hand on his shoulder. "You did a good job tonight, Thomas. It is I who thanks you," she said and released his hand.

Celeste heard the conversation and her heart swelled with pride and admiration for Quinn. She did not acknowledge Quinn's presence, however, as she walked away from the helm and leaned against the side of the ship. She stared straight ahead into the warm Caribbean night.

Jack came up, followed by Henry, who carried the wooden barrel. Jack had several tankards. "All right, men," he said, and all hands cheered as Henry doled out their reward.

Quinn nodded her thanks and stole a glance at Celeste. Jack handed her two tankards with a wink. She cautiously walked up behind Celeste and cleared her throat. Celeste did not move. Quinn winced and leaned against the side, as well.

"The weather certainly turned quickly," Quinn said and offered a glance.

"Oui, it would appear so," she replied coolly.

Quinn held the tankard in front of her. "This might warm you. It's a bit chilly," she said awkwardly and rolled her eyes. The night was balmy and warm.

Celeste took the offering and sipped the rum. "*Merci.*"

Agonizing seconds dragged on as Quinn glanced at Samuel, who was neatly twining a heavy rope back into place. Quinn glanced at Celeste and cleared her throat. "Samuel, why don't we see how fast the ship is sailing, aye?" she said in a commanding voice.

He gave her a wary look but nodded. "Aye, capt'n." He readied the rope.

Quinn stood with her hands behind her back and rocked back and forth, stealing a glance at Celeste, who hid her grin in the tankard of rum.

"Thomas, get the sandglass," Quinn ordered as he reached for the timing piece.

Quinn glanced at Celeste, who now watched. "Um, would you like to know what we're doing? I-I could explain it to you," she offered in a firm but hopeful voice.

"Oui, it seems interesting."

Quinn grinned, let out a sigh of relief, and nodded. "Well, then," she started. "The chip log is a float attached to the end of the rope, which Samuel will throw in the water. The knots in the rope are at approximately forty-seven-foot intervals. Thomas watches the sandglass that contains twenty-eight seconds of sand," Quinn explained and nodded to Samuel, who threw the float attached to the rope into the water and counted the knots as they whipped through his hands.

Celeste watched with fascination.

"Time," Thomas called out after the sand sifted through the glass. "Fifteen knots, capt'n."

Quinn nodded and Celeste smiled inwardly at the commanding pose. "You see, we're going fifteen nautical miles in one hour. Now—" As she started explain, Thomas interrupted again.

"What was the need to do this again so soon, capt'n?" he asked, scratching his head. Samuel rolled his eyes.

Quinn cringed and glared at Thomas, then offered a weak smile.

"That was very interesting," Celeste said. "*Merci.*"

Quinn was discouraged and didn't know what to say now. She wanted to take Celeste in her arms and tell her she was sorry for the words that wounded her. She said the only thing that came to mind. "I think I may still be bleeding." She winced at her stupidity and childishness. Her O'Malley ancestors must be rolling in their graves, she thought sourly.

Celeste turned to her. "Then what are you doing on deck? Why are you not in your cabin? What is the matter with you?" she said, and again, the tirade in her native tongue started.

Quinn backed up and swallowed hard as Celeste continued. Quinn glanced at Will, who silently offered his interpretation once again; Quinn gave him a threatening glare. She looked back at Celeste, who was still ranting.

Finishing her rum, she took the tankard out of Celeste's hand and promptly drank that, as well. Quinn took her by the hand and started below.

She looked at Will and nodded. "I get the general idea, Will," she said as she dragged the stunned woman off the deck.

Celeste knelt in front of her and lifted the soggy boot. Struggling, she finally got both heavy boots off the captain. "Your breeches now," Celeste said as she stood.

Quinn stood, as well, and brushed the hands away as they reached for the buttons. "I can undress myself," she grumbled as she unbuttoned the breeches and tried to peel the tight wet material down her legs.

Celeste waited patiently for as long as she could and rolled her eyes. "Mon Dieu, you are stubborn." She reached over and yanked the soaked material down the long legs.

Quinn stood there with her breeches down around her ankles. "Now what, ma'amselle?" she asked with a low chuckle.

Celeste stared at the long muscular, yet feminine legs. Gazing closer, she realized that Quinn wore nothing under the sodden breeches. She averted her eyes and looked at Quinn. "The shirt is next," she ordered as her voice trembled.

Quinn grinned as she unbuttoned the damp shirt. She winced slightly and Celeste reached behind her and eased the shirt off her shoulders. Quinn, now completely naked with her back to Celeste, stretched from side to side and grunted painfully.

Celeste watched her back muscles ripple and the firm muscles in her buttocks tense. Quinn quickly opened the drawer and pulled out a clean chemise and slipped it over her head. She turned to Celeste then and tied the top.

"I don't usually wear this to bed," she muttered with a chuckle.

"What do you usually wear?" Celeste asked innocently as she rummaged through the drawer.

Quinn raised a roguish eyebrow.

Celeste felt the color rise to her face. "P-please get into bed, Quinn." She pulled back the blanket.

Quinn eased into the bunk and Celeste covered her. "Join me," Quinn said in a low voice.

"I-I can sleep in the hammock."

"No, you will not sleep in a hammock. Sleep with me," Quinn said in a soft but firm voice. She saw so many emotions flash across the Celeste's face.

Celeste shyly turned from her and slipped out of her dress and corset. Quinn watched, her heartbeat quickening. Celeste was completely naked as she reached for the nightgown.

"Wait a moment, please," Quinn whispered, and Celeste stopped. Quinn gazed at the flawless body before her. Her milky white soft skin, the outline of her large breasts, and the lovely full curve of her hips all made Quinn's mouth water. She gazed further at the soft round buttocks and shapely thighs.

Celeste's body began to tremble uncontrollably under Quinn's intense gaze. She was thrilled and frightened at the same time. She slipped the silky material over her head and turned back to the bed. The look of wanton desire on Quinn's face made Celeste weak in the knees. She was not at all sure she could walk to the bunk.

Quinn pulled the blanket back, and Celeste put a hand to her blond hair. "May I sleep on the inside?"

Quinn nodded and Celeste scooted over her and under the covers so quickly that Quinn nearly laughed out loud. Celeste pulled the blanket up to her neck tightly.

Quinn's heart ached at the seemingly terrified pose. "Celeste," she said, and painfully lay on her side to face her. "Please, don't be afraid. Nothing will happen that you do not want to happen. Do you understand?"

Celeste held her breath and nodded. "I do not know what I want to happen."

Quinn reached over and brushed the golden locks off her forehead. She traced her fingertips along her cheek, down to her jaw, and back up again.

Celeste let out an involuntary moan as she closed her eyes and reveled in the soft touch. She felt the strong fingers against her chin as she turned her face and opened her eyes.

Quinn smiled as she searched Celeste's lovely face. "So beautiful," she whispered. She lightly brushed against trembling lips for a soft, featherlike kiss. When Celeste sighed deep in her throat, Quinn deepened the kiss, her hand cupping the soft cheek, her fingers lightly brushing her blond hair. She moved her lips slowly, reveling in the sweet, innocent taste. Quinn could not stop the deep guttural moan that escaped her as she moved closer, pulling Celeste into a strong embrace.

Celeste quivered as she felt their bodies touch. She felt the scorching kiss heat her entire being, crying out as Quinn's tongue flicked around her lips and slipped into her mouth.

Quinn rolled her onto her back, kissing Celeste passionately. She pulled back and kissed her cheek, then her tender earlobe.

"Celeste, Celeste," she whispered and felt Celeste once again tremble uncontrollably. Her hand wandered down the soft neck and caressed her shoulder through the silky material of the nightgown.

Celeste gasped as she felt the warm hand teasing her skin, fluttering back and forth across her shoulder to her neck and back again. Her body was on fire with every caress.

"Quinn, *qu'est-ce qui se passe?*" She asked in a wondrous

voice. She opened her eyes and reached up to caress the weathered cheek. "What is happening?" she asked breathlessly.

Quinn smiled down into the crystal orbs, seeing the confusion and desire in the innocent eyes.

Quinn wanted her badly. Her body ached in a way it had never before for any other. However, she saw Celeste's innocence and once again, she pulled away.

"Celeste. You are a virgin, are you not?"

Celeste, breathing deeply, nodded.

Quinn kissed her tenderly, fighting the urge to possess her.

Celeste saw the hesitant look in the dark blue eyes. "I have been with no man—or woman." She saw the sad look in Quinn's eyes. "This bothers you, *non?*"

"Someday, you will meet the man you want to marry. He will expect you to be, well, untouched. I cannot do this to you." She tried to pull back.

Celeste slipped her hand behind the strong neck and pulled her back. "You do not want me?"

"God, no. I mean yes, I want you. I don't think I've ever wanted something so much in my life. You are so young and innocent. You don't want this—"

Celeste frowned as she pushed Quinn away. "How dare you," she said angrily. "I may be young and I may be innocent, but do you think so little of me as to believe I would lie in bed with you and kiss you like some, some...whore?"

Quinn's mouth dropped as she looked down into the fiery blue eyes. "No! I don't think of you that way. My God—"

"Then how can you tell me I do not want this? If I did not, I would certainly not be in your bed right now. Oh, you are so arrogant!" She tried to pull away.

Quinn held onto her and smiled. "I meant no disrespect. I'm only thinking of your future. You know what I'm talking about."

"*Oui, je comprend, mon capitaine,*" she said with a grin.

Quinn narrowed her eyes and gave Celeste a suspicious look.

"I am young, *oui*, but I understand the way a man thinks. I know what is expected of me. I do not want to be married to—"

179

"But you're only twenty-one. You do not want a family, a husband, and home?"

Celeste reached up once again and touched her tanned face. "I want to fall in love. *L'amour.*" She pulled Quinn back down for a searing kiss.

"But…" Quinn mumbled helplessly against the warm sweet lips. She sighed heavily as she laid her body over Celeste. She pulled back breathlessly. "Your family—" she gasped as Celeste nibbled at her chin, "your life," she groaned as she felt innocent fingers touching the back of her neck. Soon, all resolve would fade away for Quinn.

"*Oui*, Quinn. Ma vie, my life. This is what I want, *votre amour.* Your love."

Quinn looked down at emotion-filled blue eyes. "God help me, I want your love, as well."

Her low voice thrilled Celeste to her very soul. "Then take it."

Quinn moved over Celeste, who was lying precariously on the brink of womanhood. Quinn kissed her deeply, her tongue slipping past her lips and into her mouth.

Celeste let out a low moan as she felt a warm hand caressing her full breast. She arched into the touch and quivered uncontrollably.

Quinn's fingers danced across the silky fabric of her nightgown. She reached up and pulled the satin ties. Slipping her hand in, both women gasped at the feeling.

"Celeste," Quinn said against her lips as her fingers worked over the hardened nipple. Celeste stretched her arm over her head, offering herself. Quinn cupped a large breast in her hand, sensually running her thumb across her hardened nipple. Her hand wandered down the soft curve of her side to her hip. She leaned in and kissed her once again as her fingers pulled up on the silky material. She gathered the hem and reached down to caress the smooth thigh.

"Oh." Celeste sighed. Her body was on fire from the searing caress.

"Easy now, love," Quinn cooed as her fingers slipped over

the top of her thighs. She parted Celeste's legs, causing Celeste to whimper once again.

So many sensations bombarded Celeste as she felt warm hands caress her—the incessant throbbing between her legs, her racing heart. It was almost too much as her heart pounded in her chest.

Quinn groaned, trying to control her urge to take Celeste as her fingers danced in the soft curls.

"Please," Celeste sighed as her legs parted farther. Her body was acting of its own desire. She didn't know what was happening. She only knew that she wanted Quinn to possess her, to take her to a place she'd never been.

"Soon," Quinn promised as she kissed her lips again.

Celeste would not, could not wait as she lifted her hips to remove her nightgown.

Quinn let out a guttural helpless groan. In one movement, she aided the frantic woman and whisked the silky material from the trembling body.

Celeste cried out as she felt warm hands on her breasts and felt a cool wet tongue flicking back and forth over her burning skin. She was naked and her body was on fire. Lying underneath another woman, who was doing things to her body that Celeste had never dreamed of, she was beyond speech—beyond reason. She allowed her body to speak for her. She let Quinn lead her wherever she wanted.

Quinn's fingers pushed back the defensive folds. She smiled at the copious moisture that greeted her loving fingers. She felt Celeste tense, her breathing stopped as Quinn slid her finger along the swollen bundle of nerves. Both women were breathing heavily as she lightly flicked her fingers over the throbbing center. Once again, she slipped her tongue into the eager mouth, flicking lightly, mirroring the action of her fingers.

Celeste was nearly faint as she arched into the touch. She jumped as she felt the fingers move farther down and instinctively tightened her inner muscles. She always wondered what it would feel like to be touched this way. Now she knew. It was heaven. She raised her hips involuntarily as Quinn pulled back slightly.

She watched Celeste as she placed her finger at the tight opening. "Celeste, look at me," she whispered and swallowed with difficulty.

Sparkling blue eyes flew open at the request and met the blue depths. "This will hurt only once, love, then I promise you it will never hurt again," she said in a soft confident voice as she pushed her finger in slowly, waiting until Celeste's inner walls accommodated the virginal intrusion.

"Please, I do not care. I want to feel you inside of me," she pleaded as she looked deep into her eyes.

Quinn smiled slightly, blinking back her tears and never losing eye contact, she leaned farther. "I'm sorry," she said sincerely and plunged her finger deep within her.

The initial pain rushed through Celeste, who cried out and arched her back. Quinn held her in a strong embrace.

Suddenly, a pleasurable feeling replaced the stabbing pain and Celeste cried out again. Quinn slowly worked another finger within and moved in long deep strokes.

"My God, Quinn. This is…" Celeste tried to talk but couldn't; her body began to perspire. She moved her hips in time with Quinn's thrusts.

"Yes, Celeste," Quinn murmured against her neck. She moved quicker, faster, and deeper.

"Oh…oh…" Celeste moaned deeply. Her body quivered, trembled, bucked, and writhed with every strong sensual stroke. She felt her body tense, felt her muscles clamp down around the intruding fingers. She couldn't breathe. Her eyes fluttered and her heart raced. "Quinn! Quinn!" she cried out helplessly, not knowing what was happening, but never wanting it to end.

"So beautiful," Quinn said as she furiously thrust now.

Celeste was clawing at her back, ripping her chemise. Quinn slipped her thumb against the swollen center and rubbed once, twice, and Celeste's body erupted into a violent orgasm.

"Quinn!" she cried out as her body twitched and bucked.

Quinn covered her mouth with her own, swallowing her cries of ecstasy. She held onto the quivering woman tightly, as she slowed. Suddenly, Celeste's body went limp as her hands loosened their hold on Quinn's ripped chemise.

Quinn, breathless and gasping, slowly pulled back. She watched the still figure and lightly kissed her dry lips.

Celeste's eyes fluttered open and tried to focus. A smiling face greeted her as she took a deep trembling breath. "*Mon Dieu.*"

She mumbled a litany of French, which Quinn was unable to understand. She heard the words, *amour* and *magnifique*, which was all she needed to hear. She kissed the warm dry lips.

Celeste moaned into the kiss, her hand caressing the strong shoulder. She felt the ripped material.

"That's why I don't wear anything to bed," Quinn said with a grin.

Celeste hid her embarrassment in Quinn's embrace. She looked up and touched the tanned cheek. "I-I want to see you, as well."

Quinn swallowed, and with the help of innocent trembling hands, she struggled out of her tattered chemise. She quickly pulled Celeste into a tender embrace after watching Celeste stare at her nakedness with petrified eyes.

"I think this is enough for now. Sleep. I think you've earned it, love," Quinn cooed.

Celeste felt Quinn's warm soft body next to her and cuddled close. As Quinn stroked her hair, Celeste reached up and cupped her face, not wanting to lose contact.

"Merci, Quinn," she said with emotion.

Quinn tightened her embrace and kissed her head. She looked down into sleepy blue eyes. "I thank you, Celeste," Quinn said as her voice caught in her throat. "Thank you."

Celeste smiled and nuzzled into her soft shoulder. "*Jamais.*" She sighed, taking a peaceful breath. "Never," she said. "Never will I forget how you love me, ma chérie," she said earnestly and finally gave herself up as the ship rocked to her sleep.

She woke slowly, her eyes adjusting to the darkness. The gentle rolling of the ship gave Celeste a sense of peace. Lying on her back, she looked over at Quinn.

Quinn was on her side, her arm protectively flung across

Celeste's waist, holding her in a strong embrace. Celeste grinned as she remembered the night. Quinn was gentle and at the same time, strong, loving her tenderly, possessing her completely. She reached up and smoothed the brown wave off her forehead, her fingers lightly tracing her jaw down her muscled neck. She grew flushed as her body once again craved this woman's touch.

Quinn let out a snort and rolled on her back. Celeste now had a full view of Quinn's body. Gently, she pulled the blanket down and took a deep trembling breath.

Quinn was a fit-looking woman. In France, all women were plump and soft, their skin milky white. Here in America, it was different. Perhaps because everyone, man and woman, had to struggle and fight. There was an air of openness, Celeste thought.

Celeste gazed at the trim figure stretched out before her. Her shoulders were broad, her waist and hips narrow, her breasts small but firm. She looked further and her breath caught in her throat as she gazed at the dark curls between the muscular thighs. She shook her head as her heartbeat quickened.

Tentatively, she reached out, but pulled her fingers back, not knowing how to touch or please Quinn. She knew she could never please Quinn as she had pleased her the night before. Oh, but she wanted to try. Her mouth watered at the sound of Quinn crying out her name.

Smiling, she touched the soft, firm belly and traced her fingers around her navel, all the while her eyes never leaving the dark triangle that beckoned her.

"Find something to your liking, *ma'amselle?*" the deep sleepy voice rumbled.

Celeste jumped slightly and pulled her hand back. She looked up into sleepy deep blue eyes and blushed. Quinn rolled Celeste onto her back; she loomed over her and kissed her. "Don't be afraid to touch me. This is new to you."

"I-I want to please you. I do not know how."

Quinn smiled and took her hand, placing it on her breast. "This is a good beginning, love."

As Celeste's fingers caressed her soft breast, sliding over the hardened nipple, Quinn closed her eyes and groaned, trying to remain calm. When Celeste brought her other hand up and cupped her other breast, Quinn moaned heavily, her outstretched arms holding her up.

Celeste looked up as the muscles in Quinn's arms tensed and quivered. She smiled as her hands kneaded the soft flesh, her nails scraping across the hard points.

Quinn groaned and lowered her head, kissing Celeste.

Celeste possessed a newfound boldness, feeling a surge of confidence trembling over her. With one hand still caressing Quinn's breast, she lowered the other down the quivering abdomen, lightly touching the moist curls. She smiled again as she slipped her fingers farther, eliciting a strangled groan from Quinn.

"God, woman." Quinn sighed as she parted her legs, getting to her knees to give Celeste the freedom to explore.

Celeste caught her breath as the wetness saturated her fingers. "Is this what you like?"

Quinn moaned and only nodded her assent as her body shivered, feeling Celeste's fingers slipping through her.

Celeste was unsure how to continue, but when her fingers slipped across the swollen center, Quinn threw her head back and cried out. Celeste watched Quinn as her fingers delved farther, sliding up and down. Soon Quinn was moving her hips in rhythm with the gentle strokes.

"Yes..." Quinn begged as she moved her hips around Celeste's fingers. She moved her hips up as she pulled Celeste's fingers into her warm depths. "God, yes!" Quinn groaned and moved her hips down around the intruding fingers.

Celeste felt her own arousal starting again as she remembered how Quinn made her feel. To be inside felt warm and soft, and she never wanted to leave. She desperately wanted to please Quinn.

Quinn arched her back and bore her hips down. Both women moaned and panted as Quinn's body broke out in a cold sweat.

Celeste looked up at Quinn's breasts swaying as she rocked back and forth. She raised her head and took Quinn's breast into her mouth.

That was all Quinn needed as she felt her orgasm tear through her body.

Celeste groaned deeply as she suckled Quinn's breast roughly. She felt Quinn's inner walls clamp around her fingers and suddenly Quinn grew still.

Quinn's body tensed and Celeste knew she was near. She remembered what Quinn did for her, so she snaked her thumb across the bundle of nerves as she continued to thrust.

"Celeste!" Quinn cried out as she shook violently. Wave after wave consumed her.

Celeste released the hold on her breast and watched Quinn succumb to her.

With a whimper, Quinn collapsed onto Celeste as her arms shook with fatigue. Celeste removed her fingers and wrapped Quinn's quivering body in a tender embrace. Murmuring words of love in her native tongue, Celeste heard the whimper and felt Quinn's body quiver through the aftershock. Celeste stroked her damp dark hair and kissed her forehead.

Quinn sighed and raised her head. "My God, Celeste, that was amazing," she said, and kissed her shoulder.

Celeste sported a happy grin and ran her fingers up and down Quinn's damp back. She pulled the blanket over them. "It is your turn to sleep now, *mon capitaine*."

Quinn mumbled something, nuzzled into a full plump breast, and fell heavenly asleep.

Chapter 21

A knocking at her door roused Quinn and she sat up. "What is it?"

"We're coming up on Jamaica, Quinn," Jack's voice called. "We have two hours, or so."

"Fine, Jack. I'll be right there," she called back. She looked over to see Celeste lying on her back, smiling happily. Her arms flung over her head, her firm full breasts partially hidden by the sheet.

Quinn returned her smile and leaned over, kissing her deeply. "Good morning, love," she murmured against her lips. "How do you feel?"

"Bonjour, Quinn. *Je suis très magnifique*," she said lazily as she stretched. She saw the uncertain look on Quinn. She smiled and took Quinn's hand, placing it on her heart. "Here, Quinn. In this place," she held her hand tight, "*Je suis très bon*. I am very, very good."

Quinn smiled, kissed her, and slipped out of the bunk.

Celeste whimpered in protest. "What are you doing?"

Quinn laughed and walked over to the basin. "I have a ship to run, my love. We're nearly to Jamaica," she said over her shoulder as she washed and dressed.

Celeste lay there, gazing at the beautiful body before her. "You are beautiful." She sighed and pulled the sheet over her.

Quinn leaned over and whisked the sheet away, causing Celeste to gasp. "You're the beautiful one, love. I have never seen such a perfect sight in all my days."

Celeste trembled, slightly embarrassed by the intense gaze.

She relaxed and stretched out seductively.

Quinn raised a challenging eyebrow. *"Ma'amselle,* do not tempt me," she warned as she knelt on the edge of the bunk.

Celeste grabbed Quinn by the shirt, pulling her on top of her. *"Ma'amselle…"* Quinn shivered as the scent of this woman wafted up to her nostrils. "I must go topside. Sleep. I'll have Henry bring us breakfast in an hour." She kissed her and scooted out of her grasp.

"Good morning, Quinn," Jack said with a grin.

It was a beautiful morning. The winds blew steadily, and the injured schooner sailed along the calm waters as quickly as it could.

"Good morning, Jack," Quinn responded heartily and took a deep breath of sea air. "It is a beautiful morning."

"Aye. It is. How are you feeling?"

Quinn glanced at him and cleared her throat. "I'm fine. Thank you. It was quite a storm," she said with her hands behind her back, rocking back and forth.

Jack nodded, doing the same. "In more ways than one," he added and scooted out of her way.

Quinn laughed as she walked the deck. Leaning on the gunwale, she closed her eyes to the morning sun and salty sea breeze. Smiling, she remembered every minute of the previous night. Quinn had been with quite a few women. However, that was physical pleasure. The night before was something different all together. Her heart was involved now.

She opened her eyes and gazed at the open expanse of water. A pang of guilt overcame her. Celeste Marchand was a young woman, perhaps too young. She knew nothing of the pleasures of a man, much less another woman.

Angry with herself, she buried her face in her hands. *What was I thinking? Celeste was innocent. Now what will happen to her?* She took her virginity. No, Quinn thought. Celeste gave it to her willingly. Though she was young, Celeste knew what she wanted.

How could she know? Quinn argued with herself. How could

anyone so young know? However, at the same age, even younger perhaps, Quinn knew. She knew she was not like other women in many ways. However, what of Celeste? Surely, she felt the same pull as Quinn. Her heart ached with the possibility of Celeste feeling the same.

"Quinn?" Henry's voice called out. "*Mademoiselle* Marchand is requesting your presence for breakfast. If you please," he said and bowed.

Quinn felt the color rush to her face; she cleared her throat and walked away. "Thank you, Henri."

As she reached for the door, she stopped and knocked.

"Come in." She heard Celeste's soft French voice and grinned widely.

Opening the door, she saw Celeste sitting at the little table, wearing a silky robe with her long blond hair pulled up and pinned.

Celeste saw Quinn and smiled. "*Bonjour.* All is well above the deck?"

Quinn let out a laugh as she bent down to kiss her, then sat down opposite her. "*Oui*, my love. All is well above *zee* deck."

"Henri is a good chef, but I must teach him how to make croissants," she said and sipped her coffee. She lathered thick bread with butter and jam.

"You can cook?" Quinn asked as she ate.

"*Oui.* I am a good cook. I had to learn at an early age."

Quinn noticed her thoughtful pose. "Why so young?"

Celeste looked up. "My mother died when I was a little girl. My father had no one. So I took care of him and our house."

Quinn reached across and held her hand. "I'm sorry. It must have been hard for you to grow up like that."

Celeste smiled and held onto Quinn's warm hand. "*Non*, I knew nothing else. When I was sixteen, Papa wanted me to marry a rich man. I-I did not want this," she said and avoided Quinn's gaze.

"Was he not handsome enough?"

"*Oui.* He was very handsome," Celeste said as she picked at her plate.

Quinn smiled. "Was he not rich enough?"

"He had considerable wealth."

"Then why didn't you marry him?"

Celeste looked up into the dark blue eyes and smiled. "I did not love him. I remember Mama telling me to wait for love, always love," she said in such a sweet soft voice Quinn forgot to breathe.

She gazed into the sparkling ocean of blue. "And have you?" Quinn asked in a hopeful voice.

Celeste's face was the picture of serenity. "*Oui*, I have found love. I find it every time I look into your beautiful eyes," she said as tears rolled down her pretty face.

The sight pulled at Quinn's heart. She walked around the table and knelt at Celeste's feet.

Celeste smiled as she searched Quinn's confused face. She reached down and laid her palm against Quinn's cheek.

Quinn leaned into the soft touch, closing her eyes.

"I know what you're thinking." Quinn opened her eyes, and Celeste was shocked to see a tear welling in the deep blue depths. "Quinn, I know I'm young, but do you not think I know my heart? *Mon père.*" She stopped, her brow furrowed in thought.

Quinn smiled at the innocent, childlike gesture.

"My papa tried to arrange several marriages for me."

Quinn sat back on her heels. "Several?" she repeated in amazement.

"*Oui*," Celeste replied in earnest. "Each one I—" She stopped and looked down at her hands.

Quinn raised an eyebrow. "What did you do?"

"I-I run away," Celeste said defiantly and looked up.

"Why?"

"I do not love those men. Papa only wanted the money he would obtain from my marriage to a wealthy man. I will not marry for money. I will not marry at all. I do not want a man." She continued, her French accent more pronounced with her rising anger, "I do not want a husband and children. I-I do not know why I feel this way, but I will not be told how to love. Not by my father or anyone."

"Not even by me?" Quinn asked in a low voice.

Celeste looked up and sported a very mature gaze. "Perhaps only by you."

"I worry that I've taken advantage of your innocence. Perhaps you should have experienced a man's love—"

Celeste rolled her eyes. "*Mon Dieu Tu es...*" She started her hand waving, rambling again.

Quinn winced, trying to comprehend the tirade. Still on her knees, Quinn looked up and reached for her flying hands.

Celeste cupped Quinn's face. "*Je t'aime,*" she insisted and smiled at the confused look on Quinn's face. Celeste thought she looked helpless; she liked the vulnerable look on the always-confident woman.

"*Je t'aime,*" she said again and pulled the befuddled face to her, kissing her on one cheek. "*Je t'aime maintenant.*" She kissed the other cheek. "*Je t'aime aujourd'hui.*" She pulled back and grinned at the stupefied woman. "*Je t'aime toujours,*" she said against the warm lips. "*Toujours.*" She kissed her, her tongue languidly gliding across the white teeth before slipping into Quinn's warm mouth. She pulled back and nearly laughed at the look on Quinn's face.

With her eyes closed, Quinn swayed back and forth as she knelt before the woman she knew she loved. She opened her eyes and gazed at Celeste. "W-what did you say?"

"Ask Will Drury," she said happily, and scooted out of her reach.

Later in the day, Celeste came topside and Quinn found her conversing with Thomas. He was expounding on his seamanship and Quinn frowned childishly as Celeste laughed with him.

"Hmm," she grunted.

Jack walked up with the map and spread it out by the helm. "Well, Quinn, the weather is with us once again. Now last year, we sailed into Kingston from the north. I think the winds are..." He stopped when he noticed Quinn was not listening.

She was trying not to watch Celeste with Thomas.

"Um, Quinn?" Jack asked.

Quinn's brow furrowed deeper when she saw Thomas lean in and say something, which Celeste thought amusing. Just then, two other men walked by, tipped their caps, and joined the conversation.

Will Drury came topside with a large wooden bucket and heaved the contents over the side. He glanced at Celeste surrounded by three laughing crewmen. Then he saw the frown on Quinn. He took a deep sad breath and started to prepare the quarterdeck for a thorough cleaning.

Quinn looked back to see Jack staring at her. "What?" she snapped.

"Nothing. I was asking about the way into Kingston this time around."

Quinn cringed at the peal of laughter coming from the stern. She was about to go aft when she saw Will Drury. She cleared her throat. "Will," she called out.

"Yes, Quinn?"

Both men glanced at each other but said nothing.

Quinn absently toyed with the map. "You, you understand French, don't you?"

He raised a curious eyebrow. "I do, yes."

"What does um, mentnah mean?"

Will scratched his head. He then nodded. "*Maintenant* means now."

She looked up. "And… ohzhoodwee?" she asked, knowing she sounded like an idiot.

"*Aujourd'hui* means today."

Jack looked back and forth, now he too scratched his head. "What about toojur?'

"*Toujours* means always or forever."

Quinn grinned slightly. "Now, today, and always," she repeated and took a deep breath and smiled. She realized both men were watching her. She quickly coughed and concentrated on the map. "Thank you, Will. That's all. Continue with—whatever you were doing."

"Yes, ma'am," he said with a slight grin.

"So… Kingston," Quinn said, shuffling the maps.

Chapter 22

When Quinn announced they were coming up to Jamaica, she could see Celeste was more than disappointed. She watched Celeste wither before her. "Celeste, you must understand."

Celeste looked up with sad blue eyes. "*Comment?*" She shook her head. "What must I understand?"

Quinn rubbed her forehead in a frustrated gesture. "Damn it, woman. You have to go back to France. Don't you want to?"

"*Non!* I want to stay with you." She ran up to Quinn, hugging her around the waist.

Quinn held on, wrapping her arms around her shoulders. "I'd like nothing more than to live the rest of my life with you." She was amazed at the declaration.

Celeste shot her head up and grinned. She tightened her hold on Quinn.

"I should have never allowed this to happen. It was selfish of me to make love to you."

Celeste pulled back and searched Quinn's sad blue eyes. "You do not love me?"

"Oh, God, Celeste. Love. What kind of life could you and I have together?" she asked angrily.

Celeste watched the woman she loved. "If we loved, we would find a way," she said in a sure voice.

Quinn took a deep breath. "I have a few things to do in Kingston. First, we'll get rooms for a few days. Then I must get the mizzenmast repaired. We'll talk of this later. We'll work something out."

Celeste flew to her and hugged her around the neck. "Merci," she said and kissed her. "Merci, Quinn." She kissed her again and again.

At the dock, Celeste eagerly looked around. Sailors were busy loading and unloading their cargo. She was amazed to see ships bigger than the *Pride of Charleston.* She looked over to see Quinn barking orders as the men unloaded their cargo down the gangplank. "Jack! Make sure there's a label on each and every carton, barrel, and crate. I don't want the disaster we had here last year."

Jack nodded and followed the men.

Quinn looked over to see enthusiasm on Celeste's face. She walked over to her. "You've never been to the West Indies, love?" she asked as she stood by her side.

"*Non,* I come only to America," she replied and looked up at Quinn. "I am glad I come."

Quinn raised a seductive eyebrow and was about to comment on her choice of words. However, she saw the innocent happy look and laughed. "I am, too. Now let's go. I'll get you settled into my rooms. I have to come back here, but don't worry. I'll dine with you tonight," she promised with a wink.

They took a carriage through Kingston. Celeste was amazed seeing so many dark-skinned people. She did not believe there were that many in all of France. Quinn sat next to her as the carriage rode down the street. She noticed Celeste's confounded gaze.

"This island was under Spanish rule for nearly one hundred fifty years. They wiped out a complete civilization, then brought slaves over to work the sugarcane plantations. Now England has it. Slavery…" she said with distain.

Celeste only nodded as she looked around. "It is so beautiful, though."

"Yes, it is. I must admit I love it here. The weather is warm all year-round. You'll find no snow in Jamaica," she said with a grin.

"Beautiful." She sighed as the carriage pulled up to a large white brick building.

Quinn hopped out and the driver assisted Celeste. Both women walked into a large foyer. Celeste dabbed her hanky to her forehead as Quinn walked up to the desk.

"Quinn Stoddard!" a woman's voice called out.

Celeste looked up to see a woman leaning against the doorway. Her skin was the color of caramel, and she dressed in the most vivid colors that Celeste had ever seen. Her dress was nearly to her ankles. She was tall and, Celeste thought, very exotic looking. Quinn grinned widely, and Celeste raised an eyebrow as Quinn rushed over to the woman.

"Miyah!" Quinn exclaimed, and the grinning woman opened her arms in welcome. Quinn wrapped her arms around her and lifted the woman, twirling her around.

"Set me down, woman," she said, laughing.

Celeste noticed an unknown accent as Quinn set her down with a painful grunt.

Miyah smiled and searched Quinn's face. "Ah, Quinlan, I have missed you," she said, and Celeste raised the other eyebrow.

"I've missed you, too. Come, I want you to meet someone," she said and took the woman by the hand. "Miyah, this is Celeste Marchand. Celeste, this is Miyah Kettering, a very old friend."

Celeste smiled and offered her hand. Miyah smiled in kind and took the offering. "It's nice to meet you, Celeste," Miyah said and eyed her expensive dress.

"*Enchantée*," Celeste said kindly.

Miyah raised an eyebrow and looked at Quinn, who cleared her throat. "She's French," she explained stupidly.

"So I gathered," Miyah said and winked at Celeste, who blushed furiously.

Miyah glanced back and forth between both blushing women and sighed. "Ah. Well, well. I will let you go. I have a customer in an hour. It was nice to meet you, Celeste," she said, and Celeste nodded. The woman turned to Quinn. "It is good to have you back, Quinn. How long will you be in Kingston?"

"Just enough to do some repairs. Your Jamaican winds split my mizzenmast in two. We're unloading the cargo now. We'll pick up supplies and whatever else is needed. We'll be here for a week at least."

"Dan Henley is back in Jamaica. You might want to do those repairs and be on your way," Miyah said seriously.

Celeste saw the worried look on Miyah's face. She looked at Quinn, who was void of emotion. "How did he get back? I thought the governor took care of that thieving slave trader."

"He did. However, with all the trading and shipping going on here, slavery is running rampant. The plantations need workers. He is allowed back for that."

"Bloody hell, what is the matter with this world? Buying and selling human flesh," Quinn said angrily.

Miyah put a gentle hand on Quinn's shoulder. Celeste raised a jealous eyebrow but said nothing. "It was talk like that, Quinn, that got him tossed off this island. You'd best stay out of his way."

Quinn laughed ruefully. "I have no quarrel with Henley. Once the *Pride of Charleston* is seaworthy, we'll set sail."

Miyah nodded and grinned. Glancing at Celeste, she leaned in and kissed Quinn. "Well, I'm sure I'll see you again," she said and sauntered off.

Quinn watched her as she walked away and caught Celeste's suspicious glare at the retreating figure. She took her by the elbow. "I'll tell you all about her," she assured her irritated lover.

The doors led to a sitting area outside, making the room look enormous. In the far corner was a four-poster bed with impeccable white sheets and a lightweight blanket. The warm Jamaican breeze wafted through the long curtains.

Quinn tossed her bag on a nearby chair.

"Is this where you usually stay when in Kingston?" Celeste asked and looked into her blue eyes.

"N-no. I usually stay elsewhere."

Celeste nodded. "I hope this is quite suitable for you," Celeste continued, never losing eye contact.

Quinn smiled through her blush. "It is quite suitable, I'm sure," she said with a cocky grin. She looked around the room and sighed. "Since the British took over, they've colonized the island. I must admit they took a good deal of Jamaica's culture away."

"The British have their hands in every country on the map,"

Celeste said, causing Quinn to chuckle.

The Americans and the French had no love for the British. Spain did—only when it benefited them, of course.

"Well, I must get back to the ship. I'll return in two hours time, love. If you need anything, there is money in my bag. I'll have them bring in a large tub, so we can bathe. I'm in need of a cool bath," Quinn said and pulled Celeste into her arms.

Celeste forgot her pique. "Hurry back, *ma chérie*." She pulled her down for a scorching kiss.

Quinn stumbled as she backed up, trying to catch her breath.

Celeste sported a smug grin as she unbuttoned her bodice.

Quinn continued to back up to the door. "I-I'll be back soon," she said in a raspy voice and bumped into the door. She made a quick awkward exit.

Celeste threw her head back and laughed at her stumbling captain.

Nearly three hours later, Quinn and the rest of her crew were sweaty, dirty, and exhausted. She wiped her face on the sleeve of her blouse.

"Good Lord, I forgot how bloody hot it gets on this island."

Jack only nodded as he drank from the water barrel. He handed Quinn a wooden mug. She nodded her thanks and gulped the cool water. "Give the men leave, Jack. However, leave two or three aboard at all times. I-I'm staying in Kingston while the ship is repaired."

Jack raised a curious eyebrow, which Quinn saw. "Mademoiselle Marchand cannot stay in my quarters while in Kingston. This is a beautiful place," she explained. "The poor girl is away from home and, and—" She stopped and glared at her first mate. "Good day, Jack. See that the men get paid. I'll see you in the morning." She turned and marched away.

"Aye, Capt'n darlin'," Jack said with a grin.

Quinn stopped dead in her tracks, then shook her head and continued. Her first mate laughed. He'd never seen Quinlan Stoddard this undone.

As Quinn walked into the foyer of the inn, she saw Miyah.

"It's been a long year, Quinn," Miyah said. "Now tell me about Celeste."

Miyah watched as Quinn grinned. "Do not tell me that little girl has a hold on you, woman."

Quinn said nothing but shrugged helplessly.

"I do not believe it. Quinn Stoddard in love?" she asked tentatively.

Quinn merely nodded. Miyah shook her head. "How did you meet?"

Quinn explained the odd situation, and Miyah laughed out loud. Quinn didn't see the humor. "Oh, Quinn. You and your crew. You are the talk of Jamaica, you know."

"Wonderful," Quinn grumbled. "Well, I'll stake my crew against any ship that sails into Kingston."

Miyah smiled affectionately at the confident timbre of her voice. She remembered when Quinn first sailed into Jamaica all those years earlier. She was young and full of herself. Quinn Stoddard was indeed an arrogant woman. To be in this man's world, she had to be. The confidence and arrogance captivated Miyah. It was a powerful aphrodisiac.

She remembered how gentle Quinn was when Miyah first told her how she started her life as a prostitute. She told her how the Spaniards abducted her along with scores of other villagers from Africa and brought them to work the sugarcane plantations. Miyah was fifteen. It was hard backbreaking work, so Miyah took the only other job offered to a woman on the island. She never expected to have a woman as a customer. Their first time together was an unbelievable experience for Miyah.

Men in general wanted their needs satisfied. They were at sea for months at a time, and when they got into port, they looked for one thing. It didn't happen very often that she was satisfied, as well.

With Quinn, it was Miyah's pleasure that satisfied Quinn. Now she looked at Quinn, who looked older and mature, as she struggled with her emotions. "Quinn, what do you think you're doing? That girl looks like she comes from great wealth."

They walked side by side down the corridor to Miyah's

room.

"She did at one point. Her father evidently squandered everything after Celeste's mother died. He's been trying to marry her off for money since."

Miyah opened her door and Quinn sat on the bed; Miyah sat next to her. "Why is she not married?"

Quinn's look was the obvious answer. Miyah shook her head. "Are you sure? How old is she?"

"Twenty-one."

"She's a baby."

Quinn let out a nervous laugh. "That woman is no baby, trust me."

Miyah laughed at the absurd situation. "Just what do you think you're going to do with her? Take her back to America? Quinn, what you and I did was one thing, but to think you can live—"

"Miyah, I'm well aware of the situation. I'm going to find passage for her and get her on the next ship for France. She'll forget this and marry some rich fat Frenchman," she said angrily.

"That is not what you want, is it?" Miyah asked. Quinn stood and paced back and forth. "You must decide. This young woman is in love. I can see it all over her face. I can see it in you, as well."

Quinn turned to her and took a deep breath. "Well, I have to decide in a week's time. It will take that long for the repairs."

Miyah walked up to her and placed a hand on her cheek. "You are in love with this woman, aren't you?"

Quinn looked into the soft brown eyes that she'd known for seven years. "Yes, I'm in love with her. I don't know how it happened or why, but I don't think I want to go on if she's not with me, and I don't see how that can happen."

"Go to her. I have never seen you like this. You must decide for your sake, as well as Celeste's," Miyah said. "She is a beautiful woman."

"Yes, she is. However, it's more than that. She's fiery and independent. She won't take any of my guff, but she cares for me. I feel it so deep."

Miyah cradled the worried face in her hands. "Then you must

find a way. Now kiss me one last time."

Quinn smiled affectionately and kissed her. When she stood back, for an instant, Quinn did not know what to say. She said nothing as she walked out and closed the door behind her.

Miyah took a deep breath and shook her head as she smiled. "Quinn Stoddard in love."

Chapter 23

Quinn tiredly walked down the hall to her room. Upon opening the door, she nearly bumped into a young man.

"Excuse me," he said, and Quinn nodded and stepped out of his way.

As she walked in, a young woman skirted past her. "Afternoon, ma'am," she said and hurried along.

Quinn stood there for a moment, then stuck her head in. "Is it safe?"

Celeste looked up and laughed as she beckoned her into the room. "I was getting settled. I hope you do not mind. I needed a few things."

"No, not at all, buy whatever you like," she said and looked at the bed. Two dresses lay side by side. "I truly hope one of those is not for me."

Celeste nearly fell over with laughter at the thought. "*Non*! I have purchased new, how you say… trousers, for you and a new blouse. I think it will go with your eyes," she said with a grin.

"You didn't have to get me anything," Quinn insisted. She glanced over to see the large basin situated by the open doors.

"They are bringing water, so—"

The knock at the door interrupted her. "Bon," she exclaimed, and Quinn laughed as she watched Celeste dash to the door.

Four young men walked in, each carrying two large buckets of water. They filled the tub as Celeste instructed them.

"You've been busy, love," Quinn said as they left. She slipped off her boots.

"*Oui*," she answered. She walked over, picked up a bottle, and poured the contents into the tepid water. She sensually swirled her fingers through it. "*Voilà*. Your bath is ready."

Quinn unbuttoned her dirty blouse and slipped it off. She unbuttoned the breeches and struggled out of them.

Celeste watched again, amazed at the strong yet soft body before her.

Quinn walked up to her and kissed her on the lips. "Thank you. No one has ever drawn a bath for me before."

"I am happy to be the first. In you go."

Quinn slid into the warm water and let out a contented sigh. She put her head back and looked up at Celeste, who slowly unbuttoned the bodice of her dress. Quinn swallowed and watched as Celeste slid the dress off and stepped out of it. Quinn smiled, noticing she wore no corset. She gave Celeste an approving nod. Celeste grinned and slipped out of her bloomers and chemise.

"Good heavens, you French wear too many clothes," Quinn said as she lay back in the lavender-scented water.

Quinn watched as Celeste walked over to the dressing table and sat down. She took her time and pinned her hair up and off her neck. Quinn's breathing was ragged as she gazed at the flawless back and the full curve of her hips as she sat at the chair. Her mouth watered as she gazed up and down the smooth expanse of milky white skin. "My God, Celeste, you are beautiful."

Celeste rose and walked up to the basin. She dipped her fingers in and swirled the water around.

Quinn reached up and caressed her full hip, running her fingers up and down the inside of her thigh.

Celeste closed her eyes and swayed at the heavenly touch. She shivered and parted her legs as Quinn slid her fingers through her damp curls. "Quinn," she whimpered. Standing in the room, naked before this woman, allowing her to touch her in such an intimate way, made Celeste's head spin. Her breath caught in her throat as she leaned forward, parting her legs farther. "I-I need to…I cannot stand any longer." Quinn relented and pulled her into the large tub.

Sitting in front of Quinn, Celeste sighed as she lay back, feeling soft firm breasts against her back. Quinn reached around with both hands to cup Celeste's full breasts as they bobbed in the water. Celeste's head fell back onto Quinn's strong shoulder as Quinn kissed the offered neck, her tongue flicking back and forth. "We'd better wash first, love, or we'll never leave this tub."

They took turns bathing each other. When they finished, Celeste stepped out of the basin and picked up a large towel. Quinn stood, and once again, they assisted each other. Then, in one movement, Quinn gathered Celeste in her arms and carried her the short distance to the bed.

Celeste looked up at Quinn with such desire that Quinn's breath caught in her throat. She knelt on the bed and loomed over Celeste. "I have never wanted anyone as much as I want you right now. You overwhelm me, love," she said and lowered her body.

Celeste was breathing in ragged gasps as she felt Quinn's strong body cover her. New sensations once again bombarded her poor brain: the sensual feel of their bodies touching in the most intimate place; their breasts compressed against one another; nipples straining with desire. *"Mon Dieu,"* Celeste whimpered as she clung to Quinn.

"Exactly so," Quinn murmured into her hair. The scent of this woman ignited her passion once more. "God, I can't get enough of you," she groaned and kissed her deeply.

Quinn woke two hours later, her stomach advising her they had not eaten. She looked down at a beautiful sight—Celeste's naked body lay sprawled across her. Her blond hair covering Quinn's belly like a gold canopy. Quinn lightly caressed her cheek. As the warm breeze blew the long curtains, Quinn tried to remember when she had been this happy and content.

Celeste sneaked into her life and now, Quinn was in love for the first time in her lonely life. What would they do? Where would they live? Could it be possible that she could share her life with Celeste? Quinn let out a sad sigh, fearing the truth: they could not. The next day, she would go and find a ship sailing for France.

She took a deep quivering breath, her heart aching at the thought of it.

"Ma chérie, what are you thinking?" Celeste whispered in the

darkness. She moved slightly and looked up at Quinn, her chin resting on her belly.

Quinn smiled and looked down at the lovely face. So young, so trusting. "I'm thinking how happy I am right now. I—" She stopped and smiled. "I'm hungry, you lustful wench." She playfully slapped her bare bottom.

Celeste screeched with laughter and rolled away.

Quinn rose and heard a knock at their door. She threw on Celeste's robe, which caused its owner to giggle, and strode to the door and opened it.

"Capt'n Stoddard. Compliments of Miyah Kettering," the owner of the inn said and waited for Quinn to move. Quinn nervously looked back at Celeste, who pulled the blanket over her head.

Quinn reached for the tray of food and the bottle of claret. "If you see Miss Kettering, tell her I appreciate her kindness."

"You can come out now," Quinn said as she struggled out of the silk robe and tossed it toward Celeste, who giggled once again and grabbed the robe.

Quinn slipped into her new clothes. "Thank you, they fit perfectly. Now come over here before I eat the entire meal."

They ate ravenously, each regaining her strength. Celeste never tasted anything so exotic. The beef was spicy but sweet at the same time. "What are these?" She stabbed a brown potato-looking vegetable with her fork.

"Yams. Sweet potatoes. They're good," Quinn said and ate heartily. She poured more wine. "We'll take them back with us. Along with sugarcane, molasses, silks I promised for—" She stopped abruptly and turned bright red.

Celeste narrowed her eyes at her. "For who?"

"A friend."

"Like Miyah Kettering?" she asked. "I am sorry, Quinn. It is none of my business."

Quinn smiled slightly and drank her wine. "Celeste, I have lived a very raucous life, and I have known a few women. It hasn't been easy, let me tell you," she said seriously. "It is not easy to find someone who shares my desires."

Celeste looked up. "I share them," she said with a challenging smile.

Quinn nodded. "Yes, you do. I am indeed a lucky woman."

"It is I who is lucky. If I hadn't run into Will and Thomas, I would be still lost."

Quinn was silent for a moment as she finished her meal. "Your father is bound to come and look for you. The people with whom you were staying, family friends, I'm sure they are sick with worry."

Celeste's head shot up; Quinn saw the fire in her eyes. "I will not go back to my father. I am of age and I will stay in Jamaica before I go back. You cannot make me. Do not even try!"

Quinn took a deep breath. She saw the determined look and relented. "We'll talk of this tomorrow."

"We will not talk of it at all. I go with you. If you do not want me, I stay here. *Ce n'est pas dificile*," she said in a firm voice.

Quinn tossed down her napkin. "It is *dificile*," she said with equal firmness. "Just how do you plan on making a living?"

"I will ask Madame Kettering," she said angrily.

Quinn's mouth dropped. She then put her head back and laughed heartily.

Celeste fumed at her arrogance. She stood quickly, knocking over the chair.

Quinn immediately stopped laughing. "I'm sorry, love."

"Do not call me that. You do not mean it!"

The litany of French started; Quinn rolled her eyes and waited. Celeste paced back and forth, wagging her finger in her direction. Quinn raised a curious eyebrow and drank her wine.

Celeste stopped and took a deep calming breath. "I am a grown woman. I may not have the life experience of you or Madame Kettering. However, I know my heart and I know yours. You can deny this if you must. I will not. I love you. If you do not want me, say so and I will make arrangements."

"Celeste, I promised you safe passage to France. I—"

"Tell me you do not love me."

"You can't possibly be in love with me—"

"Tell me. Say it and I will leave."

Quinn looked at her and swallowed hard. "I do not love you."

There was a brief moment of silence. "You are lying. You love me, I can tell," Celeste said with a light, dismissive tone. She picked up her chair and sat down. "We must think of something. Finish your meal," she ordered and poured another glass of wine.

Quinlan Stoddard obediently picked up her fork and finished her meal in stunned silence.

Chapter 24

The repair of the mizzenmast took little time. Within three days, the *Pride of Charleston* was seaworthy.

In that time, Quinn tried to convince Celeste to be reasonable. Each time, it was the same. If she said—"Tell me you do not love me" one more time—Quinn thought helplessly as she marched from their room.

She spent the entire day wandering the streets of Kingston, trying to figure out what to do. She stopped at a storefront and gazed in the window. Smiling, she opened the door.

Back in their room, Celeste pouted. She hated arguing with Quinn. *Why can't she see how much we love each other? Arrogant American. I am a grown woman. I will not go back to France and I will find a way to stay with Quinn.*

The thought of it made her body tingle once again. She flounced on the bed and smiled happily. She knew she was in love and nothing would keep her from Quinn.

She laughed openly, remembering the stupefied look on Quinn's face when she demanded—"Tell me you do not love me." Deep in her heart, Celeste knew Quinn withered at the thought of saying such a thing. She saw the love in the deep blue eyes.

She heard the door open. Quinn walked in as Celeste sat up, but said nothing, hoping they would not get into another argument.

Quinn walked over to the bed and pulled the stunned woman into her arms.

"Damn me if I don't love you completely." She gazed down into sparkling eyes rimmed with tears.

Celeste took a deep breath and wrapped her arms around the strong neck, her fingers raking through the rich brown waves. "Then I am damned, as well. For I love you... *Toujours*," she replied and pulled her down.

"Always," Quinn said in a raspy voice and kissed her.

Celeste hung on for all she was worth and returned the emotional kiss. Their lips blended sweetly, then Quinn slowly pulled back.

She reached into her vest pocket and pulled out a velvet box. Celeste stepped back and looked down. "For you, my love."

With trembling hands, Celeste took the present and opened it. She gasped as she took the necklace out of the box and held it up. "Quinn, it is exquisite."

It was a blue teardrop-shaped diamond on a delicate silver chain. Quinn took it from her and Celeste eagerly turned around, lifting her long wavy hair off her neck.

Quinn, cursing her shaking hands, reached around and fastened the necklace. She leaned in and kissed the back of Celeste's neck, her tongue lightly tracing across her shoulder.

Celeste shivered and leaned back into Quinn's warm body. She turned in her embrace and kissed her deeply. "Merci *beaucoup. Je t'aime*," she said through her tears.

"I saw it in a shop and I thought of you. I don't know why, but it seemed like it should grace your lovely neck." Quinn pulled back. "Now dinner will be here in one hour. That gives me plenty of time to give you your other present."

"Another? This is quite enough. I—" She let out a shriek as Quinn lifted her off the ground and deposited her on the bed.

She gave Celeste a look of pure lust as she unbuttoned her blouse.

Celeste lay back and smiled. She shrieked once again as Quinn leapt onto the bed.

After dinner, Quinn suggested an evening stroll along the beach. They walked side by side as the golden sun faded over the mountains. Seeing that they were alone along the stretch of sand, Quinn reached down and grasped Celeste's hand in her own.

Celeste smiled and held onto the warm soft hand. "No one has ever given me anything as beautiful as this," she said as she stroked the diamond necklace.

"The first of many, I promise," Quinn said with a tender smile.

They walked off the beach and stopped under a huge palm tree that swayed lazily with the gentle breeze off the Caribbean. Celeste leaned against the tree and took a deep soulful breath. Quinn stood in front of her and smiled.

"It is so beautiful here. I could stay here forever."

"There is nothing to do here, love. We'd have no money and no home. The Carolinas are much like this in the summertime and the winters are much milder than in France. You'll see."

Celeste looked up. "Will I?"

Quinn swallowed and moved closer, her forearm leaning against the tree, her fingers toying with a few strands of Celeste's golden hair. Searching the crystal blue eyes that amazingly sparkled even in the early evening twilight, Quinn took a deep breath. "Yes, love. You will see many summers in Carolina, and if you're a good girl, perhaps you can accompany me on certain trips back here." She kissed her cheek.

Celeste moaned as she felt warm lips against her. "If you are planning to come back to Kingston and Madame Kettering is here, *oui, chérie*, I will be joining you," she warned playfully.

Quinn laughed as she reached up to cup her soft cheek. Their eyes locked for an instant before Quinn lowered her head and captured warm sweet lips again.

Celeste sighed as she felt a hand wander down her neck, then farther where Quinn palmed her heaving breast. "Quinn," she said and caught her breath.

Quinn breathed deeply as she caressed down her hip, her fingers pulling the soft material of the blue dress up, gathering it in her hand as she continued.

Celeste was helpless against Quinn. Here in the open, where anyone could see, she once again allowed Quinn to do as she pleased—she craved her touch. She felt her dress lifted against her and suddenly, the warm fingers caressed the top of her thigh.

Quinn pulled back slightly and grinned. *"Ma'amselle,* you seem to have forgotten your undergarments."

Celeste looked up and parted her legs, opening herself to Quinn's caresses. "I have forgotten nothing. You claim we French wear too many clothes. Are you complaining now?" she asked in a seductive voice, her accent deepening.

"Never," Quinn said and leaned into her, both moaning as their bodies melded together so perfectly. Quinn slid her fingers across the top of her smooth thigh and teased the moist curls.

Celeste's body once again was not her own. Quinn controlled her with every kiss, every touch.

Quinn sighed happily as her fingers slipped through the moisture. She cupped her hand over the softness, her finger delving into the soft folds.

"Ah." Celeste sighed contentedly as her body quivered and trembled with anticipation.

Quinn leaned in farther, pressing her hand firmer against her.

"Quinn, I-I... Oh," she moaned deeply as fire ignited deep within once more. She convulsively clutched at Quinn's shoulder. She bit her lip, so as not to cry out her pleasure. "Now... now..." she whimpered her warning.

Quinn stroked her lover until Celeste writhed and jerked against her hand. Quinn murmured words of love against her hair, and as she tried to ease her hand away, Celeste clamped her legs together, capturing her in a tight embrace.

"Please, stay, *chérie.* Your gentle hand, hold me," Celeste said as she felt her knees buckle.

Quinn wrapped her arm around her waist and easily held her up.

As the warm breeze wafted over them, Celeste fought the urge to cry out her love for Quinn, she was so at peace. She prayed it would last.

Chapter 25

It was on the fourth day the tall ship docked in Kingston. Quinn and Jack had finished loading the last of their cargo. Quinn looked over to see the French flag waving from the mizzenmast and her heart sank.

As they sat eating dinner in the dining room of the inn, Quinn told Celeste of the French barque docked in Kingston. Celeste listened as she ate.

"*Non,*" she said evenly.

Quinn buried her head in her hands in an exasperated gesture. "Celeste…"

Celeste smiled happily at the poor woman's plight. "We are in love. This is final. Why do you fight this, *chérie?*" she asked, honestly confused as she cut into her beef. She liked Jamaican food.

Quinn shook her head helplessly. "I don't know, love," she answered. "I suppose I don't see how we can ever be—"

"Quinn!"

Both women looked up to see Jack dashing over to their table.

"What on earth is the matter?" Quinn asked.

"There's some fellow asking after Celeste. He's from that French barque that sailed in this morning."

Quinn stood and pulled at Jack's shirt. "What is he saying?"

"He talked to Will. He said he was looking for a young French woman who was separated from her party. He described Celeste and had her name. He's in Kingston on his way over here. He's threatening to take the *Pride of Charleston*. There were witnesses in Charleston."

Quinn tried to think quickly as she looked at the helpless look on Celeste's face. "Take Celeste to Miyah Kettering. Explain what has happened. I'll meet with these men. You never saw Celeste, tell the men. Understand, Jack?"

Jack grinned. "Aye, Quinn."

Quinn looked at Celeste and put her hand on her shoulders. "Go quickly now. Do not leave until I come for you," Quinn said firmly and smiled. "And I will come for you."

Tears flooded the crystal blue eyes as she reached up. Quinn took her hand and pushed her toward Jack. "Go now, let no one see you."

"*Je t'aime*, Quinn."

Quinn had no idea what to do next. She only knew that she couldn't let Celeste go—not now, not ever.

Miyah jumped when someone repeatedly knocked at her front door.

She threw the door open to see Celeste wild-eyed and scared along with Jack. Immediately, she knew there was something wrong. She pulled both of them in and slammed the door.

"What is it? Is it Quinn? Is she all right?"

Jack nodded and explained as Miyah ushered them into her living room. "Quinn asked that Celeste stay here until she comes for her. I'm not sure what Quinn is planning."

"Jacques, you mentioned that they are threatening to take Quinn's ship," Celeste said. Jack nodded. "Then I must go. Do you not see? I cannot let this happen. Please take me back."

"No, Celeste, let Quinn handle this. Those men didn't look like aristocrats to me."

"Well, you'll stay here until Quinn comes for you. You can take the back room and no one will know you're here. You weren't followed?" Miyah asked.

Jack shook his head. "I'd best get back. Try not to worry," he said with a smile.

Miyah reached for his arm. He saw the pleading look in her eyes.

"Don't worry, Miyah, I'll take care of Quinn," he assured her.

She nodded and kissed him on the lips. "Please take care, as well, Jack."

He searched her face for a moment. He saw the smile from long ago and kissed her on the cheek. "I will be back for you," he promised and left.

Celeste sat in a dejected heap. Miyah sat across from her, watching.

"I cannot allow this to happen," Celeste said firmly. "I must go, madame."

"And do what? Perhaps get Quinn killed? You don't know what these men are after. Trust Quinn—you do trust her, don't you?"

Celeste sat erect in her chair and met her challenging gaze. "*Oui, madame.* I trust Quinn with my life."

"Then stay here and do as she tells you. Quinn can be very forceful in situations like these."

Inwardly, Celeste did not like the fact that Miyah knew Quinn intimately. However, now was not the time for such jealousy.

Jack dashed back through the streets of Kingston and saw Quinn. She was talking with the two men from the French ship.

One man noticed Jack and pointed. "There," the man called out.

Jack walked up to Quinn, whose face was void of emotion. "Evening, Quinn."

"Did you have a good time?" Quinn asked lightly and gave him a wicked grin.

Jack adjusted his belt and nodded. "Aye, Quinn. I surely did."

One man looked at Quinn and Jack. "So you do not know who this woman is?"

"I didn't say that. I saw her, yes. She came to my ship. She had lost her party and I tried to help. However, I was bound for Jamaica and had no time. She left my ship as we set sail. What happened to her?"

"That's what we're trying to find out," the older man said.

Quinn could tell he didn't believe her. She didn't care. The next morning, they would set sail and Quinn would get Celeste from Miyah later that night.

"Who are you?" Jack asked both men. They were not French that was for sure. "You're American, are you not?"

"Yes. *Monsieur* Marchand's friends hired us to find her. They feel responsible."

Quinn gave him a wary look. "So you sailed all the way to Jamaica on a whim?"

"Not a whim. We were told she was aboard your ship when it set sail."

Quinn shrugged. "Well, my friend, you were misinformed. You may as well enjoy the weather because the wench is not with me."

"Good night, gentlemen," Jack said, and he and Quinn walked away.

When they were out of sight, Jack leaned into Quinn. "Who are they? They look like a couple of privateers to me."

"Aye, they do. Jack, get back to the ship. Make sure every man is on board and ready to sail at a moment's notice. I don't like this. Something's not right. Off with you."

"I don't like you being out here alone. I don't trust those two."

"I know, but I need you on the *Charleston*. Now listen carefully. If at anytime you think you should set sail, do so."

"Quinn! I can't sail without you."

"Listen to me. I will not lose the *Pride of Charleston* and I will not lose Celeste. Now you will follow my order. If it becomes necessary to set sail, set sail without me. The Stoddard Line is my father's life, and it's your life. Celeste is mine," she said, looking him in the eye. "Do as I say." She offered her hand.

"I will. I promise if the ship is in danger, it will sail for Charleston."

Quinn nodded and clapped him on the shoulder. "Hopefully, it won't come to that. Now go."

Jack pulled her into a strong quick embrace, then pulled

back, both stunned by the gesture. Quinn smiled and touched her friend's cheek. "Sail with the tide, my friend."

Quinn had never mentioned a kinship between them. His heart ached for what he might have to do. "If need be, the *Charleston* will, my friend," he said in a coarse voice, and walked into the darkness.

Quinn walked back to her room. As she opened the door, someone roughly pulled her into the darkness. A strong hand pushed her against the door, his forearm crushing her windpipe.

Someone lit a lantern and Quinn struggled to see who it was.

"Well, well, Quinlan Stoddard," the gruff voice said with a chuckle.

Quinn tried to focus, then saw him. "Well, well, Dan Henley. You're as ugly as ever," she wheezed.

The grin left the bearded man's face. His eyes narrowed dangerously and a wicked smile etched across his scarred features. He looked at the man holding Quinn and nodded.

As he blew out the lantern, Quinn felt the searing pain in her head as she followed the darkness.

Chapter 26

Celeste paced back and forth in the sitting room. Miyah tried not to worry, but the pacing was driving her to distraction.

"Celeste, please sit," she said. Celeste stopped and ran a worried hand across her forehead as she sat on the settee.

After a moment of silence, Celeste looked up at Miyah.

"How long have you known Quinn, madame?"

"Since the first time she arrived in Kingston some seven years ago." Miyah looked at Celeste. "You are in love with her, aren't you?"

"*Oui*, I am very much in love with her," Celeste said, and Miyah was amazed at the sudden serene look on Celeste's face.

"How can you know? You are so young, so innocent. What is it about Quinn?"

Celeste smiled, blushing furiously. "She is kind and gentle, but at the same time gruff and uncouth," she said with a chuckle. "She has compassion for her men and a love for them, as well. She is also steadfast, brave, loyal, and true. When she loves me, she touches me deep in my soul. She is so worried that she is taking advantage of me. I think it is kind and caring. She tries to be stoic, but I see the vulnerable woman in her and it pulls at my heart." She smiled and looked into Miyah's eyes. "This is why you love her, too, *non?*"

Miyah raised a wary eyebrow. Quinn was right. This woman may have been young, but she was no child. "Yes, Mademoiselle Marchand. It is exactly why I love Quinn. However, I see a deeper love in you. It is true, I love Quinlan, but you are in love with her. There is a difference. You are the lucky one. It is you she loves, you she would die for."

Celeste frowned. "I do not want her to die for me. I want her to live. Please, let us try and find her."

Miyah smiled slightly. "No, Celeste. She said to wait and we will wait."

Celeste sat back and closed her eyes. "Who is Dan Henley?" she asked, remembering the name.

Miyah rocked in her chair and stopped. "He is a filthy pig who abducts Africans from their homes like a thief in the night and brings them here and to America, selling them as slaves to plantation owners. Two years ago, Quinn found out and made quite a scene. She was an enormous help getting that pig thrown out of Jamaica. The governor exiled him, but now?" She gave a sad laugh. "Slavery is popular. There is so much money in sugarcane and molasses and he is back.

"Do you know that Quinn will only buy from the one plantation that does not use slaves? She does not get top dollar, but she told me once there was more than money sometimes," she said wistfully, remembering the conversation. She looked over at Celeste, who smiled with pride. "You are indeed a lucky woman to capture Quinlan's heart. I hope you know how precious she is."

"I do know. I will always know," she said. "I do not like this. I know there is trouble."

"Don't worry. Quinn knows what she's doing." Miyah continued to rock, hoping she was doing the right thing.

Quinn winced as pain sliced through her head. As she opened her eyes and tried to move, she realized she was standing but couldn't move. She adjusted to the dim lighting and felt her arms outstretched above her head and her wrists bound.

She heard someone behind her, and she frantically tried to turn her head and nearly cried out at the pain behind her eyes.

"You're not goin' anywhere," Dan Henley said. He walked around in front of her and set the lantern on the wooden table.

Quinn watched him carefully. He hadn't changed much in two years. He was a stout man, not tall. His longer, dirty black hair clung to his forehead as he scratched his scraggly graying beard. Dark eyes gleamed evilly in the lantern's light.

"Know where we are?" he asked.

Quinn glanced around. The room was dark and smelled musty. There were no chairs, no tables, save for the long wooden bench on which Henley now sat. She looked up to see her wrists bound to two chains, which hung from a long wooden beam. She looked to her left and saw a pair of wrist shackles dangling from the beam, as well.

Henley let out a low laugh. "I see you might have an idea. This is where I take slaves when they're uncooperative. They get that way sometimes," he said lightly. "You have to have a firm hand with those heathens."

"You're a pig," Quinn said evenly.

Dan Henley stood up and walked up to her, his putrid breath causing her to lean back in her restraints. "Do you realize how much money you cost me two years ago? All your high talk about slavery—got them all stirred up. Well, I'm back and I have my ship loaded from Africa for these plantations. Tomorrow, I'll be a very, very rich man once I sell them to the plantation owners. I have more gold and silver in my cabin than you can imagine.

"Yes, I will be very, very rich. I've been hired back. Seems there's still a good deal of money in the—how did you put it—in the buying and selling of human flesh," he said with a sneer. "Now you're going to know firsthand what it feels like. I've waited two long years and I can't believe you fell right in my lap. Those two idiots looking for that Frenchie will do anything to get her back. Now you'll tell me where she is."

Quinn laughed. "You idiot. You did all this?" She shook the chains. "I have no idea where that woman is." She moved her wrists and found them tightly bound.

Henley's eye twitched with anger. "You know, all right. I know everything that goes on, on this island. I'll ask you one more time. Where is she?"

"Apparently not everything, you ugly idiot, because I don't know where she is. And if I did, do you actually think I'd tell you?" Quinn looked him in the eye.

"Oh, you'll tell me. One way or the other. You'll tell me."

He reached behind him, and Quinn swallowed when she saw what he held up.

With all the courage she could muster, Quinn gave the ugly pirate a cocky grin. "Henley, that's against maritime law."

"But you're not at sea now, Captain Stoddard. Flogging keeps the slaves in line, and I warrant I'll find out what I need to know soon enough. Don't worry, it's not what I usually use. This won't leave much of a mark, at first. Oh, it'll hurt, believe me, but we're underground. No one will hear you. How much it hurts, well, that all depends on you." He walked around and out of her sight.

Quinn struggled for a moment, her heart racing. She gasped and a tremor of fear swept through her as she felt her shirt ripped open.

"You work like a man and sail like one. Let's see if you can take punishment like one," he said, his rotten breath in her ear.

Quinn took a deep breath and held it.

Jack paced back and forth, looking at his pocket watch. It was nearly midnight. Quinn should have come back by now. The tide was rising as the two Americans walked up to the gangplank. George Prentice accompanied them. He was the law in Jamaica since the British took over.

"May we come aboard, sir?" George asked. "We need to inspect your ship, Jack Fenton. Get Quinlan Stoddard, if you please."

"You know where she stays. She has a room at the inn. Besides, she was injured during a storm, and I'm sure she's resting. We need her fit to sail," Henry said as he walked up to Jack.

"You can search this ship, Mr. Prentice. You'll find nothing."

All three men started up the plank. "Hold on, just you, George."

George Prentice was a weak character. He was tall and slim, very proper. He walked by Jack, who joined him in the thorough search.

Twenty minutes later, George found nothing.

"You've wasted enough of my time, gentlemen. We sail with

the tide. Capt'n Stoddard has settled our accounts. The Stoddard Line is above reproach. I only hope I don't have to inform Robert Stoddard of how his ship and crew have been treated."

George swallowed convulsively. "There is no need for that. I'm only doing my job."

"And are you satisfied, Mr. Prentice?" Jack asked.

George was already making a hasty retreat down the wobbly gangplank. He nodded and waved. "Yes, I am. Gentlemen, you were misinformed. Mademoiselle Marchand is not on the *Pride of Charleston.*"

"I don't believe it. I will search the ship myself," the older man said angrily.

"You will not. We have nothing more to say to you gentlemen. We sail with the tide and I have a job to do," Jack said.

The other started for the gangplank.

"Thomas!" Jack barked, never taking his eyes off the two angry Americans and one nervous Englishman.

Thomas appeared with musket in tow. He pointed it at all three men.

George Prentice nearly fainted as both men stopped dead in their tracks.

"By my order, if anyone steps one foot on that gangplank, shoot him," Jack said and smiled.

Thomas beamed at the idea of shooting the Englishman right between his beady little eyes. He took aim right at him. "Aye, Mr. Fenton. I'd be only too happy to oblige," he said and cocked the musket.

George nearly soiled himself. He grabbed at the two men. "Come, this has gone far enough. I have done my job to the letter of the law. I will not have anyone killed on this dock."

They retreated grudgingly and Jack let out his breath. He looked over at Thomas, who was still following them with his musket. Jack rolled his eyes. "Thomas," he said. "Thomas!"

He looked at Jack. "Maybe next time, son," Jack said and patted his shoulder.

"There's always hope, Mr. Fenton," Thomas said with a wink.

Jack called Will Drury and Thomas topside. "Thomas, hand out a musket and ammunition to every man and have them stand guard. Will, you're in charge until I get back. Quinn should have been back by now. Something's wrong, I can feel it. Thomas, remember my order. You shoot any man who tries to board this ship. If I'm not back in an hour's time, take the ship a mile out and set anchor around the point to Portmore. Wait there."

All three men listened without question. Jack looked into Will's eyes. "If we are not back in twenty-four hours, sail for America."

Will blinked but never wavered. "Aye, Mr. Fenton. By this time tomorrow."

"Why don't we all go and find her?" Thomas asked helplessly and ran his fingers through his unruly red mop.

Jack regarded Thomas solemnly. "I have my orders from Quinn and you have mine. What we have on this ship must get back to Carolina."

Thomas leaned back on his musket. "I feel responsible for this whole mess. Please, Mr. Fenton, let me go with you."

"No, I need you here. Don't worry. I'm sure Quinn has got Mademoiselle Marchand and is on her way," Jack said with as much conviction as he could. "Now you have your orders."

He went below to his quarters. He knelt by his bunk and opened the bottom drawer. There he found his father's pistols and saber. He loaded both pistols, stuck them into his belt, and slid the saber into the scabbard, all the while remembering his father's words. *One day, you may need these. With all my heart, I hope you do not. Use them wisely and bravely, son, as I have.*

He was a coward once, it would not happen again, he vowed as he grasped the saber with both hands, praying for strength.

All three men were shocked when they saw the first mate armed. "Mr. Fenton, are you sure?"

"Our captain is in danger, Will. I know it. It's my duty as her first mate to find her and bring her and Celeste back here. Now you do your duty, as well."

All men nodded, watching as the first mate ran down the gangplank and out of sight.

221

Jack belted the saber and made his way down Harbour Street through Kingston. The town was eerily quiet as the warm gulf breeze cooled his skin. Nearly running the entire time, he made his way back to Miyah's home.

"Who is it?"

He heard her soft voice and whispered urgently, "Jack Fenton, Miyah."

The door immediately opened and he skirted inside, shutting the door. He felt Miyah's arms around him immediately. He was stunned as he held her for a moment, then pulled her away. Tears rimmed her soulful brown eyes and poor Jack didn't know what to think.

Several years before, they had been lovers when the *Pride of Charleston* first docked in Kingston. However, when Miyah took up with Quinn, Jack respectfully backed away.

Celeste hoped he had Quinn with him and nearly sobbed when she saw he was alone. "Jacques, where is Quinn?"

Both women saw the pistols and saber.

"Jack, what's happened?" Miyah asked as her heart sank.

Jack explained the evening's events. "I don't know where Quinn has gone, but I will find her. I don't know where to start. She would have come back if—"

"She was not in danger," Celeste finished for him and wrung her hands together.

Miyah took Celeste by the shoulders and shook her. "Listen to me. If you love Quinn as you say, stay strong for her. She needs your strength now, not your childishness. Be the woman you think you are."

For an instant, Celeste was stunned. She recovered quickly, realizing this woman was right. She took a deep breath and nodded. Miyah smiled and turned her attention to Jack.

"Jack, Dan Henley is back in Jamaica."

"Henley! Does he know she's here?"

"How can he not with her ship docked in plain sight?"

Jack paced back and forth. "He said she'd pay one day," he muttered to himself.

Celeste walked up to him and pulled at his arm. "Pay for

getting him exiled from Jamaica?" she asked urgently. Jack nodded. "Then that is where she is. With him."

Jack nodded helplessly. "But where? Where would that be?"

Miyah took a deep breath. "I remember Dan Henley when I worked the plantation. He is a sick vile man." She ran over to the chest and opened it. When she turned, she had a pistol in one hand and made sure it was loaded. She handed it to Celeste. "Ever use one of these?"

Celeste shook her head as she took the heavy pistol. She looked at the two of them and stood tall. "Show me," she said confidently.

After a moment of instruction from Jack, Miyah led them to the door. "If that pig has Quinn, I know where they are."

Quinn braced herself, knowing what was coming.

Dan Henley stood behind her, drinking rum from a large tankard. "I'll give you this, I thought you'd be crying like a wee babe."

He ran his fingers up and down the smooth skin on her back. "This will be a shame to scar such softness."

Quinn heard him leave the room and looked around; she saw no windows, no way out. She tried in vain to look behind her. She had no idea where she was, and she knew no one would be able to find her.

Chapter 27

"Where are we going?" Celeste asked as they walked down the long dirt road. It was dark as pitch without a lantern to light their way.

"The old barn. There is a cellar. If I know Henley, that's where he has Quinn," Miyah said as they neared the barn.

"What's in the cellar?" Jack asked as he looked around, making sure no one followed.

Celeste heard Miyah take a deep breath. "It's where he takes the slaves for their punishment."

When Miyah stopped, Jack and Celeste stopped, as well. "There it is." She motioned to her right.

About thirty yards away stood an old dilapidated shed. There was no one around.

"She's in there?" Celeste asked, trying to control the sob in her voice.

Jack looked around. "All right, Miyah, where's the door to the cellar? I will—"

Miyah cut him short. "I do not have time to explain. We will all go. I'm sure he's alone."

Jack nodded his assent as they walked up to the barn. The door was opened and Jack motioned that he would go first. Once in, he knew they were alone, even in the darkness. Then they heard a muffled voice.

Miyah carefully walked to the trap door on the floor of the barn. She put a finger to her lips and opened the door.

There was a staircase leading down into the damp darkness. Jack stopped Miyah's progress and went first. He took a pistol out and breathed deeply, trying to stop his shaking hands, and started down the staircase with Celeste taking up the rear.

As they got to the bottom of the staircase, they heard Henley's voice.

"You're being quite uncooperative, Quinn. I've warned you, you stubborn bitch."

They all heard the cat whistle through the air, then the cry from Quinn. Celeste put a hand to her mouth to stop from crying out.

Jack burst through the door and rushed in with Miyah and Celeste behind. Dan Henley had his hand raised for another blow.

"Henley!" Jack called out as Henley whirled around, completely surprised.

As he moved, all three saw Quinn's body arching from the sting of the whip. A lone red welt sliced across her back; her torn shirt hung around her shoulders.

Henley let out a low growl and reached into his belt, pulling out a pistol. Jack, Miyah, and Celeste all fired their pistols at once, sending Henley backward against the bench in a cloud of gun smoke. With his body covered in blood, he was dead before he hit the floor.

Celeste dropped her pistol and rushed around to Quinn.

Sweat poured from her face; her hair was matted to her forehead. Celeste reached up and brushed the hair away. "Quinn," she cried out.

"I'm all right, Celeste," Quinn said through clenched teeth.

Jack and Miyah untied her wrists from the chain. Quinn stumbled forward into Celeste's arms. "Just need a minute to get my legs back."

"Quickly, we must get out of here. I'm sure someone heard the shots," Jack said firmly. "Are you all right to move, Quinn?"

Quinn flexed her back and nodded. As they left the room, Miyah walked up to Dan Henley's body and spat. She turned and slammed the door.

They settled Quinn on her stomach in Miyah's bed. Celeste

took charge as she sat on the edge of the bed. "Help me with her shirt," she ordered, and among the three of them, they got the tattered shirt off Quinn's body.

"I tell you, I'm fine," Quinn said over her shoulder.

"I need hot water and soap." Celeste pushed the blond waves off her forehead.

Jack and Miyah left the room. Celeste sat there staring at the angry red welt on Quinn's back.

Miyah came back into the room with Jack, who held the bowl of water and clean rags.

"Miyah?" Quinn said painfully. "He's dead. He won't hurt anyone anymore."

Miyah nodded and smoothed her wet hair back. "I'm so sorry he did this to you."

Celeste fought her tears as she laid the soapy cloth against the throbbing welt. Quinn jumped as the soap stung the weeping wound. She took a deep breath and opened her eyes; she craned her neck and saw Jack standing there, smiling.

"What the devil are you doing here, Jack?" she asked angrily.

"Well, you're welcome," he said with his hands on his hips. "The ship is fine, Quinn. I had Will take her out around the point and weigh anchor there. I'll take a boat out to them in the morning. You rest. That bastard is dead now."

"You disobeyed my order."

"I did not," he said with an indignant grin. "You said if need be the *Pride of Carolina* was to sail for America. My exact words to you were—if it were necessary to set sail, it would sail for Charleston. I told you that it would. I didn't say how."

Quinn muttered as she shifted on the bed.

Miyah shook her head. "Quinlan and her crew."

"Lay still, Quinn. Jacques saved your life," Celeste said.

Quinn nodded and flinched, as Celeste soothed her injured back. "How did you find me?"

"I knew where he had taken you," Miyah said.

Quinn nodded, knowing that Henley had Miyah down there years before. "Thank you, all of you."

As she faded off, the last thing she remembered was Celeste's soft gentle hands upon her.

When she woke, her back no longer felt as if it were on fire. She looked over to see Celeste laying on her side, facing her in the bed, her hand lightly resting on her shoulder. Quinn watched her as she slept, amazed at how young she looked and how innocent. She thought of how she had risked her life for her—how they all did. It was a humbling experience, to say the least. She was indeed blessed in many ways.

As she drifted off, Dan Henley's ugly face came to mind. She remembered what he had said. He had a ship from Africa loaded with kidnapped villagers. Her mind instantly drifted to Miyah and her life. How it was brutally taken away from her and how she dealt with watching her parents whipped and beaten. It shouldn't happen to anyone.

As sleep overtook her, she tried desperately to think of a way.

Chapter 28

Celeste woke to see Quinn sitting up on the side of the bed. Tears leapt to her eyes as she saw the raw welt crossing her back, and wondered how much worse it could have been if they had not showed up in time. She hated Dan Henley, and for the first time in her young life, she was glad someone was dead. Given the situation again, she would gladly pull the trigger, God forgive her. "Quinn, what are you doing?"

Quinn looked over her shoulder. "I'm looking for a shirt."

"Lie down and rest."

"I'm fine. He barely touched me, the pig," Quinn assured her. Wincing slightly, she walked over to the dresser and opened the drawer. "Ah-ha." She pulled out a shirt.

"And how did you know that would be there?" Celeste asked suspiciously.

Quinn struggled, trying to pull the white shirt over her head. Celeste leapt from the bed to assist her. "You know the answer to that," Quinn said. She looked to see Celeste sporting a sad, dejected look.

"Madame Kettering is a beautiful woman," she mumbled, not making eye contact.

"Yes, she is."

"She is older and more experienced," she continued.

Quinn nodded emphatically. "More than you and me."

"I-I can see why you love her." She looked at her hands.

Quinn smiled broadly as she put her fingers under Celeste's chin and lifted her pouting face to meet her gaze. Sad blue eyes greeted her, and it broke Quinn's heart. "I love her, Celeste, yes,"

Quinn said, and Celeste withered before her. "But I'm in love with you."

Celeste searched her eyes, daring to believe Quinn. "You are?"

"Yes."

"And you will not send me away?" she asked as she toyed with the laces on the white billowy shirt.

"No, I will not send you away. However, I have one more thing to do and…" She stopped and grabbed Celeste by the hand.

Miyah sat at the table, drinking tea. Jack sat opposite as he cleaned the pistols, extremely glad he was putting them back in the box when he returned to the ship.

They both looked up when Quinn and Celeste walked into the room.

"How do you feel? What are you doing up?" Miyah asked angrily. "Jack, tell her—"

Jack shrugged and waved his hand in dismissal.

"I have been thinking," Quinn said and ushered Celeste to the other chair.

"Thinking about what?" Jack asked absently as he continued with his cleaning.

"That ugly bastard Henley said he had a ship loaded with slaves he picked up from Africa. I have an idea."

Both women looked up in question. Jack continued cleaning the pistols and grunted.

"I'm taking them back to Africa," Quinn said.

For a moment or two, no one said a word. Celeste rose and led Quinn to a chair. "Sit, *cherie*. Are you feverish?" She felt her cool forehead.

Quinn laughed. "No, I have no fever. I'm serious."

"And how do you intend to do this?" Jack asked as he checked the sights on the pistols.

"I'll sail Henley's ship, the *West Wind*."

Jack ignored her as he cleaned his pistols.

Quinn watched him intently and smiled. "What do you think, Jack?"

"Well, first off, I think it's a noble idea, but I don't think you can do it alone. Second, there's the *Pride of Charleston* and its cargo. Then there's Celeste and those two men. Don't forget there's Henley's death. Then—"

"I get the general idea," Quinn said dejectedly. "I don't know what I was thinking. I just cannot leave those poor people here."

"Hold on now. I didn't say it was impossible. I said you can't do this alone." Jack set down his pistols. He looked across at Miyah, who cocked her. "Miyah, how would you like to go home?" he asked and smiled fondly.

Miyah blinked back the tears that welled in her eyes. "Do not joke of that."

He reached across and held onto her hand. "I would never joke about that. I'm dead serious."

"What's your plan?" Quinn asked, noticing the tender exchange between Jack and Miyah.

"*Oui, Jacques.* Tell us," Celeste said.

Jack looked at Miyah. "We've talked of this, Miyah," he reminded her.

"That was years ago. So long ago."

Quinn looked back and forth between both friends. "Okay, what's going on? Talked of what? When?"

Jack smiled slightly. "Many years ago, before Miyah and you, there was Miyah and me."

Miyah smiled at her first lover. Jack grinned and held her hand tightly.

Celeste grinned with excitement. "*Très bon.*"

"I think I knew that," Quinn said.

"Many years ago, Miyah and I talked of someday getting her back to Africa. It was a long time ago, Miyah. Now we have a real chance. Remember the maps?"

Miyah bit at her bottom lip and nodded. She dashed over to the large chest and came back with several rolled maps. "I took these from Dan Henley's quarters when that pig had me."

Quinn and Celeste eagerly cleared the table and made room. Quinn and Jack studied the maps carefully. Celeste looked on, as did Miyah.

Quinn put her foot on the chair and leaned over the map with Jack. "He sailed into this area here... Abidjan?" she asked and looked at Miyah, who nodded.

"I was born near Sierra Leone. Our village was not far from there. Abidjan is on Côte d'Ivoire."

Celeste perked up when she heard her native tongue. "Côte d'Ivoire. Ivory Coast?"

"Ivory is in big demand. The ivory from elephant tusks is priceless," he said as he studied the map.

Quinn gave him a curious look. "I had no idea you knew this much about Africa." Jack blushed and glanced at Miyah. Quinn frowned, trying to recall all the years they had been sailing into Jamaica.

"Miyah and I have had our discussions," Jack said. "But that was before you, Quinn."

Quinn shook her head. "It doesn't matter." She looked at Miyah. "Why didn't I know this?"

Miyah offered a smug grin. "You were more interested in other things while in Jamaica."

Quinn blushed deeply and avoided the glare from Celeste. "Oh, well…" she said and cleared her throat.

"I made my choice after Quinn, and I… Well, I'm sorry, Jack," Miyah started, and Jack reached over again to hold her hand tight.

"I understand. I have no hard feelings. However, in light of the way things are turning out," he said and looked at Quinn and Celeste, "I think it's time we had a little talk. But first, let us figure out how in the bloody hell we're going to get a ship full of Africans back to Abidjan."

Quinn shook her head and studied the maps of the west coast of Africa.

"How indeed."

Chapter 29

The four sat looking at the map when there was a knock at the front door. Miyah ushered Quinn and Celeste into the back room. She looked at Jack and ripped the front of his shirt open and unbuttoned his trousers. Jack stood there stunned while Miyah kissed him deeply and tousled his thick hair.

She pulled back and looked at the shocked first mate. "Good, keep that look, Jack."

"Yes, ma'am," he croaked as she opened the door.

There stood George Prentice. "Madam Kettering. I need to talk to you for a moment."

"Certainly, Mr. Prentice, come in please." She stepped back.

As he walked in, he noticed Jack Fenton standing there. He looked up and down and grinned. "I'm sorry. I didn't mean to interrupt."

"That's all right. Jack's been here all night. It was time he got back to his ship."

Jack nodded and tried to button his shirt to no avail. George hid his grin as he cleared his throat.

"Well, as long as I have you here, Mr. Fenton, do you know where Quinlan Stoddard is?"

"I do not. She's probably back on board ship, which is where I'd better be before she skins me alive," he said seriously and shoved his ripped shirt into his trousers and buttoned them.

"Well, I will need to see her. There's been an accident. Seems Dan Henley went and got himself shot," he said and glanced at both.

"Shot, hmm. Is he dead?"

"Yes, he was shot three times."

"What has Quinn to do with this?" Miyah asked as she walked over and stood close to Jack.

"I know there was no love lost between them. I need to know where she is."

"Did you check her rooms at the inn?" Jack asked logically.

"No, I… Well, I figured she was here. Sorry," he mumbled. "Well, I best get over to the inn. Damn mess."

"Why, George? Dan Henley was a pig of the first order and you know it. This island is better off without him," Miyah said. She felt Jack put a protective arm around her as he squeezed his warning.

"I agree. Nevertheless, I'm bound at least to try and find out who killed him. Good day. I'm sorry to have bothered you." He tipped his hat and walked out.

Both waited for a moment as they heard the carriage pull away, then they dashed to the back room. The curtains in the open window blew in the warm breeze.

Celeste stood there alone.

Her back was stinging, but Quinn never ran so fast in her life. She crawled unnoticed behind the inn and through the French doors as someone knocked on the door. She took a deep breath and ran her fingers through her hair. She walked over to the basin and splashed water on her face and neck, then took a towel and answered the door. There stood George.

"Prentice, good day," she said as she toweled her face. "I was getting ready to leave. Come in."

George walked in and looked around.

"What's on your mind?" Quinn asked as she packed her bag.

"Dan Henley is dead," he said, waiting for her reaction.

Quinn turned to him with a surprised look. "Really? That's too bad. He probably deserved it, however."

"That's what Miyah Kettering said. I was over there. Your first mate was with her," he said with a smirk.

Quinn grinned and tossed the towel on the bed. "Good for him. Miyah suits him. Now did you come here to tell me Dan

Henley is dead or that my first mate is having his way with Miyah as we speak?"

George tried to gauge her reaction. "You've been in your room all night?"

"Yes, I had dinner and went to bed. I had an unfortunate meeting with my mizzenmast during a storm, and I'm trying to get my strength back."

"So you didn't kill Dan Henley?"

Quinn laughed out loud and said honestly, "No, I did not kill Dan Henley. Did someone beat him to death?"

"No. He was shot three times."

Quinn raised an eyebrow. She must remember to praise all three for their marksmanship. "Well, I can't say it's a surprise. He wasn't well liked. Now if you'll excuse me. I have a ship to get back to America."

George nodded and walked out. He turned as Quinn started to close the door. "I don't want any trouble in Jamaica, Quinn. The crew of the *West Wind* is restless. They know Henley's dead, and they think you did it. I have no proof. I'll tell them the truth. I saw you here alone and you were in your room all night. The Stoddard Line has always been above board. Whatever troubles you may have, take them to Carolina with you," he said and gave her a knowing look.

"Thanks for the advice. I'll do that."

He nodded and walked away. Quinn closed the door and stood against it, letting out a deep sigh.

"We need to get off this island," she said and packed quickly. She took the two pieces of luggage and left the inn.

Celeste paced back and forth while Jack and Miyah watched.

"She'll be back. Don't worry, she had to get to the inn before Prentice," Jack said.

As if on cue, someone knocked at the door. Quinn came in. "Good heavens, what in the world did you buy?" She let out a deep wheeze as she set the two pieces of luggage down.

Celeste was in her arms in a shot. "*Chérie*," she said and cried.

234

"Here now, what's this?" Quinn said and held on tight. "Everything will be fine, love."

"What did you tell George Prentice?" Jack asked.

Quinn let Celeste go with a tender kiss on the forehead. "I told him the truth. I didn't kill Henley," she said with a shrug and looked at her three friends. "He was shot three times."

"He deserved more," Celeste said angrily.

"Remind me—no pistols in our home, love. Now let's get back to the business at hand. How are we going to get those people back to Africa?"

Jack grinned slightly. "I have an idea. You were right to suggest taking the *West Wind*. We need to get Henley's crew off that ship long enough to get under way."

"Good idea, however, how are we going to get ten men off that ship?" Miyah asked in a dejected tone.

"Perhaps we won't," Quinn said with a sly grin. "I have a plan."

All three friends gave Quinn a skeptical look.

"I see that gleam in your eye, Quinn," Jack said warily. "The last time, we nearly lost the *Charleston* on a wager."

Quinn laughed remembering the time. "No bets this time."

She walked over to Miyah and put her hands on her shoulders. "Take whatever you need, Miyah. You are never coming back," she said and watched tears spring from her soulful brown eyes. "I only wish we could have done this years ago."

Miyah put her hand to her face and wept quietly. Quinn motioned to Jack, who walked over and engulfed the sobbing woman in a fierce embrace.

In a moment, she pulled back and Jack brushed the tears away with the back of his hand. "Now go and gather everything you need for your journey home, Miyah."

"Not too much, only what is necessary," Quinn added and avoided the smirk from Celeste.

"Come, madame, I will help," Celeste offered and both women left the kitchen.

"Okay, Quinn, how are you going to get ten men, who would like to see you swinging from a mizzenmast, to help us in this?"

Jack asked.

"Once Miyah gets her belongings together, we'll get back on the *Charleston*."

Miyah had only two small pieces of luggage. She looked around her home and smiled fondly. She looked at Quinn and Jack. "I was blessed to know both of you. You brought happiness to my miserable existence on this island."

Jack put his arm around her and picked up the luggage. "Now we can go home, Miyah," he said and kissed her.

Jack and Quinn rowed the long boat out to the *Charleston*.

"Ahoy, Capt'n," Will called out as the boat eased up alongside.

"Ahoy, Mr. Drury," Quinn called back with a grin.

All hands helped, and they finally got everything aboard. Henry smiled at Celeste. "It is good to see you once again, Mademoiselle Marchand," he said sincerely. Taking her hand, he kissed the back of it.

"*Moi aussi, Henri*," she whispered and kissed his cheek. "*Merci beaucoup*."

Quinn looked to find Thomas standing there with a look of pure dejection and guilt. She walked up to him and offered her hand.

Thomas grinned and took the offering. "It's good to have you back aboard, Capt'n."

"It's good to be back. I want to thank you for your help back there. I may still need a keen eye with a musket before this is over."

Jack settled Miyah in his quarters and Celeste happily settled back in Quinn's.

"Are we sailing, Capt'n?" Will asked.

"We are, Will, but first, we have a minor situation. Gather the crew. I need to talk to them."

All hands gathered at the quarterdeck, waiting for their captain's words. Celeste and Miyah stood back and listened.

"Men, by now you know that Dan Henley is dead. His ship, the *West Wind* has a cargo of human life. Africans were abducted from their villages to be sold as slaves for the sugarcane plantations. I'm going to see that they are returned to their home."

She stopped as the men glanced at one another in confusion.

"This means nothing to you or your pay. You will not be asked to go and do anything against your conscience. This is my duty to humankind and my conscience. As we speak, those poor people are huddled in the belly of the *West Wind*, torn from their homes and families. Now here's my plan."

She took a deep breath. "Dan Henley told me of a chest of gold and silver in his cabin on the *West Wind*. He was going to get more money from the plantation owners for the slaves. He said it would make him very, very rich. I intend to get aboard the *West Wind* and get that chest, pay off his men, and hopefully get them to sail to Africa with me."

Quinn heard Will clear his throat. She gave him a slight grin. "Something to add, Will?"

He scratched his scruffy beard in contemplation. "The crew of the *West Wind* may not be trusted, Capt'n. It's a long voyage to Africa."

"I have thought about that. However, money is a great equalizer. I'll give them an option. Take the money and sail or take the money and wait in Jamaica for another ship. I think they'll sail with me."

All this time, Jack stood there, watching his men. They were stunned. However, he saw the look of respect they gave Quinlan. He knew it was time to say something.

"Quinn, can I speak with you?"

Quinn gave him a curious look. "Speak freely, Jack. I want no secrets at this point."

Jack thought for a moment and nodded. "I don't think you should sail the *West Wind* to Africa."

Quinn frowned deeply. This is not what she expected to hear from him. "The *West Wind* must go to Africa, there's no other way."

"I agree, Capt'n Stoddard. I'm saying I don't think you should be on that voyage." He stood tall and looked his friend in the eye.

"And who do you think should sail the *West Wind*?"

Jack never lost eye contact, never blinked. "With all due respect, I think I should because we're not coming back for a long while. You have a ship to get back to America. You have a business to run. This may be your idea, but it's my life," he said and gave Miyah a fond smile.

Miyah grinned as Celeste held her hand.

"We will speak later," she said and turned back to the crew. "Once again, this does not affect you in any way. The *Pride of Charleston* will set sail tomorrow for America. Who captains the voyage back is another question. That's all," she said and all hands dispersed.

"Quinn…" Jack started.

Quinn put up her hand. "Let's get below and discuss this."

All four sat in Quinn's cabin in silence, each contemplating the future. Miyah was the first to speak.

"Quinlan, I believe Jack is right on this. If you think clearly, you will agree."

Quinn frowned stubbornly as Celeste smiled and reached for her hand. "What does your heart tell you, *chérie*? Listen to it now."

Quinn gazed into the crystal blue pools and caressed her soft cheek. She stood and took a deep breath and walked to the portal. Opening it, she looked out at the Caribbean.

My heart, she thought. All her life she had never had anyone who was concerned for her heart. In the past two months, her life was forever changed. She tried to deny her love for Celeste, but she couldn't any longer. She also knew Jack loved Miyah, and by the look on her face, the feeling was mutual.

If the situation was reversed and Celeste wanted to go home to France, would Quinn let her go? She thought of this scenario. There was no question. Quinn would follow her and live in France if need be. The thought of living without her now was repugnant.

She thought of her mother standing on the dock in Charleston when she first met her father. What would Rose O'Malley do, knowing she loved Robert Stoddard? She fondly thought of all the O'Malley women before her. What would they do for the one they loved? She knew the answer. How could she ask anything less of Jack?

"Damnable situation," she muttered as she gazed out at the sea.

She turned back to the cabin to see three sets of eyes watching her intently. She took a deep confident breath and let it out slowly. "This is how it will be. Jack and I will go aboard the *West Wind* and offer our deal to his men. I'm sure they'll take the money. I'm not sure if they'll take the voyage. Will may be right about their trustworthiness," she said and looked at Jack, who never wavered. "However it turns out, Jack, you will take the *West Wind* to Africa. I'll take the *Charleston* home."

Jack walked up to her, shook her hand, and engulfed her in a warm embrace. "Thank you, Quinn."

"It's the best thing—the right thing."

"What made you change your mind?"

Quinn looked at Celeste sitting there smiling. "If situations were reversed, I would never leave Celeste if she wanted to go back to France. I'd have a damnable time learning the language, but—"

Celeste flew into her arms and hugged her fiercely. She whispered words in her native tongue as she cried.

Quinn chuckled openly. "See what I mean?"

Chapter 30

The *Pride of Charleston* docked once again in Kingston.

"How are we going to get that chest out of Henley's cabin?" Jack asked.

"We'll take Thomas and a couple of men when it's dark. Most of them will be in Kingston. We get aboard and get the chest and get off the ship."

Jack raised a curious eyebrow. "Again, Quinn, how?"

"I don't know. I haven't thought of that yet, but we need a diversion."

Celeste was listening to the conversation. "What is diversion?"

"It means a distraction. Something to keep them occupied while Jack and I slip on board."

Miyah looked at Celeste and grinned. "I think I have just the idea. Celeste, come with me."

Both women left Quinn's cabin, leaving the captain and first mate in confusion.

Ten minutes later, Quinn heard her door open and was stunned at what she saw. So was Jack.

"My God…" His mouth dropped.

Celeste and Miyah stood there dressed in the most revealing dresses that Quinn and Jack had ever seen.

Miyah wore her native dress of many vivid colors, her breasts nearly exposed. Celeste wore her blue dress, with the bodice provocatively opened. She had her hair pinned up, rouge on her cheeks, and red paint on her lips.

Quinn's mouth dropped; her little innocent Frenchwoman

looked like a... She gulped and realized what the two were planning.

"No," she said and stood, breaking Jack from his lewd thoughts.

"She's right. You two can't go parading around Kingston—"

"We will not be parading. We will stand at the dock and distract the men while you two use the long boat to go around the other side of the ship. You climb aboard and get into that pig's cabin. Take the chest and leave the same way. It's a good idea," Miyah insisted.

"*C'est bon*," Celeste agreed with a firm nod that sent her hair precariously wobbling atop her head.

Quinn hid her eyes with her hand and groaned helplessly.

"Do you have a better idea, *Capitaine*?" Celeste asked. "We are running out of time."

Celeste and Miyah made their way down the dock, avoiding the whistles from the sailors passing by.

"Just keep walking, Celeste," Miyah said.

Finally, they stood at the gangplank of the *West Wind*. Quinn and Jack had seen most of the men leave the ship for a night in Kingston. She knew he had ten men; seven left the ship.

As Thomas and Will rowed the long boat alongside the *West Wind*, Miyah and Celeste did their part. The three remaining men stood at the entranceway of the gangplank, mesmerized by the sight.

Quinn and Jack climbed aboard and saw the backs of all three men who were completely distracted. They slipped below and found Henley's cabin. Quietly slipping in, Quinn grimaced, waving her hand in front of her face. The smell was awful.

"Good heavens, he was a pig," she said, and Jack had to agree.

"Let's get this over with. My stomach can't take much of this."

They searched the entire cabin. Jack found the chest in the large drawer under his bunk.

"Quinn, here."

She was at his side as he opened the chest. Both stared in surprise.

"My God, how much do you think is here?" He lifted the coins and paper.

"I have no idea. Let's get it out of here. C'mon, quickly," she urged, and they carried the chest up to the deck.

By now, Celeste and Miyah had all three men down the gangplank and off the ship. Quinn waved and caught Miyah's attention. She nodded and Miyah leaned into one man to keep him facing her.

Quinn hesitated as another man had his hand on Celeste's bottom and pulled her close.

Jack saw her anger and pulled her along. She glanced at him, and he shook his head vehemently. They lowered the chest to Will and Thomas and slipped down the ladder.

"Come aboard, ladies. The evening is very young," one man said as he stared at Celeste's heaving breast. She was getting nervous.

Miyah, however, had the situation well in hand. "My house is at the end of Harbour Street. Why don't you give us, say, twenty minutes? We will take you one at a time," she cooed in a sensual voice. Celeste said nothing.

All three grinned and nodded. "I'll go first," the older one said. "I'll be there in fifteen minutes."

Miyah smiled and slipped her hand down to his crotch and kissed him lightly. "We will be waiting."

Both women slowly walked away, leaving three very aroused men.

Once off the docks, they doubled back and made their way back to the *Charleston.*

"*Mon Dieu.* I was so frightened, *Madame,*" Celeste said breathlessly as they made their way up the gangplank.

"You get used to that kind of treatment."

"Never again," Jack said from behind her.

Miyah whirled around and smiled as Jack grabbed her, pulling her into his arms. "Do you hear me? No man will ever touch you again."

"Only you," she vowed and pulled him down for a deep kiss.

Celeste watched happily and looked around. "Where is Quinn?"

Jack came up for air. "She's in her cabin. Have a good rest tonight. We sail tomorrow," he said, never taking his eyes off Miyah.

Celeste opened the cabin door to see Quinn at the table, counting the silver and paper money. She was so intent on her task she didn't see her lover enter.

Celeste grinned as she walked up to her. "*Capitaine* Stoddard? Am I interrupting?"

Quinn shook her head as she concentrated. "One minute, love. I cannot believe how much money that old pig had," she said, shaking her head. She scribbled down the amount, put the coins and money back in the chest, and locked it. She then looked up.

Celeste looked nothing like the young innocent woman she met at the beginning of this unforgettable voyage. Had she looked like this, there would have been very little discussion that first night.

"Ma'amselle?" she asked and leaned back in her chair.

Celeste gave her a saucy grin and stood between her legs. Quinn leaned forward and put her hands on her full hips.

"You did a very convincing job tonight," Quinn said in a shaky voice. She reached up and untied the bodice. "For a moment there, I thought you might be—"

"Have you ever been with women like that, *chérie*?" Celeste asked as she unbuttoned the white shirt. Quinn nodded. "Would you treat her differently?"

Quinn nodded again. She reached up with both hands and opened the top of the silky dress completely, exposing the top of her breasts.

Celeste closed her eyes and swayed as the warm fingers caressed her flesh. "Show me. Make love to me as if I were one of those women." She kissed her deeply.

Quinn's arousal was skyrocketing at the thought. Her nostrils flared as she stood and ripped the bodice of the dress. Celeste gasped as the strong hands pulled at the material. With a low growl, Quinn pulled the dress from her body where it lay in a tattered heap at her ankles.

Celeste threw her head back, gasping, when Quinn kissed and bit the tender flesh of her neck. She pulled back and looked down into the sea of blue.

"You're mine, Celeste, and mine alone. Do you hear me?" she asked in a low husky voice. She buried her hands in the thick blond hair and pulled out the pins as the long hair flowed around her fingers.

"Mine alone," she murmured against her lips.

"*Oui*, Quinn, only you," Celeste whispered and gave herself up once again to the woman she loved.

Two hours later, Celeste woke to find Quinn lying on her stomach. Even in the darkness, she saw the welt on her back. She reached over and kissed her shoulder. Quinn jumped, waking instantly.

"Shh, *chérie*," Celeste cooed as she moved over her. Quinn sighed and moaned as she felt the warm lips on her shoulder and upper back. "I am so sorry."

Quinn heard the tremor in her voice. "It's all right, love. I'm fine."

"You never told him where I was," Celeste said through her tears. The thought of Quinn taking a lashing for her made her stomach clench.

"You've taken my heart, Celeste. I'm no good without you now," Quinn said fervently as she stretched out on her stomach.

"*Je t'aime*," Celeste whispered in her ear and kissed it.

Quinn groaned. "Please tell me what that means."

"It means I love you." Celeste lay on her back, high on the pillows, and urged Quinn up her breast. She held her close, stroking her hair as she hummed.

"*Je t'aime* you, too." Quinn nestled her cheek against the plump breast.

Celeste laughed and kissed the top of her head. "Your French is horrible. Now, sleep, *chérie*. I will hold you. Nothing will happen to you."

For the first time in her life, Celeste felt like a woman. Their lovemaking was incredible, that was true, but right now, she felt something more than the wonders of the physical pleasures Quinn awakened in her body. She felt like she was taking care of someone. She felt needed and loved—she felt like a woman.

"*Merci*, Quinlan," she whispered, but Quinn was already sound asleep.

Chapter 31

"Do you think they'll go for it, Quinn?" Jack asked as they made their way down the dock to the *West Wind*. The sun would not be up for several hours and Quinn wanted to get under way by then.

"I hope so," she said. "Ahoy, *West Wind*," she called up as they stopped at the gangplank.

Two men looked down from the ship. "What the hell do you want?"

"I have a business proposition for you. Where's your first mate? Who's captain now?" Jack gave a nervous look around.

"I am. Tom Dudley. Why would I want to hear anything from you?"

"Let us come aboard and I'll tell you."

They stood on deck, knowing the Africans were below in the heat. The stench was horrible.

"All right, Stoddard, let's hear it," he said, wiping his brow.

Quinn regarded him carefully. He looked beaten. Inwardly, she knew this man could not handle this ship alone.

"Now that your captain is dead, you need someone to take care of those slaves down there. How were you men to get paid?"

Tom Dudley's eye twitched for a moment. "After he sold them, we were to be paid. Capt'n Henley was going to stay in Jamaica indefinitely."

"What about the men?" Jack asked pointedly.

Tom took a deep breath. "I suppose they would wait for another ship to sign up with. I don't know," he said and looked Quinn in the eyes. "Did you kill him?"

"I did not," she answered. "That's not the point any longer. I have the means to pay your men. Whatever Henley offered you, I'll double it."

His eyes bugged out of his head. "How?"

"We did quite well this voyage, Mr. Dudley. Well?" She leaned against the wheel box.

"What's the catch?"

Quinn smiled. "I need the *West Wind* to take those people back to Africa. I need a crew. I need you."

"Back to Africa? Why? We'll get more money selling them."

"You'll get nothing. Now that Henley's dead, those plantation owners will come in and take those people. You'll be out of a ship and wages. This way, you have one more voyage and double your pay. That's my deal. You get nothing or twice what Henley promised."

Tom Dudley scratched his chin. He looked back and forth between Jack and Quinn. "Who'll be captain of the *West Wind?*"

"I will," Jack said firmly.

"Let me talk with the men."

"I need an answer now. We have provisions to take care of for the voyage. The longer we wait, the easier it is for those owners to take those people and you'll have nothing. You'll be stuck here in the blasted heat with a ship that you can't afford to sail," Quinn said.

Dudley took a deep breath, knowing she was right. He nodded and stuck out his hand. "It's a deal. I'll tell the men. When do we sail?"

"At sunrise." She shook his hand. "I have the papers drawn up. Your men will sign on with Captain Fenton and get paid when you land in Africa."

"Why should I believe you?"

Jack stepped up. "Because Quinlan Stoddard is honest, not like Dan Henley. We all know what a swine he was. You have her word and mine. Your men get what Henley offered. You get the rest when we land in Africa. Now what will it be? Are you going to use your brain?"

"Yes, I agree. I'll have the men sign up before dawn."

"Whoever does not sign up leaves the ship immediately. However, if they leave, I've decided they will still get the pay that Henley offered. I don't agree with slave running, but they are good sailors," Quinn said. "One more thing. If anything happens to those people below or to Captain Fenton or anyone else, I will hold you personally responsible. I will find you, no matter how long it takes, and I will kill you without a moment's hesitation," she said in a low confident voice.

Jack grinned as he watched the man's Adam's apple bob up and down as Tom Dudley swallowed convulsively.

Quinn had a firm grasp on his hand. She let it go and nodded. "You understand?"

"Aye, Quinn. I understand."

Quinn believed him.

It was done. By dawn, all but two men signed up for the voyage.

Jack stood on the deck of the *West Wind* and barked his orders as the men loaded the provisions for the long voyage home for the Africans. "Mr. Dudley, get those people out from that hell hole. Get them on deck for some fresh air. They need water and food."

"Aye, Capt'n Fenton," Dudley said and took two men below.

Quinn smiled and knew he would do fine. As they readied to set sail, Jack walked down the gangplank to get Miyah aboard ship. Quinn handed him a large pouch with as much gold and silver as he would need. "Guard this."

"Aye, I will."

"Quinn," Celeste said with a huge grin. "Look."

All four looked back to the deck. One by one, the homeward-bound Africans came up on deck. All looked tired and worn. All looked terrified.

Miyah laughed openly and called something in their native tongue. Men, women, and children stared at her in disbelief. Miyah nodded and clapped her hands, holding them to her chest, and repeated her words again and again.

Quinn knew she was telling them they were going home and her heart swelled with pride. She hated slavery, and in her own way, she would stop it. What happened next was anyone's guess, but at least these people were going home.

Tom Dudley and the men passed out water and bread. The African people hesitantly took the offering.

"You'd best be off, Jack," Quinn said, fighting with her emotions.

Celeste reached over and kissed Jack soundly. "*Au revoir,* Jacques," she whispered through her tears. "I am so glad to know you. Thank you for everything."

"You take care of this woman, Celeste. She needs you."

Quinn turned to Miyah, who was crying openly. She smiled and pulled Miyah into a fierce hug. "I will miss you so."

Miyah cried and held on. "I will miss you, too. I remember the young arrogant woman who sailed into Jamaica all those years ago," she said and pulled back. "You are much older but still arrogant."

Quinn laughed and kissed her on the lips. "Godspeed to you, Miyah. I will never forget you," she said with tears welling in her eyes.

Miyah smiled and touched her cheek. "You have a good life now, Quinlan. Love her as you have never loved anything or anyone in your life. Thank you for this." She kissed her one last time.

She turned to Celeste, who flew into her arms. "*Au revoir, madame.* I have learned so much from you," she cried and kissed each cheek. "I am the woman I thought I was. *Merci beaucoup,*" she whispered into her ear. "I will take care of Quinn for the rest of my life."

"I know you will, child. Goodbye," she said and let her go.

Quinn pulled Jack in a fierce hug. "Besides my father, you are the bravest man I've ever known, Captain Fenton. I'm so proud of you." She pulled back to see a stunned Jack Fenton; she gently shook him. "Now take those people home."

"Aye, Quinn. When the Jamaica winds carry you safely back to America, tell my father—" His voice caught in his throat.

"I will tell him," Quinn said. "Now go."

Jack took a deep breath and kissed her on the cheek. "I love you, Quinn."

He grabbed Miyah by the hand. She was still crying as they marched up the gangplank. Quinn and Celeste watched as the anchor lifted out of the water.

Jack stood at the helm and barked orders to Tom Dudley, who nodded and turned to the men.

Soon, the sails of the five-mast barque fluttered before they captured the wind. The *West Wind* slowly sailed out to sea. Jack and Miyah stood at the stern and waved.

Quinn and Celeste waved in return. "She's going home," Quinn said as they watched the ship sail eastward. She put her arm around Celeste and looked down. "It's time we did the same, love."

Celeste grinned happily. "Will I like living in Charleston?"

"*Oui*. You will love living in Sharleston. My mother will love you. She can now know all the latest fashions from Paris."

"Where will we live?" Celeste asked as they walked to the *Pride of Charleston*.

They marched up the wobbly gangplank. She looked at Will. "Well, Mr. Drury, you're the first mate now. Get the *Pride of Charleston* under way and back to America."

Will was stunned for a moment. He took a deep proud breath and nodded. "Aye, Quinn," he agreed, turned, and bumped into Thomas.

Quinn closed her eyes briefly. *My crew*.

"Thomas, get aft, you young fool," he said affectionately and ruffled the boy's hair.

"Aye, Mr. Drury," Thomas said with a smile.

"I'll be in my cabin, Mr. Drury," Quinn informed him.

Quinn closed the door to her cabin. "Now where were we?"

"I asked you where we will live in Charleston."

Quinn nodded and walked up to the chest on the table. She opened it and sifted her fingers through all the gold and silver. Celeste stood by her and her eyes grew large as she looked into the chest.

"*Mon Dieu*. I thought you gave this to *Jacques*," she said and touched the silver coins.

Quinn laughed. "I gave him enough to live like a king in Africa with Miyah as his queen. Henley was a scoundrel of the first order, love. He never paid his crew, and he stole whenever he had a chance. It is justified that those people will go back to their homeland on his thievery. Jack will pay the men for their voyage, handsomely I might add. Those men are used to being treated poorly by Henley. Jack will show them respect, they'll do fine. If that doesn't work, there's always their pay. Money is a great equalizer, love." She sifted the gold and silver through her fingers. "This, my little minx, is ours. I intend to vulgarly spoil you, *ma'amselle*." She pulled her into her arms. She placed a gold coin in her cleavage.

"I intend to let you, *Capitaine*," Celeste assured her. "What about my father and those men?" she asked in a worried voice.

Quinn shrugged and held her tight. "I'll pay him. If need be, we'll write him and tell him you've married some rich sea captain. He'll leave you alone, love. This is good, *n'est-ce pas?*" Quinn asked with a cocky grin.

"*Oui. C'est très bon.*"

"There is one other thing I'd like to give you, love," Quinn said as she reluctantly slipped from Celeste's warm embrace.

She walked over to her chest and threw back the lid.

Celeste watched curiously as Quinn held a cloth package in her hand. She remembered seeing this when Quinn had given her the dresses.

Quinn sported an affectionate smile. She polished the gold brooch with the cloth. "This was my mother's. It has been passed down through the generations by O'Malley women."

"O'Malley?" Celeste said the name slowly.

Quinn nodded with a fond smile. "My mother's name. You see, supposedly it all started with Branna O'Malley many centuries ago. My mother said she was a warrior who fought tenaciously for her love and her family. On her deathbed, she gave it to Mairéad O'Malley, a niece. It's been handed down to an O'Malley in each generation since. I'm supposed to give it to my daughter," she said and laughed nervously. "This, my love, is not to be. I want you to have it. It's part of my soul, therefore, it's part of you."

She pinned the brooch to the crying woman's dress. Quinn then lowered her head and kissed the brooch.

Celeste reached up and held Quinn to her breast as she kissed her dark hair. "*Merci.* You honor me too much. I am so proud of you for what you did for those poor people. You gave them back their lives—their destiny. Your ancestors, all the O'Malley women, are looking down from heaven with pride. I will wear it always," she promised in a quiet voice. She cupped the tan face and lifted it to meet her gaze. "I love you."

"I love you, too. I don't know what will happen, but I will always love you," Quinn vowed as she kissed away each tear.

Later that night, they stood on the deck of the *Charleston.* Quinn placed Celeste at the helm and stood behind her. The starry night was warm as they steered the schooner through calm waters.

Celeste leaned back into the warm body she could not, would not live without. "*Je t'aime,*" she said as she held onto the wheel.

Quinn reached around, placing her hands over Celeste's, and kissed the back of her neck.

"Always," Quinn whispered in her ear.

Celeste smiled serenely as she gazed into the night. She thought of her life before Quinlan Stoddard. She barely remembered it now. She thought of Quinn's ancestors living and fighting for love and family. It was her life now. She smiled and caressed the gold brooch. She would live and fight for Quinn with every ounce of her being.

Neither woman knew what this new life would mean for her, but it mattered little.

As they reveled in the warmth of the Caribbean night, they felt the freedom of the Jamaica winds guiding them over the never-ending sea, leading them to their future.

Epilogue

"That was quite a story, Kath," Branna said wistfully. She sat back and glanced around the cottage that she had known since she was a girl. She remembered how she and Reagan would play outside when they were children; she could almost hear their laughter.

Kathleen smiled and took a deep breath. "It would seem they had quite a life, Branna. The O'Malley women all fought so hard... And the women they loved could do nothing but love them in return." Then she laughed quietly. "You O'Malley women have a way with you. Reagan sees that in you. She loves you, and if you'd just open your heart, you'd see that you love her, as well."

Branna opened her mouth and Kathleen raised her hand. "If you say one more word about pigs..."

Branna chuckled and blushed horribly. "It's what she does for a living, Kathleen. It's not even about Reagan. Listening to all these stories, maybe I'm supposed to be doin' something grand." She sat forward looking at Kathleen. "You know what I'm talking about. Look at your life with Seana. You did something great during the war." She stood and paced back and forth in front of the fireplace. "Look at Branna. My God, seven centuries ago, she wielded a sword and fought like a warrior. And what about Quinlan?" she asked and looked at Kathleen again. "She captained a schooner and sailed to Jamaica and set slaves free. What have I done?"

"Branna," Kathleen started and smiled. "Those O'Malley women—Branna, Seana, Quinlan, they had the adventurous spirit of your ancestors. Do you know how many lived quiet lives, how they loved and raised their children and loved their husbands just

Kate Sweeney

as Seana loved me?" She put her head back and sighed. "It's not that you wield a sword or sail the Jamaica winds, or even do your part during the war. It's not only what you do, darlin', but how you love. Your ancestors fought and forged a life out of that love. That's your legacy—what's handed down through generations is love. Seana was so excited to find relatives here in Ireland after the war. We settled in this place, and we lived a quiet peaceful life. We watched you grow and were so proud of you when you went to university." She chuckled quietly. "Seana had a soft spot for Reagan."

"I know," Branna said, sitting on the hearth again. She looked down at her hands. "It's not that I don't love her. I-I do."

Kathleen raised an eyebrow. "And have you told her this?" Branna shook her head but said nothing. "Why not, darlin'?"

Tears streamed down Branna's cheeks as she looked up. Kathleen's heart broke. Oh, these O'Malley women, she thought.

"I'm not sure I have the strength that my ancestors had," she whispered through her tears. "I have little Rose—"

"Who Reagan adores," Kathleen interjected.

"I made such a mistake with Timothy. I-I don't want to do that again."

Kathleen let out an exasperated sigh. "You're an O'Malley. Haven't you been listening? You have their blood flowing through your veins." She stopped and rubbed her forehead. "I'm tired of fighting with you, and if you're not careful, Reagan will grow tired, as well. You either love her or you don't."

There was a knock at the door. Branna sighed as she walked to the door. Kathleen's heart ached for the younger O'Malley, just as it ached for Seana all those years ago. "They'll be the death of me," she whispered and put her head back.

"Branna, I need to talk to you," Reagan said in a low voice.

"Come in, Reagan," Kathleen called out.

She walked in and stood in front of Kathleen. "I'm sorry, Kath. I don't want to disturb you, but you might as well hear this, too." Kathleen heard the resignation in her voice. Reagan looked at Branna. "I'm done, darlin'. I can't do this anymore, though I'd fight forever if you loved me."

Kathleen looked at Branna, who wiped the tears from her eyes. "Reagan, there's so much that scares me—"

"Do you love me, Branna?"

Branna could only nod as she wiped the tears away.

Reagan stepped up and faced her. "I know what scares you, darlin', but if you just take my hand," she said, and Kathleen's heart broke when she heard the quiet plea in Reagan's voice. "I promise I'll give you all the time you need. We'll work through it together."

Branna took a deep quivering breath. Reagan smiled and offered her hand. "I washed it," she said with a crooked grin.

They both laughed quietly as Branna took her hand.

Reagan cleared her throat. "I'll get rid of the farm. I'll—"

Branna's head shot up. "You'll do nothing of the kind."

Reagan was stunned. "B-but you—"

"That's your life. It's been in your family for generations. How can you just give it up? I won't let you do it. Not for me, not for anyone. We'll just have to deal with the pigs," Branna said and winced. "Somehow…"

Reagan gave her a cautious glance. "You're gonna drive me crazy, aren't you?"

Branna raised one eyebrow. "I'm an O'Malley."

They stood there facing each other for a long moment. Kathleen looked from one to the other and rolled her eyes. She took her cane and rapped Branna on the backside. Branna jumped and Reagan pulled her into her arms.

"Tell me," she whispered, as tears rimmed her blue eyes.

"I love you, Reagan. I've always loved you," she said in a quivering voice. "I don't know why I fought it for so long. All my life, I think I've loved you. I just didn't know my own heart. Then when I went away to Dublin to university, I met Timothy and well, you know what happened."

Reagan held her at arm's length. "Little Rose happened, and she's a blessing. You belong to me. We belong together as a family. I love you and Rose."

Branna took a deep breath. "You must know, I'm terribly stubborn and I—"

Reagan grinned. "Say that again."

Branna frowned in confusion. "What? I-I'm stubborn and…" She stopped when she saw the wide grin and blushed to her roots. She reached up to caress her cheek. "Reagan," she whispered fondly. "My own. I love—" Her next words were muffled by Reagan's tender kiss.

Kathleen gently cleared her throat. "Reagan, sit down. Branna, go into my room and bring the box on my dresser. It's time."

Branna cocked her head in confusion, but rose and walked out of the room.

Kathleen stared at the peat fire as the glowing bricks flickered and danced. She looked around the cottage, and her tired mind wandered back all those years before when she and Seana came to this place after the war. She remembered how they lived and loved; oh, how they loved.

Kathleen looked at Reagan. "She's an O'Malley. You'll have your hands full."

"Don't I know it," she agreed. "Seana used to tell me stories about all of them from Branna to Quinlan."

Kathleen was surprised. "I had no idea."

"I drew great strength from those stories," she said with a wicked grin. "Seana told me all about the O'Malley women."

"She did, did she?" Kath gave her a suspicious glance. "And I suppose Seana told you about the heather?"

She laughed and nodded. "She was a hopeless romantic."

Kath's smile spread across her face. "That she was."

"Here it 'tis, Kath," Branna called out and presented the old box to Kathleen, who looked up with a teary eye and smiled.

"Open it, please. My hands are no good."

Branna sat on the hearth next to Reagan and opened the box. She took out the soft linen cloth and cautiously opened it. She looked at Kathleen.

"This is…" She took out the gold Tara brooch and gently held it in her hands.

"Yes, handed down from your namesake throughout the O'Malley generations, finally coming to Seana. It was her wish that your mother should give it to you when the time was right,"

Kathleen said and looked at both women. "That time is now." The tears fell down her old weathered cheek. "They're both gone now. If you have love, you have the best of everything. Seana and I knew our love was as constant as the twilight—the best of everything that the heavens would allow."

"Twilight's own magic?" Branna wiped the tears from her cheeks.

Reagan reached over and gently held her hand. "It's almost that time of the evenin' now," she said softly and kissed Branna. "Our twilight, Branna."

Kathleen nodded and laid her head back and closed her eyes. "It's time."

"I'll wear it always and hand it down to our daughter, as well, Kath. I promise," Branna said, looking at Reagan, who was stunned. "Rose is ours, Reagan." She kissed her tenderly and turned back to Kathleen. "Can I help you to bed, Kath? It's getting late and you look so tired."

Kathleen opened her eyes and smiled. "No, darlin'. I'm content right here. Go on with you now. Reagan, take this woman in your arms and never let her go. Branna, be strong, be true to the O'Malley."

"I will, and our daughter will know of her ancestors—all the O'Malley women who lived, loved, and fought for what they believed." She took the afghan and covered Kathleen, who closed her eyes and smiled. "My daughter and my daughter's daughter will know." She gently kissed her forehead. "Good night, Kathleen."

Reagan tucked the afghan around Kathleen and kissed her cheek. "I promise, as well, Kath. I've learned from Seana. Thank you."

"We'll be right outside. Reagan and I need to talk a little." Branna patted her hand.

They quietly walked out of the cottage and closed the door. Kathleen let out a deep tired breath and fell peacefully asleep.

"You did just fine, Kath," a soft voice called out.

Kathleen opened her eyes and smiled. "I promised you I would, Shawneen."

Seana stood in front of her and grinned. "I know you did," she said affectionately. "I understand Branna finally admitted she loved the pig farmer." She held out her hand to Kathleen. "They're hogs, and Reagan loves her," Kathleen said with a tired smile. "And you told her about the heather, didn't you?" She reached up and took the warm soft hand she remembered all those years before.

As she stood, she expected the ache and pain that usually followed. However, she easily stood. She glanced in the mirror above the fireplace. Her hair was no longer white; red hair now shimmered in the fire's light. Kathleen looked down at her arthritic hands only to see the soft skin of her youth.

"I'm so sorry you had to spend these years alone," Seana said.

"I haven't been alone. I've had your family about me," Kathleen replied softly. "But my bed has been lonely, Shawneen. Where are we goin'?"

Seana put her arm around her. "To meet the in-laws." She led Kathleen through the cottage door and into the twilight.

The End

About the author

Kate Sweeney was the 2007 recipient of the Golden Crown Literary Society award for Debut Author for *She Waits*, the first in the *Kate Ryan Mystery* series, which was also nominated for the Lambda Literary Society award for Lesbian Mystery.

Her novel *Away from the Dawn* was released in August 2007 and *Residual Moon* was released in May 2008. She is also a contributing author for the anthology *Wild Nights: (Mostly) True Stories of Women Loving Women*, published by Bella Books.

Born in Chicago, Kate resides in Villa Park, Illinois, where she works as an office manager—no glamour here, folks; it pays the bills. Humor is deeply embedded in Kate's DNA. She sincerely hopes you will see this when you read her novels, short stories, and other works by visiting her Web site at: www.katesweeneyonline.com. E-mail Kate at ksweeney22@aol.com.

Other Titles from
Intaglio Publications
www.intagliopub.com

Accidental Love by B.L. Miller	ISBN: 978-1-933113-11-1	$18.50
An Affair of Love by S. Anne Gardner	ISBN: 978-1-933113-86-9	$16.95
Assignment Sunrise by I Christie	ISBN: 978-1-933113-55-5	$16.95
Away From the Dawn by Kate Sweeney	ISBN: 978-1-933113-81-4	$16.95
Chosen, The by Verda Foster	ISBN: 978-1-933113-25-8	$15.25
Code Blue by KatLyn	ISBN: 978-1-933113-09-8	$16.95
Cost of Commitment, The by Lynn Ames	ISBN: 978-1-933113-02-9	$16.95
Compensation by S. Anne Gardner	ISBN: 978-1-933113-57-9	$16.95
Crystal's Heart by B.L. Miller & Verda Foster		
	ISBN: 978-1-933113-29-6	$18.50
Deception by Erin O'Reilly	ISBN:978-1-933113-87-6	$16.95
Define Destiny by J.M. Dragon	ISBN: 978-1-933113-56-2	$16.95
Flipside of Desire, The by Lynn Ames	ISBN: 978-1-933113-60-9	$15.95
Gift, The by Verda Foster	ISBN: 978-1-933113-03-6	$15.35
Gift of Time by Robin Alexander	ISBN: 978-1-933113-82-1	$16.95
Gloria's Inn by Robin Alexander	ISBN: 978-1-933113-01-2	$14.95
Graceful Waters by B.L. Miller & Verda Foster	ISBN: 978-1-933113-08-1	$17.25
Halls of Temptation by Katie P. Moore	ISBN: 978-1-933113-42-5	$15.50
Heartsong by Lynn Ames	ISBN: 978-1-933113-74-6	$16.95
Hidden Desires by TJ Vertigo	ISBN: 978-1-933113-83-8	$18.95
Journey's of Discoveries by Ellis Paris Ramsay	ISBN: 978-1-933113-43-2	$16.95
Josie & Rebecca: The Western Chronicles by Vada Foster & B. L. Miller		
	ISBN: 978-1-933113-38-3	$18.99
Murky Waters by Robin Alexander	ISBN: 978-1-933113-33-3	$15.25
New Beginnings by J M Dragon and Erin O'Reilly		
	ISBN: 978-1-933113-76-0	$16.95
Nice Clean Murder, A by Kate Sweeney	ISBN: 978-1-933113-78-4	$16.95
None So Blind by LJ Maas	ISBN: 978-1-933113-44-9	$16.95
Picking Up the Pace by Kimberly LaFontaine	ISBN: 978-1-933113-41-8	$15.50
Preying on Generosity by Kimberly LaFontaine	ISBN 978-1-933113-79-1	$16.95

Price of Fame, The by Lynn Ames	ISBN: 978-1-933113-04-3	$16.75
Private Dancer by T.J. Vertigo	ISBN: 978-1-933113-58-6	$16.95
Residual Moon by Kate Sweeney	ISBN: 978-1-933113-94-4	$16.95
Revelations by Erin O'Reilly	ISBN: 978-1-933113-75-3	$16.95
Romance For Life by Lori L Lake (editor) and Tara Young (editor)		
	ISBN: 978-1933113-59-3	$16.95
Sea Captain and the Lady by Vada Foster	ISBN: 978-1-933113-89-0	$16.95
She Waits by Kate Sweeney	ISBN: 978-1-933113-40-1	$15.95
She's the One by Verda Foster and B.L. Miller		
	ISBN: 978-1-933113-80-7	$16.95
Southern Hearts by Katie P. Moore	ISBN: 978-1-933113-28-9	$14.95
Storm Surge by KatLyn	ISBN: 978-1-933113-06-7	$16.95
Taking of Eden, The by Robin Alexander	ISBN: 978-1-933113-53-1	$15.95
These Dreams by Verda Foster	ISBN: 978-1-933113-12-8	$15.75
Tomahawk'd by Diane S Bauden	ISBN: 978-1-933113-90-6	$16.95
Traffic Stop by Tara Wentz	ISBN: 978-1-933113-73-9	$16.95
Trouble with Murder, The by Kate Sweeney	ISBN: 978-1-933113-85-2	$16.95
Value of Valor, The by Lynn Ames	ISBN: 978-1-933113-46-3	$16.95
War Between the Hearts, The by Nann Dunne		
	ISBN: 978-1-933113-27-2	$16.95
With Every Breath by Alex Alexander	ISBN: 978-1-933113-39-5	$15.25

Printed in the United States
124639LV00001B/73-75/P

9 781933 113951